WONDER

WONDERFALL, BOOK THREE

BIX BARROW

Cover designed by Alexandria Corza

eBook ISBN: 978-1-964616-16-2

Print ISBN: 978-1-964616-17-9

BOOK DESCRIPTION

Does it still qualify as a mating of convenience when one partner is all in? Asking for a vampire friend...

Simon:

Look, I get it. It's a shock when some random vampire shows up out of the blue and says you're his mate. I don't blame Reno for not welcoming me with open arms. He's had a lot of responsibilities thrust on him in the last few years, and this mate thing is too much on top of all that.

But me? I have no doubt Reno's the one I've been waiting for. I've been trying to find my mate for decades, enduring years of loneliness as I struggled to complete my mission.

I'd love nothing more than to give Reno the time and space he needs to get to know me and embrace our mating. There's just this one teeny, tiny, deadly issue: Wonders are in danger, and as a Seer, Reno's in a unique position to find the ones hunting them so I can take them out. Being mated will boost both of our abilities, so when Reno agrees to complete our bond, I'm relieved and ecstatic.

At least until he tells me it can only be temporary.

Reno:

FFS, fine. I'll do the bonding thing, but only because Wonders are dying and Simon and I need the enhanced skills we'll get. Yes, he's easy on the eyes and a super nice guy. He'd make a great mate for anybody who's in the market for one, but that's not me.

Two years ago, I took on the District Monitor role short-term. But there's still no replacement, and I'm constantly barraged by texts and calls from the Wonders. I had to quit the job I loved, and I barely have any time to myself. Now I'm supposed to be thrilled because some guy says we're mates? No, thank you, I don't need another obligation. We'll sever the bond after the danger is over. Simon isn't happy, but he promised.

Soon I'll be a free man again, and Simon will find someone else he's compatible with. We'll both get what we want.

As long as we survive this fight.

Wonder is a medium-angst contemporary paranormal romance with psychics, magic, suspense, humor, found family, a dramatic rescue, and... is that Ms. Jackson? HEA guaranteed!

AUTHOR MISCELLANY

AUTHOR'S NOTE

Before each chapter is a short flashback scene from Simon's life before we met him in Seer. These are in chronological order, though there are significant time skips between some of them. If bouncing back and forth between Simon's past story and his present story makes your brain unhappy, I recommend reading the flashbacks first before reading the main chapters.

And, for the record, the bathroom scene was Beck Grey's idea.

The farting scene was all mine.

If you find any typos or continuity errors in this book, please email me at bixbarrow@gmail.com. Reporting errors through Amazon does not trigger an alert to the author.

ACKNOWLEDGEMENTS

A big thank you to Lewis, my go-to for car questions.

Thank you so much to the following members of my Facebook group, Bix Barrow's Boom Boom Room, for helping me with all the TV and movie references: Shelly S., Paul G., Denise W., Bieke D., Meadows L., Lee B., Nancy C., Yvonne D., Susan B., Colleen F., Becky A., Ken S., and Shannon J.

Thank you to Alexandria Corza for the beautiful cover!

Thank you to Amy Pittel for the always amazing professional beta reading!

Thanks to Beck Grey, Lee Blair, and Dani Gainer for beta reading and brainstorming.

Love as always to the Sparrows!

CONTENT WARNINGS

- Violence, including hand-to-hand combat and use of bladed weapons, claws, and guns.
- Frequent mention of off-page kidnapping of people who are never found or who die in captivity
- On-page attempted kidnapping of side characters who end up remaining free
- Side characters are held captive but are freed
- A side character is malnourished and physically weak from his time in captivity
- Description of scars on a former captive from restraints and multiple vampire bites over a long period of time
- On-page death of villains by beheading, loss of magic, and sudden expansion of an internal object
- Off page deaths of villains by grenade, beheading, and other unnamed methods
- A side character is thrown out of a window

- A side character (not a vampire) is beheaded on page
- A side character is ill with AIDS and passes away off page
- Vampire characters drink blood from consenting, non-consenting/mesmerized, and deceased characters
- Vampire characters are shot in the head but the wounds are not fatal
- A character cuts his own wrist in order to feed a vampire

WONDER

KNOYDART PENINSULA, SCOTLAND – MARCH, 1946

"My king, the Guards will arrive with the prince this afternoon." I put my right fist against my chest and gave a half-bow.

Some of the tension in his face eased. "Thank you, Siomon. Sending him to Canada during the war was the correct decision for his safety, but I have missed my son. Even so, I'll be relieved when he is in saoghal breith with his mother."

I doubted Prince Nicol felt the same way. He'd lived on Earth all twelve years of his young life, since the king and queen had not wished to be separated from him, though the human war had caused that to happen anyway.

But Earth had become too dangerous for people from our dimension, so the king had made the decision to permanently close the portal between the two worlds. Over the next few months the Elves, plus myself and the Royal Guards, along with any Wonders who wished to accompany us, were heading home to saoghal breith. The queen, pregnant with Nicol's younger sibling, had already left, but King Domhnull and his advisors would stay to make sure everyone who wanted to go home got through the portal before it was closed.

"Your Majesty, here is the final list of Wonders who have asked to cross." Adair, King Domhnull's dèideag dìon and closest advisor, handed him a short stack of typed pages.

The king thanked him before turning to me. "Sìomon, please bring the prince here as soon as he arrives." He made a wry face. "I have no doubt he'll want to express his opinion regarding leaving Earth, and I'd rather have it out with him here before he causes his mother undue stress at home."

I smiled. "Being a parent is not for the faint of heart. I will bring him to you straight away." I bowed again and turned to leave the receiving room.

Before I'd taken two steps, the king cried out, and I whirled around, claws at ready, looking for the threat. King Domhnull clutched his chest, his face ashen.

"My king!" Adair and I rushed forward as he started to collapse, but I didn't reach him.

My magical core recoiled as my connections to several of the Guards were cut, and I doubled over myself. "The Guards with the prince!" I staggered upright even as more connections were ripped away. Desperately I clung to my connection with Ciorsdan, determining her location before she too was killed. My colleagues, my team. Some of them my friends. I clamped down on my grief and anger. When I could speak, I addressed King Domhnull, "They were approximately twenty miles north of Glasgow. I will be on my way as soon as I can gather a team of Guards." He knelt on the ground, his face in his hands. I dared to reach out and touch his shoulder. "I will find out who did this. It will not go unanswered."

CHAPTER 1
RENO

TIA ESPERANZA'S CAR WAS IN MY DRIVEWAY WHEN I GOT HOME, and I wasn't proud of how much swearing came out of my mouth as I pulled in next to it. And of course she'd already gone inside.

I hauled myself out of my SUV, feeling every one of my forty-six years as I stood up. All-night stakeouts were no fun, especially when the person you were following didn't leave their lover's apartment until late morning. I leaned across the driver's seat and grabbed my backpack. After I got rid of Tia —in the gentlest, kindest way possible—ate something and slept, I'd write up the results of my investigation and send the report and photos to my client. Unlucky bastard.

I pulled open the door, and the unmistakable smell of tamales hit me. "Tia?"

"In the kitchen!" She said something else I couldn't make out, and then I heard laughter. Fuck. All three of them were here. Too bad I hadn't slept last night; I might've had a vision to warn me they were coming.

My phone chimed with a text, and the muscles in my back tightened with irritation. It could wait, along with the others

I'd missed while I was driving. If a situation was urgent, they'd call.

I dropped my backpack on the couch as I walked through the living room. When I could see the kitchen island, I stopped cold. Tia and her two best friends, Rosita and Soledad, were all frowning at me, shaking their heads and *tsking*.

Normally I would've gone over and kissed their cheeks, but I'd learned at a young age to stay out of reach when elderly women were pissed at me. Especially when they were holding kitchen utensils. "What are those looks for? And why are you cooking here? Is something wrong with your stove?"

They were in the middle of the assembly stage, which meant they'd been here for at least an hour, maybe more if the chicken and shredded pork I could see hadn't already been cooked before they arrived. It was barely 11:00 a.m.

Tia snorted. "There's nothing wrong with my stove." She pointed a damp, droopy corn husk in my direction. "But you're in big trouble."

I frowned. "Did I forget to do something?" It wasn't her birthday.

She threw up her hands, the corn husk flapping in the air. "Yes! You forgot to tell me you were nesting!" Rosita and Soledad exchanged disappointed head shakes.

My mouth dropped open, and I blinked. "Huh? I'm not nesting." No way. Even if I'd wanted one, I was too old to have a mate dumped on me.

She threw the corn husk onto the counter, where it landed with a pronounced *thwack*, then she pointed toward the door on the far side of the living room. "You told me you'd rearranged your office. You added another desk and two bookcases."

I rubbed my forehead, wishing I'd slept before this conversation. "I rearranged the office to add a table, yes. I wanted room to spread out evidence or photos."

She held up her right hand, her pointer finger aimed toward the ceiling. "The office." She extended another finger and gestured with her left hand toward the living room. "A new coffee table. With storage inside. Empty."

It was more of an ottoman, but whatever. "Yes? I haven't gotten around to filling it yet." I didn't know what would go into it, but it'd been on sale, and more storage was always a good thing.

Tia glared at me and extended a third finger. "You put furniture in the attic."

I folded my arms and glared back. "It was finished out to be a guest suite when I bought this place. I finally got around to making it into a real one."

"For who? You already have a guest room."

I gave her a disbelieving stare. "You know how things are right now, especially this close to the border. People might need a place to stay out of sight."

Tia grudgingly acknowledged this but still extended a fourth finger. "Fine. But how do you explain your bedroom?"

I felt my face flush. I should've known she'd go through the entire house. "I was updating the other rooms, and I had enough extra budget to do my bedroom."

The three of them exchanged raised eyebrows before facing me again. Soledad tapped her chin. "*Mijo*, you bought a larger bed, you painted the walls that soft blue, and the new bedding is gorgeous."

I ground my teeth together and didn't respond.

She glanced at the others and went on. "The overall impression the room gives off is... romantic."

I breathed slowly in through my nose and out through my mouth. "It's my bedroom. It's supposed to be soothing and restful. I'm sorry to disappoint you, but I'm not nesting." I stared at the tamales-in-progress, and understanding struck. "You're making tamales for my nonexistent mate?"

Tia lifted her chin. "Nonexistent only because you haven't met them yet. That new refrigerator you think we didn't notice in your garage needs filling. You can deny it all you want, but I know nesting when I see it."

I stifled a sigh. "Okay, well, you do what you need to do. I've been up all night working, so I'm headed to bed."

I ignored their clucks of dismay over my job and left the kitchen. I trudged up the stairs to the bedroom. Hopefully the three meddlers would be gone by the time I woke up.

———

Standing in the middle of a two-lane rural road, I faced a mailbox next to a driveway entrance. The sun was halfway down toward the horizon. It might've been morning, but the quality of the light made me think afternoon. The mailbox sported metallic stickers that spelled out "1018". The driveway led to a large two-story house. The yard was overgrown, and the place would've appeared abandoned except for a dusty white van parked in front. It was too far away for me to make out the license plate.

I was moving, whizzing past the house, a decrepit barn, and a couple of corrals on the verge of falling down before I stopped at a thick forest of trees and shrubs. Just far enough inside the foliage to be hidden, a man holding a cell phone crouched on the ground and stared toward the house.

The man's face was a blur, so he wasn't someone I'd met or seen a photo of. He was white, skinny, and his auburn hair was tied up in a bun. He was wearing a small daypack with the handle of what was probably a machete sticking out of the top.

A twig snapping had the man whirling around. He rose up, his forearm blocking a knife thrust from a big white guy with black hair. Fuck, I hated knife fights.

Auburn Hair twisted away and moved back until he had enough room to reach over his shoulder to pull out his machete. Except it wasn't a machete. It was what I'd only recently learned was a mek'leth. A fucking Klingon sword.

Which meant this guy was Simon, and he was a vampire. And if he was fighting the other guy, that one was a vampire too.

I woke up with a gasp. Quickly I grabbed my phone, and, ignoring the twelve texts that had come in since I'd been home, I opened the notes app. Activating voice-to-text, I dictated everything I remembered about the vision.

Based on the position of the sun through the window, I had roughly an hour to get to Simon if my vision was happening today.

A quick look at Google Maps told me there were hundreds of addresses in my area using the numbers 1018. Shit, that would've been too easy.

I put the phone on speaker and dialed Cal. He was the closest thing to a computer expert I knew. He didn't answer. Fuck. I pulled up my texts and sent *Emergency please call*. He was probably working, but he'd step away to help with this.

I threw on a t-shirt and jeans, along with boots suitable for tromping through the woods. As I was opening my gun safe, Cal called.

"Hey, thanks for getting back to me. I had a vision. That friendly vampire, Simon? He's found at least one of the other vampires, and they're going to fight. I need help finding the location."

Cal cursed. "And of course he didn't call us when he tracked them down. Okay, no worries. Let me get to my computer. Do you know when it'll happen?"

"My best guess is in about an hour."

He put me on speaker. "What's your vision radius?"

"A hundred miles or so." Hopefully it wouldn't be that far away, though, because I'd never make it in time. I described the house for Cal as I strapped on my shoulder and ankle holsters. I threw on a long-sleeved shirt, leaving it unbuttoned to disguise the outline of my gun. Then I put together a change of clothes for Simon, since knife fights were never clean. My stuff would be too large for him, but at least he'd be able to be seen in public.

Downstairs, Tia and the others were gone, but they'd left a plate of tamales in the fridge for me, bless them. I scarfed down the food in between emptying my backpack and reloading it with a first aid kit, the clothes for Simon, and some bottles of water.

All the while Cal was silent, only the occasional click of his keyboard letting me know he was still on the line. Just as I ran out of things to do, he said, "Okay, I'm sending you five map pins. Let me know if any of these are the house you saw."

It was the third pin. Fifty-three miles away, so I'd be cutting it close. Cal said he'd send the location to the Hunters, in case any were in the area, and he'd text Simon that I was on the way. I thanked him and hung up as I got into my car.

As soon as I was on the road, I called Tucker.

"Well, if it isn't Veronica Mars."

"Yeah, yeah. Hey, are you off duty right now? I could use some backup." Tucker had not only been my best friend since elementary school, but he'd been my former partner on the police force, both before and after we'd made detective. Even more pertinent to today's fuckery, he was an enormous cougar shifter.

"Shit, sorry, but I'm on duty. What're you headin' into? Can it wait? I'm off in four hours."

"Fuck. No, unfortunately it can't wait. I had a vision. Remember those vampires everyone was talking about? Turns out they're in our backyard."

"Shiiiit."

"Yeah, no kidding."

"Let me see if Ma's available. I can send her to meet you."

I grunted. "Yeah, I'd love it if she could come. But remind her that one of the vampires is on our side. He's got reddish hair and a Klingon sword." Tucker and his mother, Shirley, were the only cougar shifters in the area we were aware of. His mom might be pushing eighty years old, but she'd still make mincemeat of a vampire. "Let me know and I'll text her the location. Even if she can't be there right away, I'm sure there'll be some cleanup to help with."

"Got it. I'll let you know."

We hung up, and a few minutes later Tucker texted that his mother could join me. She'd arrive twenty or so minutes later than I would, though. I hoped we were both in time to help Simon. At the next stoplight I texted the address to Shirley and Tucker, with a caution for Shirley to enter from the rear of the property. A couple of months ago, Simon had said there were four vampires left who were involved in kidnapping and possibly killing Wonders. Until I ascertained otherwise, I had to assume the other three were in the house or close by where Simon was.

My phone buzzed with several texts while I drove, but I'd have to read them when I stopped. The traffic gods were kind, and I made it to the address a little over an hour after leaving home. Even so, I felt in my gut that I was too late. I drove by the house, and the front was exactly like my vision —white van, no signs of life.

I turned at the next crossroad and slowed down near the property backing up to my destination. It was another run-down farmhouse, but this one had a chair on the porch and chickens dotting the yard. Shit. The next one looked more accessible—no people, no animals, but the yard was completely exposed to the neighbors and the street.

I parked and jumped out, swinging my backpack over my shoulder and shutting the car door as softly as I could. Ignoring my desire to break into a run, I walked casually toward the house, veering at the last minute to walk around it instead of up to the porch. The trees were much closer to the house here, so I picked up speed and ran until I was safely hidden within them.

My phone buzzed again. Shit. I pulled it out of my pocket and put it on silent, taking a few seconds to scan the messages. The usual requests for help from Wonders—they'd have to wait. Shirley was on her way; Tucker would be here as soon as possible after his shift was over, and... Shane. Shane was one of the East Texas District Monitors, and he was driving from Houston with Ms. Jackson, who had demanded to come here.

Later I'd worry about why a sentient Elven artifact had chosen today to visit. Right now I had other priorities.

I continued as quietly as I could, making my way south and west, hoping to end up at the edge of the woods near where Simon had been in my vision. I kept my eyes peeled for that other vampire too. The last thing I wanted was to run into him. Despite my police training, I was a Seer, not a Hunter. My skills were geared toward closing my eyes and sitting still. I wasn't built to take on a vampire with super speed and strength.

Grunts and cracking twigs came from up ahead. The fight had started. I hurried forward as fast as I dared, pulling my gun from the shoulder holster.

One of them started talking. "You won't die. You're like one of those Earth cockroaches, always showing up."

I could see them now. It'd been the black-haired vampire who'd spoken.

Simon gave him a cheeky grin. "You ever watch that show *The Boys*?"

What the fuck?

The other vampire hesitated. "What?"

Simon's body... dissipated. He turned into fog, but not into a cloud like Cal and Greg had described seeing. Simon's fog became a very small straight line, and he speared into the other vampire's open mouth.

The vampire jerked back, his eyes going wide. He put his free hand over his mouth and raised his knife to cut into the fog.

Then the fog was gone, and Simon was back in his human form, right in the middle of the other vampire's neck. I only caught a brief glimpse of the vampire's head separating from his body before he and Simon both fell to the ground in a heap of blood and gore.

I turned away until I got my nausea under control. When I felt steady enough to look again, Simon had rolled over onto his back. He wiped his face and licked the blood off his hand. *Eww.* Fuck, I needed to get over his unconventional fighting style and find out where the remaining vampires were. I holstered my gun and walked forward, not hiding my footsteps.

Simon jerked his head toward me, his expression wary. I was startled at how young he appeared. Even though I was used to how slowly shifters aged, this guy had to be over a hundred years old at least. He looked maybe twenty-five.

When he met my gaze, his eyes widened, and he smiled like I was the best thing he'd seen all day. He flexed his right hand, which was positioned in a fist over his belly, almost like he was holding something.

What the hell was up with this guy? Hopefully there weren't any more vampires in the woods to hear us, because I couldn't stop my frown. "That was fucking disgusting."

His smile vanished. "But effective. Mostly." He made a face and let his hand fall to his side, revealing the hilt of a knife sticking out of his gut.

"Fuck!" I ran forward and dropped to my knees next to him. "What do you need? I have a first aid kit, but I don't think...."

He shook his head. "Don't worry about it. I'll heal eventually, but—"

"Oh, right. Vampire." I yanked off my overshirt and shoved my wrist in front of his face. When Shane had described the rogue vampires' attack on the dryad grove in Marble Falls, he'd said Simon had needed to drink blood after expending energy fighting. It had to be the same when he was injured.

He pushed my arm away. "No. You'll need your strength. The *luchd-òl fola* will know Tormod is dead. One of them might come to find out what happened, and the remaining two will be packing up to leave." His eyes lasered into mine. "If they get away, they'll take one or more of the captives. You have to disable their van." He jerked the knife out of his stomach with a grunt and dropped it at his side. "This has to end today."

"Shit!" I wadded up my shirt and pressed down on the wound. Simon's eyes had closed and he was even paler than before. His hair had fallen out of its bun and was spread over the grass in a halo around his head. Which was a fucking useless thing to notice right now. "If I go deal with the van, who'll fight off the vampire that's coming?"

His eyes popped open. "I will. But I need to feed from Tormod's body, if you would do me a favor and bring it over here."

I looked over at the headless corpse and swallowed down the bile in my throat. "Um, any particular part you need to reach?"

He put his hand over mine on top of the shirt and smiled faintly. "Thigh or groin will have the most blood still."

I couldn't help but notice our magics resonating with each other like they were long-lost friends. I pulled my hand away. "Got it."

I used the dead vampire's mostly clean pants to drag him next to Simon. Then I picked up the knife, slick with Simon's blood, and sliced away the fabric on the closest thigh and hip so he wouldn't have to work to get to the skin. "Uh, do you need me to cut into him for you?"

His eyes crinkled as he smiled. "Kind of you to offer, but no, thanks. I'd appreciate it if you could hand me my mek'leth before you go." He pointed and I saw the Klingon sword lying in the grass a few feet away. Right.

I went to get it, and when I brought it back to him, Simon had managed to sit up.

"What's your name?"

"Oh!" I felt my face get hot, which was... weird. "Sorry, it's Reno. Reno Torres. Um, Cal said he would text you to let you know I was coming."

He shrugged. "Sorry. I had all my notifications turned off. I was only using my phone to track the van." He smiled, which made his face that much prettier, even with the blood spattered all over it. "I'm Simon, but you seem to know that already. Nice to meet you. Now, if you don't mind, please go disable the van."

Moving as quickly and stealthily as I could along the fence line of the property next door, I mulled over the biggest hurdle I was facing to disabling the van. I wasn't a car guy. I didn't spend my weekends cleaning carburetors or whatever it was Tucker was always doing that involved grease and rolling under the car. I preferred to spend my free time—at least when I had some—either kayaking in the bay or playing video games in air-conditioned comfort.

What I knew about disabling a vehicle was limited to what I'd learned from movies and TV shows. If I let the air out of the tires, the vampires could still drive away on the rims. I didn't have any sugar to put in the gas tank, and I wasn't sure where the distributor cap was, even if I could open the van's hood without anyone noticing.

When I was even with the front of the house, I crouched down behind some of the neighbor's shrubs and pulled out my phone to call Tucker.

"Hey, hang on." I heard him speak to someone, then he came back on the line. "Everythin' okay?"

I kept my voice as low as I could. Tucker's shifter ears would hear me. "Not yet. Can you tell me how to disable a van? Silently, if possible. I don't know if it's locked."

"Does it look old or new?"

I examined what I could see of it. "Old, I think."

"If you're lucky, you'll be able to open the hood without needin' the key."

"You mean stick my fingers under the hood in front until I find the latch?"

"Exactly. Otherwise you'll have to open the driver's door and find the hood release button."

That sounded time-consuming, and the van might be locked. Fuck. "Okay, say I get the hood open. What then?"

"Just open it far enough to stick your hand in there. Yank out any wires or hoses you can reach, and remove any caps or fuses you feel."

Shit. "The van's parked facing the house. I'm not sure I can get the hood open without them seeing or hearing."

He blew out a breath. "It's the most effective and fastest option. If you want to be quiet, you can't slash the tires, because the inner tube will burst. Lettin' the air out through the valve will take too long."

"Shit."

"Yeah, you can try blockin' the exhaust pipe, but whatever you put in there will most likely get blown out by the air pressure when the engine turns on."

I looked around. "Would rocks be heavy enough?"

"Only if you wedge 'em in there really good."

I resisted a hysterical giggle at the innuendo my brain wanted to make. Refocusing, I frowned. "It wouldn't be airtight."

"No, but the van'd have trouble getting' very far. If you can open one of the doors, you can remove the fuses. But you'll need to find out where the fuse box is, and that might take a good minute."

I ran my hand over my face. "Fuck. I'll start with the exhaust and see how I feel about opening the hood."

"Please be safe."

"Thanks. You're the best, Tucker."

"You're buying the beer later." He hung up.

I found some decent-sized rocks almost under my feet next to the fenceposts, so I grabbed some likely-looking options and stuck them in my pants pocket. I crept around the fence and braved a run to the vampires' house, my hand clamped over my pocket to keep the rocks from clacking against each other. I crept along the front of the house, ducking under the windows and hurrying past the front door, until I could sprint to the rear of the van.

I took a photo of the license plate and sent it to Tucker just in case. Then I pushed three rocks into the van's tailpipe as hard as I could without making a ton of noise. I wasn't sure they'd stay, but it was better than nothing.

I heard raised voices in the house. Fuck. I crouched down by the rear passenger tire, the one furthest from the windows, and held my breath until the voices went quiet. The front door didn't open.

If I was going to try to raise the van's hood, I needed to do it sooner rather than later.

Wishing I believed in Tia Esperanza's religion, I crab-walked forward until I was next to the front tire. Peeking over the hood, I couldn't see anyone through the windows. Hopefully the vampires were occupied at the back of the house.

I didn't let myself think, I just jumped to the front of the van and felt under the edge of the hood for the release lever. *Yes!*

The hood popped open with a small thunk, but unless the vampires in the house were listening for it, I didn't think they'd have noticed. I held the hood up only as high as I needed to get my left arm inside, then I started pulling on things. Some stuff I couldn't budge, but other things came loose. I counted in my head, resolving to be done after thirty seconds. Except right as I counted out *twenty-nine*, I found what had to be a fuse box. Ten extra seconds scored me a handful of fuses.

I lowered the hood but didn't bother latching it. Even if the vampires noticed the van had been messed with, they still wouldn't be able to drive it.

The yelling in the house started up again, and I could make out the words, "Move it! Come on!" I pocketed the fuses and ran for the side of the house, intending to head around the corrals and back to the trees.

The vampires would see me if they looked out any of the back windows or if they came out the front and went to the passenger side of the van. They were faster and stronger than I was, and if I didn't make it to the trees before they saw me, I was screwed.

I gave up on being stealthy and ran.

TWENTY MILES NORTH OF GLASGOW, SCOTLAND – MARCH, 1946

There weren't any bodies. A few spatters of blood, but no bodies. The five estate cars I'd sent to meet Prince Nicol and his party at the airfield were parked by the side of the road, every door open. Drops of blood were visible here and there on the road, but not enough for anyone to have bled out. A few bullets had punctured the upholstery inside two of the cars, but there were no corresponding bloodstains indicating someone had been wounded or killed.

All five Guards who'd been driving had pulled over, then every Guard plus Prince Nicol had been forced or manipulated into exiting their vehicles. Kinnon had been in charge of the Guard contingent. I'd been training him to take my place as Captain one day, and I could not imagine a scenario where he would've allowed all five cars to stop and for every single Guard inside to get out. It went against every security protocol.

Some of the grass by the road appeared disturbed, so there may have been a fight. But, based on how quickly all of their connections had been severed, my Guards had been overpowered in minutes. Twenty-nine Guards, plus Prince Nicol.

I breathed in and out, pushing down my anger and grief. I couldn't be emotional yet. I had to be the Captain of the Royal Guard and determine what had happened and who had killed my people and the prince.

But where were the bodies? Why take the bodies? I thought uneasily of the Nazi experiments on Wonders during the war, but none of them had happened in Britain, and most Nazi scientists had been relocated to the United States by now.

Mairead came out of the woods on the west side of the road. "Nothing to indicate anyone tried to get away in this direction, Captain."

"Same over here." Peadar shook his head as he picked his way across the grass. "I'd say they weren't expecting it. Someone pretending they needed help, perhaps."

Perhaps. But that still didn't explain the violation of our standard procedures. One car might have stopped to render aid, but not all five.

The Guards I'd brought with me stood watch at either end of the grisly line of cars while I searched each one for clues. Prince Nicol's luggage was in the boot of the first car, but he wouldn't have been riding in that one.

I was searching under the second row of seats of the third estate car when I saw what looked like a small statue on the floor. I pulled it out. "Oh, hello." Prince Nicol's dèideag dìon was in the shape of a small cat curled in on itself with their face hidden. Hope flared. Had they seen anything? I leaned over. With the car door open, they would've been able to see part of the road from their spot under the seat.

I held them to my chest and stroked their runes carefully. I hadn't interacted much with many of the dèideagan dìon. I knew they were sentient, and only the rich and powerful Elves had the resources to create them for their children. They served first as companion, and later, as they Became alongside the child they'd been given to, as protector and advisor. This one was still small, so

Prince Nicol must not have found them interesting enough to interact with regularly. Typically a child of twelve Earth years would have a dèideag dìon twice this size.

Unless... unless the dèideag dìon had given their magic to protect Prince Nicol or to keep him alive. They would've lost mass as their magic went to the prince.

I stroked them again. "You're safe. I've got you. You remember me, right? I'm Sìomon. I lead the Royal Guard. Can you tell me what you saw?"

After several seconds the dèideag dìon moved, stretching out to display more surface area. Its runes flashed. **Guards cut own connections. Took prince. Traitors.**

CHAPTER 2
SIMON

I'D FOUND HIM! I'D FOUND HIM AT LAST! GIDDY WITH JOY, I LET myself watch Reno—my mate!—for a few seconds as he left the cover of the trees to duck behind the fence separating this property from the neighbor's. I'd almost given up hope of the Seer's vision from all those years ago coming true, but here he was. The thin but already strong and bright mate connection stretched between us. I didn't think he'd noticed, so I'd wait to tell him after we'd finished here today.

He was probably in his forties, with graying dark hair, stunning brown eyes, and a stocky, barrel-chested frame. His ass was just as nice as the Seer had promised. He had several strong connections, mostly friends and family, with a few others that were more like distant acquaintances. I'd have to ask why he'd made those connections. I couldn't wait to get to know him.

But before anything else I needed to heal myself so I could fight off whichever one of the remaining three *luchd-òl fola* was coming to find out what happened to Tormod. After that, Reno and I could take out the other two and rescue the captives.

I tore into Tormod's thigh, and the magic of those he'd fed from sparkled on my tongue and eased the pain from the knife wound. At least I had my answer as to whether Prince Nicol was still alive. His magic was unmistakable for anyone else's.

As to what decades of captivity had done to him mentally and physically, well, that could be dealt with after I'd rescued him.

I drained what was left of the blood in Tormod's body, then I took my shirt off and dropped it on the ground. It was drenched in blood, and I didn't want to make it any easier for them to track me. My wound wasn't quite closed, but it was getting there. I got to my feet and carefully leaned over to pick up the mek'leth and Tormod's blade.

I left the small clearing and eased into the trees, trying not to make a sound. The birds and insects went silent, and I didn't think they were reacting to me.

I chose a spot a few yards from the clearing before going still, listening for footsteps or clothing brushing against a leaf. Only luck had me looking in the right direction when Ciorsdan stepped out from behind a tree and fired her gun.

I misted just in time, but I wouldn't have the energy to do it again. I reformed right in front of her, too close for her to shoot. Bullets wouldn't kill us, but a head shot took too long to recover from.

She dropped the gun to block my mek'leth with her forearm. I was slow bringing Tormod's knife up, and she punched me in the stomach, right over my still unhealed wound. Fuck. I gasped at the pain and dropped back, which gave her the space to draw her blade.

She appeared fit, but her hair was long and she hadn't put it up to keep it out of her face. She was wearing a threadbare t-shirt, cut off sweatpants, and some ancient Air Jordans. For comfort or because they couldn't afford anything new? I'd never been able to find that they kept any bank accounts.

As expected, Ciorsdan only had two connections. Marcas and Roibeart. Time to deal with them after I killed her.

She moved to the side, looking for an opening, and I shook my head. "I can tell you haven't been training regularly. Relying on a gun, and not having a backup weapon ready?" I *tsked*.

She bared her fangs. "You always were a sanctimonious asshole." She stepped to her left, no doubt trying to get me to move with her, which would put the sun in my face.

I smirked. "We both know you can't take me down." Which was a bit of an overstatement, if I was completely honest. I was tired from the fight with Tormod, shifting into mist twice within minutes, and healing. Ciorsdan and I were probably evenly matched at the moment. But that would only change my strategy, not the outcome. I'd win this fight. I had Reno as well as Prince Nicol to motivate me now. I would not lose.

She mirrored my grin. "Oh, but I will. And I'll celebrate by drinking from Nicol. I'll tell him how close you got to rescuing him, but, so sad, you—"

A big tawny cat leaped from behind a large shrub and tackled her, knocking her to the ground. They were huge, their body covering Ciorsdan's full length and then some. They had short fur over their undulating muscles and claws as long as my fingers. The faint shimmering outline of their human form overlaying their cat form told me this was a shifter.

Before Ciorsdan could bring up her blade, the cat's enormous fangs flashed as they sliced into her neck and ripped out her throat. They froze, blood dripping from their mouth and chin.

They looked up at me, scrunched up their face, and gagged like they were trying to hack up a hairball.

"Yeah, that's the magic from the people she's drunk from. The captives."

I moved forward cautiously, my mek'leth held out to the side and Tormod's knife dangling loosely from my other hand. Ciorsdan wouldn't die unless I cut off her head, but would the cat let me?

The cat, or I guessed I should say mountain lion, grimaced again and jumped away, leaving Ciorsdan to me as they frantically rubbed their chin and cheeks in the grass.

I made quick work of separating Ciorsdan's head from her body, then I wiped the mek'leth and Tormod's knife off on her t-shirt. The mountain lion licked their paw and swiped it over their face.

"Thank you for your help. I'm Simon. I need to go find my— Reno. There are two vampires left. I wouldn't mind some company if you don't have anything better to do?"

The cat nodded and stood, flexing their big claws into the grass and dirt and swishing their tail back and forth. Their ears pricked up and they moved swiftly through the trees toward the edge of the woods. I followed, mek'leth held ready.

It wasn't the other vampires running toward us, but Reno. My heart lifted to see him unharmed. His face relaxed with relief when he saw the mountain lion, but he didn't stop running until he reached us, whirling around to see if he'd been followed. No one was visible. "Everything okay?" He reached out a hand to rub the mountain lion's ears, and they brushed their head along his hip.

I stifled my jealousy. The connection between them was a blend of familial and friend. The shifter was no threat to my mating. "Sure is. There are only two vampires left." Merely saying those words was a dream come true, but I didn't have time to dwell on my elation.

"Yeah, I heard them in the house. The van isn't going anywhere, by the way. How's your injury?" He made a face at the barely healed wound in my stomach.

I shrugged one shoulder. "Good as new." Of course I didn't have a ton of energy left, but I wasn't about to tell Reno that.

He raised a skeptical eyebrow at me. "Uh huh. Oh, this is Shirley." He gestured at the mountain lion shifter. "She's a friend of mine."

I smiled at her. "Nice to meet you, Shirley." She made a little chirrup sound I interpreted as agreement before turning around and vanishing into the trees. "Um, should we follow her?"

"No, she would've made that clear. She'll be back. I asked her for her help when I knew I was coming here." He waved a hand toward the house. "The two of them have been shouting, but I haven't seen them outside."

I nodded. "It'd be easier if we could ambush them when they're packing the van, but they'll probably be carrying at least one captive, and I don't want to deal with a hostage situation." I took a deep breath. "Not to mention they might kill the captives they can't take with them."

Shirley reappeared, holding Reno's backpack in her teeth. "Shit. Thanks, Shirley." He took it from her, then dug inside and handed me a bottle of water. He opened one for Shirley and took another for himself. "So we need to move fast. How many captives do you think they have?"

I frowned at the farmhouse. "Anywhere between four and eight. I vote we see if we can sneak in through the back door."

Reno pointed at the fence. "Okay. We can use this for cover like I did before and climb over when we're even with it." He ran his hand through his hair. I couldn't wait to find out how soft it was. "We'll still be pretty exposed for a hundred feet or so as we run across the yard."

I smiled approvingly. My mate was quite intelligent. He gave me an odd look, but I ignored it. "I agree. It's the best plan we have."

We put the empty water bottles in Reno's backpack, then we crept as swiftly and carefully as we could across the open space to the neighbor's fence. Reno and I ducked down as we ran along the fence toward the house.

When we were even with the back porch, we climbed over the fence. I pulled out the mek'leth and Tormod's knife again, and Reno gripped a gun with both hands.

We eased onto the porch as silently as we could, but the boards still creaked and groaned. I held up a finger. I could hear Roibeart saying, "We don't have time for that. Let's go!" He sounded like he was on the ground floor.

I barely used any breath to whisper, "They're both still inside but they're getting ready to leave."

Shirley crouched down, and Reno gave me a sharp nod. I tested the door handle, but it didn't turn, dammit.

The time for stealth was over. I stood up and kicked the door right next to the handle, putting all of my strength into it. It crashed inward, taking some of the doorframe with it. I rushed through.

Roibeart was directly across from us, shouting as he ran for the front door. I dodged around the kitchen table and jumped over the tattered couch in the living room to get to him. Shirley broke off and ran for the stairs.

"Go with Shirley!" I pointed Tormod's knife in her direction, hoping Reno would comply. I was used to fighting *luchd-òl fola*, but the other two were not.

Roibeart opened the front door and ran to the left, toward the van. I was only seconds behind him when I got outside.

Multiple voices shouted from upstairs, and there was a banging sound, like Reno and Shirley were trying to break down a door. Roibeart hesitated near the van, looking up as a person fell out of the open window above him and landed with a thump, unmoving and with their limbs splayed out.

This was not someone who had jumped under their own power. They hadn't tried to land on their feet or even hold their arms out for balance.

Marcas followed, though he leaped through the window intentionally, landing gracefully beside the unconscious person. I forced myself to keep my attention on the *luchd-òl fola* instead of checking to see whether it was Prince Nicol on the ground as I suspected. He'd be the one they took with them over any Wonder or magic carrier. Please let him have survived the fall.

Roibeart and Marcas stood next to the van, claws out, with several feet between them. Of course it was just my luck to face the only *luchd-òl fola* who remembered their training when I wasn't in any shape to win against two of them.

I waved my mek'leth in their direction. "It's over. You might as well surrender." Hey, it could work.

Marcas scoffed. "You can't take both of us." Shit.

Roibeart moved another step away from Marcas, probably positioning for a dual assault.

I held up Tormod's knife. "Tormod and Ciorsdan would tell you differently."

"We can see your injury. You're weak." Roibeart watched me carefully. He'd put on weight, and I was betting he wasn't as fast or nimble as he'd once been.

I snorted. "Tormod's blood gave me back everything I lost and more." I was pleased to see Roibeart's uneasy expression.

A louder bang came from above, and the voices who'd been shouting earlier now chorused in variations of, "Save Nicky!" or "Get Nicky!".

I heard Reno cursing but Shirley leaned out of the window first, growling when she saw us below.

I smirked at Marcas and Roibeart. "Think you can take me plus a mountain lion shifter? Oh, and Reno up there has a gun. At this distance, he can't miss."

"Hey, FYI, the cops are here," Reno called out.

I didn't take my eyes off the two *luchd-òl fola*, but it was hard to miss the SUV pulling into the driveway, a flashing red light on the dashboard. Fuck, this was a complication we didn't need.

The driver's door opened, and a male voice called out, "What's goin' on here?"

Roibeart and Marcas glanced at each other, then turned and ran down the driveway, passing the SUV at a speed the officer or whoever he was would have no hope of matching. They crossed the road and hit the trees, changing to mist form just before I lost sight of them.

Ignoring the cop, I fell to my knees next to Prince Nicol, who was indeed the person who'd been thrown from the window. He wasn't moving, and blood was seeping from the back of his head where it had hit the ground. "Nicol!" I couldn't use his title here, in front of so many who didn't know. He was older, of course, fully adult. But he was small, shorter than any Elf I'd ever met, and frail and malnourished. The scrubs he wore gaped at his neck and arms. His skin was covered in bite scars and marks from restraints.

Even worse, his magical core was dull and barely moving. When I pressed my fingers to his throat, his pulse was hardly detectable. My entire chest constricted. "No, no, no. You can't die on me. You can't."

KNOYDART PENINSULA, SCOTLAND – MARCH, 1946

"No." King Domhnull held up a hand. "Nicol is dead. I felt it."

"But, Your Majesty, you're aware my kind can manipulate connections. Any one of the Guards with Prince Nicol could've severed his connections to you and everyone else. It would feel the same as if he'd died."

My gut—filled with rage and betrayal—was telling me Kinnon had to be responsible for the attack. He would never have allowed the entire contingent to stop and get out of their cars at once, unless he'd been the one to order it.

I held up the dèideag dìon. "We have a witness. If I could take a team of Guards—"

He scoffed. "Look how small they are. Nicol obviously didn't care for them while he was away, and they haven't Become enough to know what they're saying." Beside him Adair nodded in agreement.

I opened my mouth to explain my theory about the dèideag dìon giving their magic to Prince Nicol, but the King made a slashing motion with his hand. "Enough. Nicol is dead. Searching for his killers won't bring him back. It will only delay the portal closing. We must focus on getting the last of the Wonders through the portal *and the magic gifted to the humans as planned. Then we'll never have to see this abominable world again."*

CHAPTER 3
RENO

WHEN I MADE IT TO THE TOP OF THE STAIRS, SHIRLEY WAS shoving against what appeared to be a bedroom door. Inside I could hear several voices, all shouting about someone named Nicky. I hoped these were the captives, because at least they were alive. Except maybe poor Nicky.

I had Shirley stand to the side while I kicked the door with my foot a few times with no result. I didn't want to shoot the lock, because if I missed, I might hit one of the captives.

She shifted into her human form. "Let's do it together. Hips and shoulders. On three."

I positioned myself to be first into the room so Shirley would have time to shift after the door opened. We slammed into it together, and it finally broke free. I stumbled inside, gun first, and behind me Shirley changed back into her mountain lion form.

The room was big, probably originally two bedrooms with the connecting wall knocked out. Two rows of cells, each for a single person, lined the room. Instead of bars, crisscrossed heavy-duty metal wire kept the captives inside, certainly to prevent small shifters from escaping. Five of the cells were occupied, and the door to one of the empty cells stood ajar.

The prisoners all pointed at the open window. "Help Nicky!" "He took Nicky!"

Shirley got there first, and I rushed to join her. Simon was facing off with two men, one of which was the guy from downstairs when we'd burst into the house. Next to them a man lay on the ground. He was some sort of Wonder, but his magic core was almost lifeless, and I couldn't tell what species he was. His eyes were closed, and blood pooled under his head. Physically he reminded me of the photos I'd seen of concentration camp survivors, gaunt and with his head shaved. I glanced back at the other captives, and while they were wearing similar scrubs, they weren't emaciated or shaved bald.

"Can you see him? Is he okay?" The woman in the nearest cell, an emu shifter, gripped the wire of her cage anxiously.

I grimaced. "He's not conscious. I think he hit his head."

Simon was threatening the other vampires with Shirley and me, so I turned back to the window. When I saw Tucker speeding down the road toward us, his dashboard light flashing, I grinned. I yelled down to the vampires, "Hey, FYI, the cops are here." Let them think Tucker was human. Not even vampires would want to come to the attention of the human authorities.

Simon didn't need me to help him take down the vampires, as they ended up running off. Fuck, that'd probably come back to bite us in the ass, but at least we had all the captives.

I holstered my gun before facing the room. The cells were stark and horrifying. All but the one with the open door contained only a cot, a toilet, and a TV blaring some reality show. The open one, which I assumed was where Nicky had been kept, had the same toilet and TV, but the cot had restraints hanging off each corner. What the hell? Vampires could make you stand still just by looking at you. That poor, emaciated guy needed restraints in addition to his cell door? What the hell was he?

Shirley, returned to her human form, had found some keys and was trying them on the first cell, which held an imp whose human form was a small wiry man with black hair.

I waved to get everyone's attention. "Hey, everyone. Just so you're aware, the last two vampires who were holding you captive got away, but all the others are dead." They looked at each other uneasily. "Don't worry, we'll keep you safe. As soon as we get you free, you can call your families and get looked over, um, medically." Shit, I hoped the Hunters Cal had called were bringing somebody. "I'm Reno and this is Shirley. Outside is our friend Simon, who's a vampire, but he's not like the others. He's helping your friend Nicky right now."

This caused some anxious whispers that I couldn't hear over the TVs. One of the men, a buffalo shifter, said, "He won't feed from us, will he?"

I shook my head. "No. He does drink blood, but several Wonders set up a system where people voluntarily donate, and he gets the blood in bags."

The emu shifter put her hand to her neck. "How can we be sure? I—I don't want to be around another vampire."

Shit, who could blame her? "Hey, if you don't want to talk to him, you don't have to. But he's the one who tracked down those assholes who kidnapped you, and he's the one who killed all the rest of them."

She dropped her hand and looked away. "Oh. Um, I guess...." The others whispered some more.

The mountain goat shifter in the fourth cell asked, "Where are we, anyway?"

I could've slapped myself. "Sorry. You're about an hour outside Corpus Christi, Texas. Don't worry, we'll make sure you get back to your homes."

Shirley got the first cell open. "Why don't y'all wait here until we've got everybody out, and we'll go downstairs together?"

The imp nodded as he walked out into the room. He glanced at the window like he wanted to see what was happening, but he shuffled over to the door to the hallway instead. "Did you say the police are here? The humans?" He crossed his arms. They were dotted with scars from bites, and he had the same marks on his neck.

"It's only Shirley's son, Tucker. He's a mountain lion shifter too." They all relaxed. "What are your names?"

"I'm Thomas." The imp walked over to the wall next to the door and unplugged a power cord. Immediately the light in the cells changed as the TVs turned dark. The quiet was a relief. "They kept the TVs on all the time to try to keep us entertained so we'd be quiet."

Shirley let the next person out, the buffalo shifter who'd spoken earlier. He thanked her. "My name's Arlo. Ma'am, I've memorized which key goes to which cell, if you'll let me...?"

After Shirley handed him the keys, he made short work of opening the rest of the cells. The other three captives were Ophelia, an anaconda shifter; Morris, the mountain goat shifter; and Anika, the emu shifter. They'd been kidnapped over a period starting seven months ago with Anika and ending two months ago with Morris and Thomas. After they all hugged each other, they hovered near the door, seeming hesitant to leave the room.

Shirley took charge. "Let's go outside. We can check on your friend Nicky and get some sunshine while you call your loved ones. We'll figure out somewhere for you to spend the night tonight, and tomorrow we can work on gettin' you home." This was met with universal cheer, and they eagerly followed Shirley into the hallway and down the stairs. None of them seemed to have any trouble walking, and they appeared uninjured except for the bite scars they all carried.

At the bottom of the stairs, I detoured to retrieve my backpack, which I'd left on the back porch. Nicky would need the first aid kit. Outside, the former captives all rushed over to hover a few feet away from Simon, who was holding Nicky's hand. My heart contracted oddly, as if I had... feelings about Simon comforting this guy. Which didn't make sense. I barely knew Simon, and Nicky definitely needed someone to hold his hand right now. Up close, his wrists were bruised from his restraints, and he was literally covered in bite scars. I didn't want to know what was under his scrubs, but his arms, neck, feet, and even his cheek were marked up. Some of the scars looked old, and Wonders generally didn't scar at all.

I frowned. What kind of Wonder *was* Nicky? Physically he appeared human except for some pointy ears, but lots of Wonders had those.

"Do we have anything to brace his neck?"

Simon shook his head. "I felt along his spine and I didn't hear any bones grinding together like they would if there was a break."

I winced at the thought of someone who wasn't a doctor manipulating an injured person's spine, but Nicky was a Wonder. They healed pretty damn quickly. Well, usually. His magic was weak, and the scars said he'd endured what amounted to torture for a long time. I unzipped my backpack and handed Simon the mylar blanket.

He unwrapped it and spread it out over Nicky's still body. "I'm mostly worried about his head wound."

Tucker, wearing the button-up shirt and jeans that were his version of a work uniform, trotted up carrying his first aid kit as well as a bundle of clothing. He handed the clothes to his mom, nodded at the former captives, then knelt down next to Simon. "Hi, I'm Tucker. I called Doc Aguilar, but he's out of town. Any ideas on who else can help?" Simon blinked at him and Tucker said, "He's a horse shifter and the local veterinarian. It's the best we can do for a doctor 'round here, but we're out of luck today." He opened his first aid kit, and I set mine down beside it.

"Maybe not." I pulled out my phone. "Shane texted earlier. Ms. Jackson wanted to come here. Hang on." Ms. Jackson had healed someone a few months ago, and I hoped that was why they were on their way. They didn't have visions like I did, but they'd exhibited some psychic powers of their own.

I opened Shane's text thread. There was an unknown number included, so I guessed that was Ms. Jackson. A couple of months ago on Discord, Shane had told the other District Monitors and me that Ms. Jackson could form humanoid hands while in their animal-shapes. Hopefully I wouldn't have to see that, but it was nice to know they could text.

ME:

> Two vampires got away, but we rescued six hostages. One is injured badly. What's your ETA?

My phone buzzed almost immediately, but it was my text conversation with Cal instead of Shane or Ms. Jackson.

CAL:

> Well???

ME:

> Six captives rescued, but one needs medical attention. Two vamps got away. The rest are dead.

CAL:

> At least we got the captives. The Hunters should be there in an hour or so. I'll check to see if they have anyone with medical training.

ME:

> Shane's on the way with Ms. Jackson. Hopefully they can do their healing thing.

I pocketed my phone. "The Hunters will be here in about an hour. I'm waiting to find out when Shane and Ms. Jackson will get here."

Simon thanked me absently. He was focused on Tucker carefully wrapping Nicky's head in gauze.

Tucker finished and sat back, frowning. "I hope Ms. Jackson can at least figure out if your friend here broke any bones, so we can move him somewhere more comfortable."

Simon shook his head. "The sun is good for his magic." He gazed up at the former captives, who were huddled together staring worriedly at the man on the ground. "He calls himself Nicky?"

As one, they took a step back at being addressed. Arlo swallowed and said, "Yeah. He would only talk when the vamps —I mean the other vampires—were asleep or out of the house. If they heard him, they'd come in and drain him straight away. They never let him get much energy back, but they didn't do that to the rest of us. We weren't tied up like Nicky either."

Simon nodded but didn't speak, looking down to where he held Nicky's hand. I couldn't take my eyes off the picture he made, with the sun highlighting the reddish glints in his hair as it fell to his shoulders. He wore a silver pendant but was otherwise bare chested. Tia would have said he needed some more meat on his bones, but I had no complaints. Most of all it was his expression that made it difficult to look away from him. His face held worry, which I would have expected, but it also held grief. Maybe that had to do with whatever shared history Simon and Nicky had.

Maybe one day he would tell me.

I cleared my throat. "Um, while we wait, does anyone want to help me search the house? We could also use some water for everybody, and food, if there's anything in the kitchen."

The former captives shifted on their feet and didn't meet my eyes. Yeah, okay. I could see why they didn't want to go back inside. Anika raised her hand. "Can I borrow a phone instead? I'd like to call my husband."

Fuck. "Shit, I'm so sorry." I pulled out my phone, unlocked it, and held it out to her. "If you see a text from someone named Shane, let Simon here know how far out they are." I looked at the other former captives. "If any of you can't remember the phone numbers you need, call a guy named Cal Steadham. He's in my phone. He'll help find them for you."

Simon fished in his pocket and held out his own phone. "Here. I don't need it right now. This way two of you can call at a time." None of them moved toward him, but they all gazed longingly at the phone. I walked over and took it from Simon, then handed it to Morris, who was closest. He thanked me.

Apparently Simon's care for Nicky didn't override his being a vampire. Hopefully they'd come around in time.

Simon turned to me. "Can you save any paperwork or computers you find? I followed them here by putting a tracker on their van. I'd like to know how they rented or bought this house. They have to have a bank account somewhere and that may help us track down Roibeart and Marcas."

"Of course."

He gave me a sad smile, so different from the cocky ones he'd worn earlier. Before he saw Nicky. How did Simon know Nicky?

Tucker stood up, dusting off his knees. "I'll help search."

Thomas came over to us. "I don't have anyone who I need to call right away. I don't want to go upstairs, but I'll search the kitchen."

Shirley, now dressed, said she'd help.

Tucker and I headed for the second floor, intending to work our way down. I showed him the room the captives had been held in, and he shivered. "This is awful. How long was Nicky in here? He's definitely the worst off."

"I'm not sure." I'd been part of enough updates about the vampires that I knew they'd been kidnapping Wonders for decades. Other than Nicky maybe, the captives we'd freed today had to be replacements for others who hadn't made it.

We searched the cabinets in the room, but they only held cleaning supplies. At the end of the hall were two bedrooms, each with two twin beds. There was no desk, but we found one laptop and a folder of papers I took to read through later.

On the first floor was another bedroom, this one with a queen-sized bed. Whoever had rated this room had another laptop plus a stack of what looked like accounting journals.

We didn't find anything else of interest. They didn't have much besides clothes, food, a TV, and gaming consoles. When the Hunters got here, we'd have to go check the two dead vampires in the woods for cell phones.

Tucker and I took our meager findings out to his car. Thomas and Shirley had moved the dining table out of the kitchen and loaded it with bottled water, sodas, and snacks. Nicky was still unconscious.

Anika walked over. She gestured toward the other former captives, who were still hanging out near Simon and Nicky. "Thanks for letting me use your phone. Ophelia has it now. I told Simon and Shirley, but someone using a number you didn't have in your contacts texted you that they would be here soon. You had a bunch of other texts come in, but based on the previews they didn't seem related to this." She circled her finger to encompass everyone.

I thanked her, and Tucker and I went over to Simon. My gaze lingered on the pale skin of his back, admiring how his muscles flexed. Shit. "Any change?"

He shook his head, keeping his eyes on Nicky's still form. "No."

"What about you? Do you need to feed?" I knelt down next to him.

He met my eyes at last, a tired smile gracing his face. I could've stared into his golden eyes for days. "Thanks for checking, but I'm good for now. Are you okay? You didn't get hurt, did you?"

My face felt hot, and I stifled the urge to run my fingers through my hair to make sure it was laying flat. "Nah, I'm fine." Fuck, what was I, in middle school again?

I looked down at Nicky. I was kneeling by his feet, which stuck out from the end of the mylar blanket. Other than the bite scars, the skin on his soles was soft. No calluses. I tugged at the hem of his scrub pants. The scars were everywhere, and his ankles were scabbed and bruised from the restraints on his cot. "How long did they have him?"

Simon didn't respond, so I glanced up. He was gently tracing the tip of Nicky's ear with one finger. He dropped his hand and let out a huge sigh. "Since 1946. He was twelve years old."

ABERDEEN, SCOTLAND – AUGUST, 1946

I thanked the brownie, and he shut his door—rather firmly—behind me. I got into the Ford Anglia the king had allowed me to keep and made my way back toward the main road.

Hundreds of years. Wonders had been regularly vanishing for hundreds of years, and we'd never realized. The brownie's story matched the others I'd heard, varying only in the length of time since the disappearances had taken place. I felt sick thinking of the rotting pestilence at the heart of the Royal Guard. This wasn't a few bad apples egging each other on as a whim. This was entrenched generational behavior. A club, a cabal. And all the members were vampires. My species.

When I was young, long before I'd left the Elven dimension, the vampire community had been up in arms over an Earth book, Dracula by Bram Stoker. My kin were either amused or horrified that one of our kind would be portrayed as feeding directly from sentient people. Theories abounded as to how the author had come to know of our species in the first place—some of the details were too accurate to be coincidence. But what if that author had witnessed, or known someone who'd witnessed, a real vampire feeding from a Wonder?

I'd never suspected my people, my colleagues, could do such a thing, but obviously they had. What signs had I missed? There had to have been signs.

I'd led the Royal Guard for the past twenty-seven years. Maybe most of the guards who'd vanished with Prince Nicol had never been people I'd enjoyed spending time with off duty, but they'd all been completely professional. They'd done their jobs and done them well.

So I wouldn't suspect them. So the king wouldn't suspect them.

And when Wonders had reported loved ones missing, the only investigations had happened locally. Word had never reached the king, had never reached me.

If King Domhnull hadn't decided to abandon Earth and close the portal, we still wouldn't know about it.

I grimaced. There was no we. I was the only one who knew, the only one who'd ever know. The king was back home behind the closed portal. I wondered how many of the luchd-òl fola, the blood drinkers as I had named them, had returned with him. Surely there were more in their club than only those who had taken Prince Nicol. The Wonders in our home dimension were not safe, just like those here on Earth were not safe.

I'd sent thirty-six Royal Guards to meet Prince Nicol, his tutors, and his four Guards when they'd arrived in London. Kinnon had announced there wasn't room for everyone to return in the estate wagons. He'd put the Prince's Guards immediately on leave, then he'd chosen seven of the Guards he'd brought—and I'd cleared those seven of any involvement in the kidnapping—to stay behind with the tutors and travel by train back to Scotland. When I reviewed the names of the remaining twenty-nine Guards, I'd been able to trace strong friendships between all of them. I was certain none had been killed. They had all participated. Twenty-nine Guards had betrayed their king. Betrayed their prince, their people, and me.

Ordinarily, tracking such a large group would be easy, but these were vampires. Vampires trained to be Royal Guards. So far I hadn't found a trace of them, so I'd resorted to looking for missing Wonders. I hadn't expected to find evidence like this though.

I glanced down at the passenger side footwell to make sure my carryall was still secured. I kept a journal of my findings, though I didn't know who I'd ever show it to. The bag also held Prince Nicol's dèideag dìon. The king had wanted to destroy them, but I'd asked to keep them with me on Earth. He'd been relieved to have them out of his sight.

As adamant as he was that Prince Nicol was dead, the king had hated my decision to stay on Earth to find out what had happened and why. But in the end, he'd allowed it, deciding it was a tribute to his late son.

In addition to the car and a good amount of money and jewels, the king had left me with a generous supply of fuil-bheatha, the life-giving serum the Elves created so we vampires did not have to feed from other sentient beings. But I was running low, and with the portal closed, there would be no replenishing it.

Soon I would have to drink from Wonders. I'd have to become like the luchd-òl fola myself.

CHAPTER 4
SIMON

RENO'S BEAUTIFUL BROWN EYES FLEW WIDE WHEN I TOLD HIM how long Nicol had been held captive by the *luchd-òl fola*. His expression went slack in horror, and he dragged his gaze over Nicol's wasted-to-nothing body.

I could tell when he made the connection.

"Is he an... *Elf*?" His voice was pitched low, and only Tucker was close enough for his shifter hearing to catch Reno's question.

Tucker, whose blond hair matched Shirley's, took a step toward us, but I put my forefinger to my lips. "Yes, but we need to keep it quiet. He's the only one left on Earth."

Reno swallowed. "They... they kept him alive all this time? Is his blood special or something?"

I sighed, taking Nicol's bony hand in mine again. "In the Elven dimension, vampires eat regular food but also receive doses of a serum made from the diluted blood of Elves who donate it to maintain us. This allows vampires to avoid feeding on other citizens, the Wonders. It's considered offensive to even ask to drink someone's blood, and it's a crime without consent." I gave Reno a crooked smile. "I ran out of the serum within months of the portal closing, so I can say with authority that blood from the source is a thousand times more potent than the serum. And Elves have even more magic than Wonders or magic carriers, so...." I shrugged.

Reno dropped from his knees to sitting on the ground. "Are you saying these vampires stayed behind when the portal closed so they could keep drinking blood from *people*?"

"Yes. They were Royal Guards, part of a contingent assigned to escort Nicol—Nicky—to the portal. They cut Nicky's connections and their own so everyone would think they were dead."

Tucker scowled. "And the other Elves just left Nicky behind without lookin' for him?" His voice rose, and Reno shushed him. "Sorry," he muttered.

I grimaced at the memory. "At the time it wasn't well-known that vampires could manipulate magical connections. We kept it quiet so other species wouldn't fear us. When the King felt his connection with Nicky torn apart, he assumed it could only mean death. I tried to explain I thought Nicky was still alive, but he didn't believe me. He did let me stay behind, though."

"Hold up." Reno put his hand on my bare arm. Our magics flared, and he jerked it back. "Are you saying Nicky was part of the Elf royal family?"

I looked around to make sure no one was paying attention. "Nicky is—was—the Crown Prince. The King and Queen's firstborn child."

Tucker squatted down on Nicky's other side. "Holy shit. And that's who they chose to kidnap? Seems risky."

I shook my head. "They made it seem like an attack. The King believed what he was supposed to believe."

The mountain goat shifter came over and, barely making eye contact, handed my phone to me. "Thank you. It was good to talk to my husband again." He sniffled and wiped his eyes with the back of his hand. "I thought he'd have decided I was dead and moved on, but he said your friend Cal let everyone know about the kidnappings. He's starting the drive down tonight from Tulsa to pick me up." He glanced warily at me before dropping down to kneel next to Tucker. "Sorry, I'm Morris."

"Simon. I'm glad your husband will be here soon."

He smiled, then he reached out and touched Nicky's shoulder. They were connected, and I was glad Nicky had had people who cared. "I don't feel right leaving Nicky like this though."

I leaned toward him but quickly retreated when Morris flinched. "I knew Nicky before he was captured. I promise I'll make sure he's okay. If you leave your phone number, or your husband's, with me and Reno, we'll have him call you when he feels up to it."

He nodded and swiped at his cheeks. "I need to go home and bond with my husband again." He rubbed his chest. "I miss him so much."

"We understand." Reno's gaze was soft with sympathy. Damn, he was so pretty. "Don't feel guilty leaving. You need to get your life back on track, and I'm sure Nicky would tell you the same thing."

The anaconda shifter walked over, put her hand on Morris' back, and knelt down beside him. "Hi, I'm Ophelia," she said to me. I introduced myself, making sure to remain as still as possible. She hugged Morris. "Nicky always told us not to worry about him, to take care of ourselves first. You know he meant it."

Morris snorted. "He was always quoting the scene from that movie *A View from the Top* where the flight attendants all recite the line about putting the oxygen mask on yourself before helping someone else."

Ophelia laughed. "And then he'd try to get us all to shout at the vampires that we wanted our *warm nuts*." They exchanged grins before looking fondly down at Nicky.

Reno sat forward. "Well, he doesn't have to take care of himself anymore. He has us to help him get back on his feet. I'm sure he'll want to stay in touch, so we'll set up a group chat for all of you so you can check on him and make sure he's doing okay."

I beamed at him. My mate was so caring.

Tucker stood up and started walking toward the road just as a silver SUV came into view. It turned into the driveway, and he stopped to wait.

Reno stood as well. "It's Shane and Ms. Jackson."

I squeezed Nicky's hand in relief. Ms. Jackson would make sure Nicky didn't have any broken bones or a brain bleed.

I hadn't seen the *dèideag dìon* in months, so it made sense that they'd Become beyond the animal forms they'd been using back then. But I was shocked when they exited the car in a human shape. It was an impressive leap in their evolution. They also had several strong friend connections they hadn't had before.

"Um...?" Reno and Tucker both stared at Ms. Jackson as they walked swiftly toward all of us. Shane followed at a much slower pace.

Ophelia and Morris scrambled to their feet. "Is that Misha Collins?"

I blinked and reassessed Ms. Jackson's appearance. "Hah. No. Ms. Jackson has chosen that form to represent themselves for now. You may see them in a different form later."

I ignored the muttering as all of the former captives went to stand in a group by the table. Ms. Jackson gave us all a brief wave before sitting down cross-legged on the other side of Nicky's head from me.

"Thanks for coming, Ms. Jackson. This is Nicol, but he's going by Nicky now. You were originally his companion when you were both young. Do you remember?" They hadn't remembered me when we'd met again a few months ago, but they'd had a much closer relationship with Nicky.

"No." They examined Nicky's body. "He will require a long convalescence." They met my eyes. "Is he safe from the other vampires?"

I made a face. "Not yet. Two still live."

They nodded and looked down at Nicky again. They reached under their rune-covered trench coat and dug their fingers into their side, pulling out a handful of their essence, which glittered in the sunlight. Gently lifting Nicky's head, they smeared the essence over the bloody spot and rubbed the remainder over his chest.

I looked up as Shane told Reno that Ms. Jackson would need to eat soon.

"Shit, they're not the only one. Hey, Shirley?"

She'd been speaking to Anika by the snack table, but she walked over immediately. "What's up, hon?"

Reno gestured at Nicky. "Any idea what foods would be easy for Nicky to digest when he wakes up?" He glanced at me. "Shirley used to be a nurse."

She frowned. "Soup. Broth. Small quantities frequently." She turned and addressed the former captives. "Is he vegetarian?"

They shook their heads. "No." Thomas scowled. "And there's no reason for him to be so thin. Those fuckers never gave Nicky as much food as the rest of us got. And he was always tied up, so it wasn't like we could toss him some of ours."

Ms. Jackson's expression turned sad, and they ran their hand over Nicky's forehead.

Shirley put her hands on her hips and turned her head to consider the snack table. "We've got some puddin' cups and applesauce we could try him on, but he'll need protein."

"On it." Reno tapped at his phone, then lifted it to his ear. "Hey, Tia? Do you have any of your *caldo de pollo* already made?" His shoulders relaxed. "Yeah? Would it be too much trouble for you to run some of that by my house? I've got a crime victim who's not in good shape."

My mouth curled up. I had the best mate anyone could ask for.

As if he felt me watching him, Reno glanced up and met my eyes. He gave me a puzzled smile but said into the phone, "I'm going to ask if he wants to stay with me, and that'll probably mean three or four people total. I can let you know. Your tamales will be much appreciated." He dropped his head forward and pinched the bridge of his nose. "No, Tia, sorry to disappoint you."

Nicky's fingers flexed in mine, and I whipped my head around to stare at him. His face had a little more color, and his breathing was stronger. His magic even threw off a few sparks, and I could see a faint outline of his core.

I looked over at the former captives. "Can one of you come

over here, please?" I jerked my chin toward Nicky. "He's waking up. He'll want to see a familiar face."

"Yes!" Thomas rushed over and sat on the ground next to Ms. Jackson. I kept my hands in plain sight and gave him a nod of thanks.

"The rest of you, please give him space until he gets his bearings, okay?" They all agreed, hanging back but watching intently.

Nicky squeezed my fingers again. Ms. Jackson stroked his head right as his eyes opened. He blinked and squinted up at them. "Castiel? What...? Am I dreaming?"

Thomas patted Nicky's leg. "Hey, Nicky. You're okay. We're free now."

He frowned. "Thomas?"

"Yeah, it's me." He waved a hand around. "Look! We're outside!"

Nicky blinked again, glanced at the sky, then focused on me. His eyes went wide, and he emitted a high-pitched keening sound. He raised up on his elbows and tried to scoot away from me. "No! No!"

Oh, shit.

LONDON, ENGLAND – SEPTEMBER, 1946

I steeled my nerves and approached the wolf shifter I'd been following for the last twenty minutes. We were alone on the street, and I assumed he was headed back to his lodgings from the pub where I'd noticed him.

I only had two doses of the serum left, so I needed to start feeding from people before I was desperate. London at least had a fair number of Wonders, though I hadn't seen any of the newly minted magic-carrying humans yet.

I was still getting used to not having any connections. My magical core felt oddly empty. I didn't know anyone back in the home dimension without connections, and I was ashamed to say in my former life I would've been suspicious of someone who walked so alone. But I had no choice. I couldn't stay in one place long enough to form friendships.

Brief interactions, like the one I planned to have with this shifter, were all I could allow myself.

"Excuse me."

He whirled, his hands raised, ready to transform into claws.

I lifted my own hands, but mine were in an I'm-no-threat-to-you gesture. "I'm sorry to startle you. I saw you at the pub, and it's so rare to run into someone else like us."

He allowed me to approach, probably trying to figure out what kind of Wonder I was. When I caught his gaze, I immediately put him in thrall. He dropped his hands to his sides. "Thank you. I'll only take a little, I promise."

He was taller than me, so I used his wrist. It seemed less personal than biting someone's neck anyway.

I'd tried to imagine what it would be like, but I wasn't prepared for how I instinctively knew how to find the most prominent blood vessel, or how easily my fangs cut into his skin. The heat of his blood wasn't a surprise. I'd stabbed too many people over the years not to expect that. But the taste. The taste was amazing. A deep, rich flavor with sparkly fizzy notes from his shifter magic.

I didn't know how much I'd taken when I suddenly came back to myself. Shit. I didn't want to leave him half-drained. What if he had a laborer's job and needed his energy? Hastily I licked the wound to promote healing. The tear in his skin would appear days old by morning.

I kept hold of his arms but stepped back to look him in the eye again. "You had a little too much to drink at the pub, but you'll be fine in the morning after you have a good breakfast. You won't remember running into anyone on your way home."

The shifter nodded sleepily. I turned him around to point him in the direction he'd originally been headed, then I moved to the shadow of a doorway. After a pause of several seconds, the shifter's body jerked like he'd been startled, and he began walking. He hummed a little before singing "It's a Pity to Say Goodnight", which the crowd had been belting out drunkenly in the pub we'd been in earlier. His gait was a little unsteady at first, but he found his stride and hurried on his way.

I licked my lips. The guilt I felt at taking the Wonder's blood without asking warred with my pleasure at the taste. Would other Wonder species taste different? I suspected the blood of Elves, with their powerful magic, would be much more potent. And Elven royalty, like Prince Nicol, had to be even headier.

I'd never know what had made the luchd-òl fola *try blood from the source the first time, but it was frighteningly easy to understand why they'd become addicted to it.*

I'd have to be careful it didn't happen to me.

CHAPTER 5
RENO

WELL, WE PROBABLY SHOULD'VE SEEN THAT COMING. NO MATTER how well Nicky had known Simon back in the 1940s, after what he'd been through, it was no wonder he'd seen a vampire instead of his friend.

I stood up and rushed around Simon to put myself between him and Nicky. Ms. Jackson had wrapped their arms around Nicky's upper body, so as he pushed away from Simon he was pretty much climbing into their lap.

I knelt down and waved to get Nicky to look at me. "Hey, Nicky. I'm Reno. I'm the acting District Monitor here. You're in Corpus Christi, Texas, and you're safe. Your friends are safe too. Thomas is right here." I pointed.

Thomas knew how to take a cue. "Nicky, these are the good guys. They rescued us. You know, like Han and Luke rescued Princess Leia."

I wouldn't have expected that statement to affect Nicky, but it did. He stopped struggling and his expression eased. He repeatedly glanced between Thomas, me, and Simon.

I scratched my jaw, trying to figure out what to say. "Simon might be a vampire, but he didn't have anything to do with your kidnapping, and he's been trying to find you for, uh, years." I wasn't sure if Nicky knew how long he'd been held captive, and right then wasn't the time for him to find out.

Thomas stepped in again with another *Star Wars* reference. "Yeah, remember how in *The Force Awakens*, at first you think Finn is exactly like all the other stormtroopers, but he turns out to be a good guy? Simon's like Finn."

Simon kept his face friendly. "I'm glad to see you, Nicky. I'm sorry we couldn't kill Marcas and Roibeart today, but we got the other two. And we'll keep you safe while you recover and get your strength back up."

Nicky looked down at Ms. Jackson's arms circling his chest. He tilted his head to see them. "Misha Collins?" His tone was bewildered.

Ms. Jackson shook their head. "No. I'm just using this form for now. I should probably alter it as it seems to attract attention."

He blinked. "You can change shape? Like Odo on *Star Trek: Deep Space Nine*?"

Ms. Jackson hesitated. "I haven't seen that show. I will put it on my list." They lifted one hand from Nicky and pulled their phone out of their pocket. We all watched them type one-handed for a moment.

Nicky didn't appear any more enlightened when he looked back at the rest of us. I told him, "This is Ms. Jackson. As they said, they can change their form."

"I'm going by Jackson now." They tucked their phone back in the pocket of their trench coat.

"You are?" Shane stepped forward, then stopped. "Uh, that's great, Jackson. Thanks for telling us." I guessed they hadn't discussed it on the three-hour drive from Houston. He waved. "Hi, Nicky. I'm Shane. I'm another District Monitor."

Uncertain of what to do next, I was grateful when Shirley came over.

"Hey, Nicky, I'm Shirley. That big blond goof over there is my son, Tucker." She crouched next to Thomas. "How does your head feel? Any aches or pains? You took a nasty fall."

"I did? I don't feel anything." His eyes seemed to land on the window above us before darting away to look in the other direction.

Shirley ignored this. "Are you thirsty or hungry?"

His eyes shot back to her. "You'll let me eat?"

My entire body froze. Simon made a low whining sound.

Shirley, bless her, just smiled. "Yes, whenever you want. You can't have too much all at once right now, but we'll get you back to eatin' full meals as soon as possible." She turned her head and gestured, and Anika came over with a bottle of water and a single-serve pouch of applesauce.

Since Nicky was still propped up against Jackson, Anika handed him the water while Shirley tore open the applesauce pouch. I was relieved to see Nicky had enough strength to hold the water bottle on his own.

"Incoming!" Tucker pointed toward the road. Three large black SUVs turned into the driveway.

"Must be the Hunters." I got to my feet, which was harder than usual because my muscles were stiffening up. As I walked past Simon I patted him on the shoulder—on his *naked* shoulder—and I immediately felt like a dumbass for doing it. Our magics were still resonating, so I decided to blame it on that. But magic didn't cause the feel of his warm skin to linger on my hand.

Dominic Shaw, the guy in charge of the Hunters in Texas, was in the first SUV. I'd seen him on Zoom calls before, but never in person. He was big, probably as tall as Simon but with muscular shoulders and a military bearing. He shook my hand, and, once all of his crew gathered around, asked me for a summary of the situation. I didn't mention who or what Nicky was, only that he'd been held captive for many years. I introduced Jackson to the Hunters as Jackson walked past us on the way to Shane's SUV. The Hunters all stared, but nobody said anything about Jackson's appearance or human form.

When I'd told the Hunters everything I knew about the vampires, Dominic gave me a businesslike nod. "Thanks." He pointed at some of the Hunters. "You four search the house and grounds. Parkerson and Chen, determine the direction the escaped vampires were moving when they went foggy, and head into the forest thirty minutes in that direction to see if you can pick up any scent or tracks. Ross and Fortunata, you're with the captives. Check in with Shirley over there." He turned back to me. "We've arranged for rooms at a hotel for the captives, and we'll post guards. We have some burner phones for them to use to talk to their families."

"Okay. I need to see what Simon wants to do, but I'm going to invite Nicky and him to stay at my house." Tia would murder me if I let Nicky stay anywhere else, and I knew Simon would want to be close to him. My brain helpfully pointed out that I wouldn't mind being closer to him either, but I shut the thought down.

Dominic stood taller and narrowed his eyes at me. "He'll be safer at a hotel."

I straightened my spine right back at him. "He's been a prisoner long enough. Plus he's malnourished and will need small meals every few hours. But why don't we ask Nicky where he wants to go, seeing as he's an adult and everything?"

Dominic swept his hand out in an *after you* gesture. "By all means."

I marched the ten or so feet over to where Nicky was still lying on the ground, but he'd fallen asleep. Simon was still sitting with him though. "Hey." He looked up at me and smiled. Fuck, the man was gorgeous. I wished our magic wasn't resonating so strongly, because I'd have loved to see if he was interested in a hookup. But doing that when we were resonating was tantamount to making a commitment. "Uh, the Hunters have hotel rooms, but I thought you and Nicky, and probably Shane and Jackson, could come stay with me tonight. I've got the room, and my tia made soup and tamales."

Simon's smile got even wider, a reaction weirdly out of proportion to my offer. "I would love to. Thank you. I'm sure Nicky would prefer staying at your house to a hotel." He'd probably heard my entire conversation with Dominic, so he'd known what I was going to ask before I said anything.

I stuck my hands in my pockets. "Great. Um, obviously the priority is keeping Nicky safe, but maybe tomorrow we can also strategize about how to track down the two runaway vamps." I darted a glance over at Dominic. "Assuming the Hunters don't find them tonight, of course."

Simon lost his smile, and his entire body slumped. "They changed to their mist form. The Hunters won't be able to follow them. And you should warn the Wonders in the area. The vampires will need to feed." He looked down at the sleeping Elf. "But more than anything they'll want Nicky back."

Fuck. Nicky was way too weak to be used as bait, but if we waited, the vamps would attack Wonders for their blood. And without anywhere to hold them captive, they wouldn't bother keeping their victims alive.

I opened my Discord chat with the local Wonders. There were over thirty messages—some private, some not—that I barely glanced at. Bernard Laurent's daughter could wait to tell her boyfriend about the campaign, and I'd check out Anjelica Rios' disguise for her passport photo in a day or two.

I quickly composed a message telling everyone that there were vampires on the loose and not to go anywhere alone. I asked them to please spread the word and to let me know if they saw or heard anything. Fuck, why couldn't this District have a real DM?

Jackson, having eaten a large quantity of snacks, was napping in the back of Shane's SUV. I looked around for Shane, intending to invite him and Jackson to stay with me tonight. Before I found him, Anika broke away from the group of ex-captives and came over to us, a blanket wrapped around her.

"Reno?" She glanced back at the others, then seemed to steel herself. "Can we get your phone number?" She met Simon's eyes. "Um, both of yours, I guess? We don't know if our old numbers are even still working, but we want to stay in touch with each other. Nicky's staying with you, right?"

I nodded. "Makes sense. I'm happy to share everybody's numbers as they get them."

She nodded and produced a paper napkin. I told her my number, and Simon told her his. I ended up putting his in my phone as well, since I'd probably need it over the next few days.

Before Anika could leave again, Simon held up a hand. "You and the others are pretty thin on connections after what the, uh, other vampires did to you. Would you like to add me and Reno?"

I raised my eyebrows. Shit, that was generous, and actually a good idea.

She hesitated but then nodded firmly. "Yes, please, if you really don't mind." She turned and waved the other former captives over.

I ended up sitting on the ground next to Simon, and Shirley and Tucker joined us. We made a sort of connections assembly line. All of the former captives already had connections to Nicky, fortunately, since I would've hated to wake him. Simon and I had formed a connection earlier this afternoon, so we were covered.

Simon told each of the former captives that he wouldn't be offended if they didn't want to create a connection with him, but all five said they wanted to. Arlo and Ophelia were a little hesitant to take Simon's hand, but once the connections were formed, they were smiling and relaxed.

The Hunters took Thomas, Arlo, Ophelia, Anika, and Morris to a local hotel for the night. All of them avoided touching any of the Hunters, but they didn't seem in distress, talking excitedly about what food they wanted to have delivered. Morris' husband would pick him up at the hotel in the morning, and the other four would be returned to their homes tomorrow. Two Hunters were staying to guard the vampires' house and search it more thoroughly. Neither Tucker nor I mentioned the laptops and papers we'd found. I didn't feel at all guilty giving Simon first crack at them. He could pass them on if he wanted to.

Dominic came over as Tucker and I were discussing how to go pick up my, Simon's, and Shirley's cars. We'd all parked on the next street.

The Hunter looked down at Nicky. "Reno said Nicky here's been held captive for a long time. We'd like to cross him off whatever missing persons list he's on. Do you know where he's from?"

Simon hesitated, then said, "He was taken in Scotland. I'll talk to him about whether there's anyone there he wants to notify."

Dominic was unimpressed. "What's his last name?"

Simon shrugged. "I'll ask when he wakes up."

I turned away so I wouldn't laugh. When Dominic finally gave up and stomped off to bother someone else, Tucker caught my eye and grinned. For all he worked for the police department, he'd always enjoyed watching someone give the finger to people in authority.

Shane stayed with Nicky while Tucker drove me, Shirley, and Simon to our respective vehicles. Simon had a minivan of all things. Though it probably blended in better than something like the vampires' van, and he could sleep in it if he needed to.

I invited Shirley and Tucker to have dinner with us, but Shirley wanted to go home, and Tucker went with her. Simon met me back at the vampires' house, where we loaded a still-sleeping Nicky into one of Simon's rear seats, which could be reclined to lay almost flat. His cargo area was full of plastic storage containers, some knitted blankets, a yoga mat, and what looked like a mini fridge.

Shane, with Jackson still sleeping in his back seat, and Simon followed me to my house. As we pulled onto my street, I saw

Tia Esperanza's car in the driveway. "Fuck." I should've known she'd stay to meet the crime victim I'd told her I needed to feed.

I pulled in beside Tia's car, and Shane and Simon parked in front of my house. I got out and trotted over to help Simon with Nicky, but he already had the man in his arms and only needed me to slide the minivan's door shut.

Simon carried Nicky as if he didn't weigh anything. I did *not* have any feelings about seeing Simon holding someone—not someone *else*, just someone—in a bridal carry. It was the most efficient option after all.

Shane and Jackson met us on the way to the front door, and I held up a hand. "Fair warning, my aunt is here. She'll feed us, but she's also nosy as hell. You don't have to tell her anything you don't want to."

Shane snorted. "We're lucky my grandmother wasn't visiting when Jackson asked to come here." He glanced around. "Though it's probably only a matter of time."

Shane's grandmother was dead, but she'd hung around in ghost form. One of Shane's partners, Rory, was a Medium, and Shane had the ability to see ghosts now too. Rory's grandfather was also passed on but still part of the family.

I opened the front door and ushered everyone inside. "Tia?"

"In the kitchen!" She hurried into the living room, gasping when she saw Nicky in Simon's arms. "Oh, the poor thing!" She pointed at the ground-floor guest room. "I made sure there were fresh sheets in that room, and the attic is ready for guests too. *Hola*, I'm Esperanza."

Simon beamed at her. "Thank you for cooking for us. I'm Simon, and this is Nicky." He carried Nicky into the bedroom.

Shane and Jackson introduced themselves. Jackson had altered their appearance slightly, no longer looking exactly like Misha Collins, and they were now wearing jeans and a plain black t-shirt. Tia stared a little, probably noticing Jackson's unusual magic, but she didn't ask any questions, thank goodness.

I pointed up the stairs. "Um, I've got another spare bedroom in the attic, but there's only one bed."

Jackson shook their head. "I can sleep anywhere in one of my other forms, so don't worry about me."

"I'll take the attic then. I'll go get cleaned up and be right back." Shane headed upstairs.

I didn't know where to have Simon sleep. The couch was a sectional made up of four recliners, so he could sleep there if he wanted to be close to Nicky. Or he could share my bed, since it was a king, but that was a recipe for me waking up with my morning wood pressed against Simon's body without his consent. Screw it, we'd figure it out later.

Jackson looked around, seeming uncertain about what to do.

"You can wash up in the kitchen if you like." They seemed relieved to have instructions. I followed, intending to wash my own hands. I really wanted a shower, but it would have to wait. "Tia, do you want me to set the table?"

"Please. You can make a salad when you're done with that. I need to warm up more tamales."

I showed Jackson how to chop tomatoes and carrots for the salad, which they took to with great enthusiasm, if little skill. Esperanza eyed them like she was itching to show them how to hold the knife properly, but she must've decided she had bigger concerns and went back to stirring the soup. Shane joined us, sitting at the kitchen table since the kitchen itself was too crowded already.

Simon came out of the guest room. "Hey, Nicky's gonna need a bath somehow, and clean clothes."

I frowned. "He's not the only one." I pointed at Simon's less than clean jeans and his blood-smeared chest. "Shit, I'm sorry. I had a change of clothes in my backpack this whole time. Do you want them now? And my stuff'll be huge on Nicky, but it'll do for tonight."

Simon looked down at himself. "Sorry. I didn't realize how dirty I am."

I snorted. "It was well-earned. None of us are complaining."

He gave me one of those over-bright smiles. On anyone else it would seem fake, but it made me feel like I'd... exceeded his expectations, maybe?

He waved a hand toward the front door. "I have enough clean clothes in the minivan, though if I could borrow your washing machine tomorrow, it'll save me a trip to the laundromat."

"Of course. I figure you and Nicky'll be here for a good while, so make yourself at home. I'll go find Nicky something to wear."

"That boy needs to eat before anything else. I've never seen anyone so skinny. Our dinner can wait." Tia grabbed a mug from the cabinet, then dropped in a couple of ice cubes before ladling some of the soup into it. "Are any of you going to tell me what happened to him?" She glanced deliberately from Simon to Jackson. "Seems like something important's going on."

Fuck. I ran my hand through my hair. "Those vampires everyone's been talking about? Simon ran them to ground an hour outside of town. They had six captives, including Nicky. The others are okay, but they'd had Nicky for a long time."

She narrowed her gaze at Simon. "You're the vampire who's been helping, yes?"

He squared his shoulders. "Yes, ma'am."

She put a spoon into the mug and handed it to him. "Here. The boy eats first, then he can have a bath. If he feels well enough afterward, bring him out to sit at the table, or he can lie on the sofa. It's not good for him to be shut away from everyone."

Simon gave Tia a weird little bow with his free hand clenched into a fist and held over his chest. "It shall be done." He turned to go but hesitated. "Reno, maybe you should come with me, in case he gets scared about me being a vampire again."

Crap, good point. "I can do that. Let me grab the clothes for him." I dashed upstairs to my bedroom and picked out a t-shirt, some boxer briefs, and a pair of basketball shorts. Hopefully the elastic would keep everything from falling off of him.

Nicky was still asleep, his body small under the quilt. The bandages were gone from his head, but his hair was matted with blood. We'd have to change the sheets again once we got him clean. Simon gestured at me to wake Nicky, and he stood back a little holding the mug of soup.

I sat on the edge of the bed. "Nicky? Can you wake up? We've got some soup for you." When he didn't respond, I touched his hand.

Nicky exploded into motion, sitting up and knocking my arm away, punching at me with his other hand.

"Fuck!" I barely got my elbow up to block his strike. I dove off the bed onto the floor. When I looked back, he was panting, wide-eyed and with his fists up.

"Peace, Nicky. I'm Simon, and that's Reno, remember?" He held up the mug. "We didn't mean to startle you. We brought you something to eat."

Nicky blinked, then lowered his fists. "I'm sorry."

I climbed to my feet. "No, it's my fault. I should've remembered what you've been through. It's natural for you to be uneasy. You're at my house. This is my guest bedroom." Shit, I hoped there was a therapist nearby who was part of the campaign. I waved toward Simon. "My aunt made some chicken and vegetable soup, if you'd like to try it."

He looked at the mug. "I've never had that before. It smells good."

Simon handed the mug to him, and Nicky pulled the spoon out, examining it like it was a novelty. His face twisted as if he were trying not to cry. "I haven't been allowed any utensils since...." He shook his head, then dipped the spoon into the soup.

My throat went tight. "You can have all the utensils you want now. Knives, forks, whatever." Feeling odd about looming over him, I sat on the chair in the corner of the room. Simon moved to lean against the doorframe.

Nicky's hand was too shaky to use the spoon effectively, but he got one mouthful in with it. He smiled. "This soup is amazing." He ended up sipping the remainder directly from the mug. When it was gone, his expression was almost mournful.

"There's more, but why don't we get you a bath first?" I pointed toward the bathroom across the hall.

Nicky's mouth fell open as if I'd offered him a million dollars. "A bath? Like, in a tub?"

Oh, fuck, my heart. I didn't want to consider how they'd kept Nicky clean. "Yeah, and there's a shower too, for when you're stronger and can stand up."

Nicky allowed Simon to carry him to the bathroom. I offered to wait outside while Nicky relieved himself, but he asked me to stay. I guessed he was nervous being alone with a vampire, even a friendly one. Too bad I wasn't the sort of magic carrier who had super strength, but Nicky would get used to Simon over time.

When I helped him remove his scrubs, I braced myself to see additional bite scars. But there were many, many more than I'd anticipated. He hardly had any unmarked skin, including his scalp. My stomach roiled at the realization of why his head had been shaved. He was so thin I felt like he would break if Simon dropped him.

Other than his pointed ears and his eyes, which had purple irises and vertical pupils, Nicky could pass for human. He didn't have any body hair at all. Had he even gone through puberty? I had no idea about the life cycle of Elves, but if he'd been this malnourished for all those decades, he might not have been able to experience puberty on time.

I forced myself to keep smiling and show Nicky how to use the pump on the bottle of shower gel. He inhaled the honey-suckle scent and eagerly used the washcloth to spread it all over himself, including his head. Simon and I didn't correct him. He could use the shampoo next time.

We ended up draining and refilling the tub twice before Nicky deemed himself clean. He was tired afterward but didn't want to be alone, so we got him set up on the couch with a blanket and a pillow. Tia fussed over him, and Nicky gazed at her like she was the most amazing person he'd ever met.

Simon retrieved his clothes from the minivan and took his own shower. After changing Nicky's sheets, I cleaned up as well.

The others were waiting for us at the kitchen table. They'd been sharing a plate of quesadillas Tia must've whipped up. Shane had a glass of wine in front of him, as did Tia, but Jackson was drinking water.

When she saw Simon, Tia popped up out of her chair. "Simon, dear, do you eat human food too, or only blood?"

He smiled at her, but it wasn't the over-the-top smile he'd been giving me all day. "I eat regular food as well. Thank you for checking though."

She nodded. "Okay, and do you need blood this evening?"

I froze. Oh, shit. He'd expended a lot of energy today. He probably did need blood. I vaguely remembered someone posting in Discord about a blood bag drive for Simon, but that wouldn't have been local.

"I already had some, ma'am. I got a bag out of the little fridge in my minivan."

I scowled. "You need to move those to the refrigerator in the kitchen. What if your minivan's battery runs down? Plus it's more convenient."

I got another megawatt smile. "Thank you, Reno. I'll go get them after dinner."

Tia urged us to sit down and eat. I was tired, but I forgot that she wouldn't be. We were halfway through the meal when she started. "Simon, what are you plans for after this?"

He cocked his head and his eyebrows scrunched up. "After what?"

She waved her fork in the direction of the couch. "After the last of Nicky's kidnappers are... dealt with. Are you and Reno planning to stay here, or do you call somewhere else home?"

My head shot up. "Tia Esperanza! What the hell?" I should've known if I brought houseguests home so soon after my renovations, she'd decide one of them was my mate. However, when I turned my head to apologize to Simon, he wouldn't meet my eyes.

"Simon?"

He sighed and finally looked at me. "I'm sorry, Reno. There hasn't been a chance to talk to you about it."

"Excuse me? About *what*?"

NICE, FRANCE – NOVEMBER, 1949

The Seer worked out of the back room of a tiny nightclub on the outskirts of Old Town. I hadn't been sure exactly what abilities King Domhnull had instructed his emissaries to give the humans, but the Wonders whispered that some of the new magic carriers were starting to make themselves known. As soon as I'd heard rumors of a true Seer, I'd paused my search for the luchd-òl fola and looked for the Seer instead.

In Paris I'd lucked out, running into a bear shifter who'd met the Seer herself. I'd come straight here.

The Wonder at the door—a gargoyle in his human form—was less than impressed by my request to see Madame Vivienne, but a fistful of francs made him suddenly cooperative. "You'll have to wait. She has another guest. Have a drink or two at the bar, and someone will come for you when she's ready."

I kept my eye roll to myself. They wanted me to spend more money. No matter. Everyone was trying to get by. I ordered a Sidecar, which I'd become fond of in the past few years. I didn't dare drink more than one though, because I needed to feed and I'd get drunk way too fast. I hated feeding from Wonders without them agreeing to it, so I only took enough to get by. Which was stupid for someone who needed to be able to fight, but so far I hadn't been able to convince myself to take more than I needed in any particular moment.

The bartender left me alone to watch the guy at the piano listlessly singing Hank Williams' "Lost Highway" translated into French.

After about twenty minutes the bartender came back and pointed at a curtained alcove to one side of the stage. I paid for my drink and left him a generous tip. I still had some of King Domhnull's gold and jewels left, but selling them made me more memorable than I was comfortable with. A year or so ago I'd learned to find underground gambling rooms in large cities. It was easy enough to mesmerize a human into playing badly. I made sure to only prey on those who could afford it, and I'd had no trouble staying flush with cash.

Madame Vivienne was younger than I'd expected. She wore a cream silk evening gown with a lace shawl around her shoulders. A black silk turban with a blue gemstone in the center was wrapped around her head, and a matching gem graced the choker that mostly covered her prominent Adam's apple. She sat at a small table draped with more silk, and a shallow bowl of water sat in the center.

"Come in. Please sit." Her voice was low, with an affected highbrow accent. She gestured regally at the chair opposite hers, and I sat as she examined me. Her eyebrows went up. "I have not met your kind before."

"I am no threat to you, madame. I need your help." I smiled reassuringly as I set my small pack on the floor beside my chair. Most of my things were back at the inn, but I preferred to keep my money and the dèideag dìon with me.

She spread her arms wide with a theatrical flair. "Show me some francs, and my visions will come."

"Will British pounds do instead?" I offered her a ten-pound note, and her eyes lit up. Since the war, francs were worth less and less on an almost daily basis.

She plucked the money out of my fingers and tucked it into her bosom, then she laid a gloved hand, palm up, on the table. I put my hand in hers, and she closed her eyes. After a few seconds, her eyes darted back and forth behind her lids. Her fingers tightened on mine, and her expression turned grim.

About two minutes later, she let go and sat back in her chair as if exhausted. Her voice was even lower now, more dramatic. "My vision came to me in two parts. First, your companion must follow a different path than yours." She tilted her head down toward my pack. "Put them into the keeping of the flying fox." She placed her hands palm-down on the table and didn't say anything more.

I narrowed my eyes. "That's not how visions work."

She lifted her head so she could look down her nose. "I'm the only Seer in France. This is how *my* visions work."

I raised an eyebrow. "Before the portal closed, I was part of the Elven King's Royal Guard. I've worked with Elven Seers for longer than you've been alive. When the magic was granted to you, it would not have been altered so."

She sat up, relaxing and losing her dramatic affectations. "Well, don't tell any of my other customers. I need the repeat business." She reached under the table and brought out a bottle of cognac. Then she produced two glasses. She poured for each of us, and when she lifted her glass in a toast, I copied her.

She downed half of drink in one swallow. "I don't know what that is in your bag, but it's got magic like a person. In my vision I saw you giving it to a young-ish American man. He was a fox shifter, and you were in a bar, I think. He mentioned he was taking a plane to New York City in the morning, and you told him your friend there would keep him and his family safe."

Well, that was interesting, but it didn't help my mission. "Thank you for telling me. What was the second thing you saw?" I took a sip of cognac and waited.

She shook her head. "I didn't get a lot of detail, but there were flashes of blood and traveling. Lots of time passed. When it stopped, you were sitting in a bed. You were smiling, and you said, 'It's finally over.'" She sounded the words out carefully. "Those are English words?"

"Yes."

"Good. I hope I repeated them correctly. After you said those words, your mate hugged you."

I hadn't expected that. I set my glass down gently. "I'm sorry. Did you say my mate? The only ones of my kind left on Earth are those I have to kill."

She waved a hand dismissively. "Such thinking is so limiting. The Wonders have already discovered that on Earth, mates can be anyone with magic. Your mate will be someone like me, a human who received magic from the Elves. The bond between the two of you was unmistakable. I couldn't see his face, of course." She gave me a wink. "But I promise you his backside was quite shapely."

I tried to wrap my head around this. I wasn't opposed to having a mate who was different from me, but in the Elven dimension mates were always—always—from your own species. Luckily, I found all sorts of people attractive. But the idea that I could even have a mate was stupendous. I'd given up so many dreams for my mission, I hardly dared believe it was true.

She drained her glass. "You'll need your mate by your side before you complete whatever quest you're on, but it'll be a long, long time before you find him."

CHAPTER 6
SIMON

I WAS NOT PREPARED TO HAVE THIS CONVERSATION, ESPECIALLY not in public. But if Esperanza could see how strong the connection between me and Reno had grown, he was sure to notice it sooner rather than later.

Bracing myself, I pointed at the thick, glowing mate connection and traced it with my finger. I felt Reno's denial before he said anything.

His mouth dropped open. "It... it wasn't so strong earlier!"

I tried to keep my voice even. "No, but our spending time together today, especially when we were taking care of Nicky, fortified it." I clenched my hands together in my lap. "I'm pretty sure it's permanent now."

He pushed his chair back from the table. "Connections don't grow that fast. I didn't agree to this. I'm not in the market for a mate." He made a jerky cutting gesture and stood up. "I need some air." He strode to the back door and went outside. The porch light was on, and I saw him walk to the far end of the yard.

It was irrational for me to feel hurt by his reaction. He was tired and mentally drained like I was, and he'd had the news of our mating dumped on him without warning. But I'd been anticipating this moment since I'd met that Seer in 1949. I'd never even considered my mate wouldn't be as happy to be with me as I was to be with him.

"Um, congratulations?" Shane gave me a wry smile. "He just needs some time. It's been a hell of a day."

Esperanza snorted. "He's stubborn. You'll have to fight to convince him. He's been nesting for the past couple of months, but he refused to admit it."

Jackson was frowning. "Why didn't he know it was a mate connection when it was created? They appear completely different from the other kinds."

Shane shook his head. "Only District Monitors can detect the different types of connections. Other magic carriers see all connections as kind of golden and sparkly, even their own. The strength and the romantic feelings are what tell them a particular connection is a mate connection."

Jackson looked to me for confirmation, and I shrugged. "Vampires can see details about any connection, so I wouldn't know."

"Interesting. I knew magic carriers had limited abilities, but... *hmmm*." They started eating again.

I peered out the back windows, but I couldn't see Reno. I turned to Esperanza. "He doesn't want to be bonded?"

She sighed. "His parents didn't give him the best example of what a mated partnership could be like, and then as he got older he decided he wasn't destined to have a mate anyway. I think he told himself he didn't want to be mated so it wouldn't hurt as much." She gave me an encouraging smile. "Changing his mind will be a challenge, but he's worth it."

"I have no doubt." I looked out back again. No sense in avoiding it. "I'm going to talk to him." I pushed back from the table. "Thank you for dinner. Um, I'm not sure how long this will take, but Nicky probably needs to eat again."

Esperanza patted my hand. "We'll take care of him."

"Thanks." I stood up and tugged at my shirt to straighten it. Taking a deep breath, I walked to the back door, slipping through before shutting it behind me.

"I'm over here." His tone sounded resigned.

I'd never had a connection this strong before, but—even without the hours and hours of study I'd done in my youth— I instinctively knew how I could push a feeling of reassurance and affection through to Reno. If I thought he'd be receptive to it, of course. Unfortunately now was not the time.

I walked around a stand of shrubs to the right to find him sitting in an Adirondack chair in front of an empty fire pit. He waved at the chair next to him, so I went over and sat down.

He rubbed his chest where our connection emerged. "You've known all day, haven't you?"

"Yes." I looked up at the stars overhead. The light pollution wasn't so bad here, this close to the ocean. "In 1949 I met a Seer. They told me my mate would be a magic carrier, and I'd complete my mission with him by my side. When you came into the woods to help me, I knew." I hesitated. "I'm sorry I didn't tell you, but it seemed like something better discussed after... today." I waved my hand in a vague gesture.

"I understand that part. I just...." He sat forward. "Wait a minute. The Seer had a vision in 1949 about *now*?"

I smiled. "She was one of the people who got their magic directly from the Elves. Their abilities were stronger than today's magic carriers."

"Huh." He shivered, and it wasn't due to the summer night air. "Look, I know you've been waiting all this time, but—"

I held up a hand. "But you've just found out. I completely understand. We can keep a little distance between us for a while. Will that work?"

"For now. But, Simon, to be completely transparent with you, I don't *want* a mate." Even though Esperanza had warned me, the statement still sent a spear of pain through my heart. It must've echoed through the bond, because he winced. "I'm sorry. It's got nothing to do with you. I never felt like I was missing out on anything being single, and at my age...."

I was exhausted, and I didn't have the mental fortitude to hear this right now. I stood up. "Thank you for telling me. I'm going to go inside."

He didn't say anything as I walked away.

In the living room, Nicky had another mug of soup, and Jackson sat next to him while the opening credits of an episode of *Star Trek: Deep Space Nine* played.

Shane was in the kitchen putting dishes in the dishwasher. "Hey. Esperanza went home. She said to tell you if you need more room for your blood, there's a second refrigerator in the garage. She'll be back in the morning to see if we need anything for Nicky." He glanced behind me at the closed back door. "How did it go with Reno?"

I made a face. "He doesn't want a mate."

Shane sucked in a breath. "Shit, man, that's rough."

"Yeah." I ran my hand through my hair. I was so tired. Before I forgot to do it, I went out to the minivan and emptied my little fridge. I was down to two bags of blood, which would probably be gone in the next day or so, based on the amount of energy I'd be expending looking for Marcas and Roibeart.

I'd have to contact Levi, the dryad who for some reason had taken it upon himself to get involved in my well-being. He'd organized blood donations everywhere I went, so I never had to mesmerize anyone anymore. I owed him a great deal.

I snorted to myself. What I really owed him was a phone call. He never let more than three days go by before he wanted an update on where I was and what I was doing.

Something to worry about tomorrow. I put the blood bags, along with the other snacks I'd had in the minivan, in the fridge in the garage, in case anyone would be grossed out by seeing the blood. The fridge seemed brand new, and I remembered Esperanza mentioning Reno had been nesting. Had he bought this for me? Maybe his magic knew we were mates, even if his brain wasn't ready to accept it yet.

I wandered into the living room, and Nicky nudged Jackson. "Hey, can you pause the show, please?"

Obligingly they pointed the remote at the TV and the image on the screen froze.

I forced a smile. "How are you feeling?"

He smiled back. Maybe the dim lighting in the room was hiding how fake my expression was. "Better, thanks. Um." He looked down at his mug and ran a finger around the rim. The marks from his restraints stood out starkly on his skin, even among the multitude of bite scars. He glanced at the TV and back to me. "I don't really want to be all alone in that guest room after... everything."

Shit, I should've thought of that. I nodded encouragingly. "Understandable. Would you feel better if Jackson stayed in there with you?" I didn't think he'd want me for a roommate, considering I was a vampire.

He shook his head. "I asked Jackson if they'd mind sleeping out here with me, and they said they would." He pointed at the TV. "I'm used to having that on all the time."

"Ah. Got it. Whatever makes you comfortable, Nicky. But, if that's the case, do you mind if I sleep in the guest room instead?"

"It's all yours." He gave me a little grin. "I won't fight you for it like Greg and Marcia on *The Brady Bunch*."

I chuckled. "Okay, thanks." I left the room, my heart aching for Nicky, who'd had to grow up watching other people experience life on television. As soon as he was healthy, I would help him experience life for himself.

I fell asleep making a mental list of things he might like to do once he was well. It helped me avoid obsessing about Reno.

———

I woke up before dawn, so I got my yoga mat out of the minivan. In the backyard I went through my usual sun saluta-tion sequence then a short but much needed vinyasa flow. When I was done, I could smell bacon and hear voices talking softly in the kitchen. Reno and Tucker. My connection to Reno was still as solid as it had been last night, which was a relief. I had to hope Shane was right, and all Reno needed was to get used to the idea of us being mates. Or even just *having* a mate.

For decades I'd been looking forward to meeting my future mate, but he'd only been what my imagination could create. Now that I'd met Reno and knew he was a good man, caring and protective, not to mention sexy as fuck, I was all in. Fully smitten. He might not be ready to be mated right now, but I'd had plenty of practice waiting to get what I wanted. I'd stick close and treat him the way he deserved. The magic pointed people in the direction of their mates, but it was up to us to fan the flames and create the romance.

I went back inside and greeted Reno and Tucker on my way to the guest bedroom. Reno met my eyes briefly before looking away. I kept smiling. This was a marathon, not a sprint.

After I showered and got dressed, I returned to the living room. Nicky was on the sofa eating oatmeal, and Jackson was next to him in their panther form, sleeping on their back with their paws in the air. Nicky was wearing clothes that fit him, so Tucker must've brought those over. I waved at Nicky, and he waved his spoon back at me before returning his gaze to the TV.

Shane had joined Reno and Tucker at the table, and Esperanza was stirring something on the stove.

"Good morning." They all greeted me, and Reno actually gave me a nod. I passed the table and went into the kitchen. "Esperanza, do you need help with anything?" I'd only occasionally had access to a decent kitchen, but I could do prep work like nobody's business.

"No, thank you, *mijo*. I'm making some hot chocolate for Nicky. If you want coffee, the mugs are in the cabinet above the coffee maker. Your breakfast is in the oven."

I leaned over her shoulder. The rich chocolate and cinnamon smell was intoxicating. I found a mug and filled it halfway with coffee, then I took it over to the stove. "Is there enough to spare for me?" I gave her my best puppy dog eyes, and she laughed and knocked her shoulder into my arm.

"You are trouble, aren't you?" She lifted the pot and carefully poured some of the hot chocolate into my mug.

"*Mmmm*. Thank you." I bent down and kissed her cheek. What the hell? I froze for half a second, but I managed to straighten up and take my mug to the table. The last person I'd kissed, even on the cheek like I'd just done to Esperanza, had been Davi, multiple decades ago. But this kiss had been unconscious, like my magic already recognized Esperanza as family.

Reno watched me with an unreadable expression as I set my mug down at the empty seat next to Tucker. I couldn't feel anything through our connection. Had he already learned how to block it?

I went back and got my plate out of the oven. After complimenting and thanking Esperanza, I sat down and focused on eating. I'd need to figure out how to obtain more blood, because I'd have to consume my last bag before nightfall. After a few minutes, Jackson came over, yawning and swishing their tail, and hopped onto the chair on my other side. I gave them a piece of my toast, and they purred.

Tucker pushed his empty plate away. "I was tellin' Reno and Shane that I spoke to Dominic this mornin'. The Hunters he sent after the runaway vamps couldn't find the trail."

I sipped my coffee and nodded. "I didn't expect them to. Marcas and Roibeart would've stayed in mist form as long as they could." I glanced over to the living room to make sure Nicky was occupied with the TV. "Which means they burned a lot of energy. They'll have to feed as soon as possible."

Reno pulled out his phone and set it on the table. "How far could they get in mist form before they had to rest?" His phone vibrated with a text, but he swiped it away, pulling up a map app instead.

"Maybe twenty miles on the outside."

His head shot up, and his whole body went tense. He kept his voice low. "That's not far enough for them to have followed us here, but could they have waited around and seen our cars?"

I gave what I hoped was a reassuring smile. "Even if they did, they've never had much in the way of computer skills. They wouldn't know how to hack into the state's database to find your address from your license plate."

He relaxed. "Okay, good."

Esperanza came out of the kitchen. "I've got my bridge club luncheon today, but let me know if you need help this evening. There's more soup in the refrigerator, and I also left a container of beans and some tortillas for Nicky to try." She kissed Reno's cheek, then Tucker's, then mine. I managed to refrain from putting my hand over the spot, but I wanted to. She patted Jackson on the head and waved at Shane, stopping on her way to the front door to reach over the back of the couch to hug Nicky.

Reno watched her fondly as she left before turning to me. "Hey, I hope you don't mind, but I looked through those papers we found at the house. They're in my office if you want to see them." He made a face. "The laptops are password-protected, but hopefully you can get around that."

"I can try." I raised my eyebrows. "Did you find anything interesting in the papers?"

"I found a bank account. Since the early 2000s they've been using an account in the name of Monique Grafton. I'm guessing she was one of their victims back then." He darted a glance toward the living room. "I don't really want to ask Nicky about her though."

I grimaced. "I'll do some research. It probably won't make any difference whether or not he remembers her."

"Agreed. I also found a sort of ledger of jobs and who brought in what money. They did a combination of day labor and fencing stolen items. And they were squatting in the house. The owner went into a nursing home, and the property was being foreclosed on. That shit takes years, and even in Texas squatters have some rights. Even if one of the neighbors had reported them, they weren't in any danger of being forced to move any time soon."

Tucker groaned. He elbowed Reno. "Remember those people we had to roust out of that house near the bayfront that one time?" He looked at me. "This was back when we were patrol officers. This crew of four people had moved into this empty house and packed it with boxes and shit. When we finally got the approval to remove them from the premises, Reno and I had to chase them through this maze of crap. It was fucking frustrating."

I frowned. I didn't know what Reno did for a living. I knew he was the acting District Monitor, but in Texas it was an unpaid position. I turned to him. "Are you still a police officer as well?"

He shook his head and sighed. His phone buzzed with another text message, and he turned it over. "No. Tucker and I had both made detective. We were partners. I fucking loved that job."

Tucker reached over and put his hand on Reno's back. "You're still doin' some good out there, Magnum, P.I."

I cocked my head. "You're a private investigator now?"

He nodded, frowning down at his phone, which vibrated again. "My cousin Daniel, Tia's son? He was the District Monitor here. He passed away two years ago from a heart condition. And other than the DMs who already have Districts,"—He pointed at Shane—"there aren't any magic carriers with District Monitor-type skills in Texas that we're aware of. But somebody had to step up and help the Wonders." He turned his phone over and tapped it, not looking up at us. "The demands aren't compatible with shift work, so I couldn't remain a cop."

My heart hurt for him. I still couldn't feel anything through our connection, but his entire posture seemed defeated and depressed. He shrugged. "I don't love the PI work, but it's flexible, and usually it's interesting. But the Wonders need a real DM." He glanced toward Nicky and lowered his voice again. "I keep thinking there's a Wonder somewhere who's scared because they're facing down two vampires, but I won't know because I can't feel anything even if I'm connected to them."

Shit. I wanted to help my mate. But how?

"Reno." Shane reached out and put his hand on Reno's wrist. "You can't think like that. You can only do what you can to the best of your abilities. The Wonders in this District are better off having you than they would be without you, and you know it." I fought down the urge to bare my fangs at Shane for touching my mate.

Reno ran his other hand over his face. "I know. It's just, I never wanted to be DM. I mean, I never thought it was *possible* for me to be DM, so I never even considered it. But having to act like a DM and not having the innate ability to be good at it? It's fucking with my head every single day." He pushed his chair back and stood. "I've been up for hours. I'm going to go take a nap and hope I have a vision about where the vampires are. Not that I can call a vision, but maybe if we all cross our fingers it'll happen. I love being a shitty Seer, exactly like I'm a shitty DM." He walked swiftly out of the room, heading for the stairs.

I half-stood, wanting to follow him, but Tucker shook his head. "Let him breathe a bit. He's under a lot of stress, and he'll feel better after a nap, whether or not he has a vision."

Reno's phone vibrated again. He'd left it behind. "Should we check that?"

"Nah." Tucker grimaced at the phone. "The Wonders'll call if it's an emergency. He's got them trained that much at least." He shook his head. "By the way, the vampire's van was stolen in Missouri two years back. The plates are stolen too, but from up near Lubbock a few months ago."

"So nothing to help us there."

"No. Unless you find somethin' on the laptops, we're kind of at a dead end."

Beside me, Jackson morphed into their human form. Today they'd altered their cheekbones, and their hair was a little longer. They still wore the jeans and black t-shirt they'd had on last night. "Since we are not required to be anywhere at the moment, could someone help me learn to use this human form?"

"Uh, I've got the day off today, but what exactly would that entail?" Tucker's tone was more than a little apprehensive.

Jackson's eyebrows scrunched up. "I'm not exactly sure. In my other forms, the rear legs bent in the opposite direction, and all four limbs were used for locomotion. Today is only my second day in this form. I have managed walking and sitting, but I feel unsure of my steps, and I don't know how to grasp things with my hands while also walking."

Tucker's face lit up. "Hand-eye coordination and movin' around. Let me run out to my car. I have just the thing to help."

He went outside right as Shane got a phone call. "It's Pia," he told Jackson. "She's pretty freaked out about us being in danger." Shane's adopted daughter, who he shared with his two partners, had witnessed a vampire attack a few months ago. One of her other fathers had been taken captive before Shane and I, with Jackson's help, had rescued him.

Shane picked up his phone to answer it, but Jackson held up a hand. "You should go home. You're more valuable as a DM and a father than as a fighter."

I nodded. "I agree." Shane could go into combat mode, which Reno couldn't, but I didn't get the impression that Shane had been in many fights. Reno, however, had experience from his time with the police.

Shane gave me and Jackson a thoughtful look as he answered the call, then he walked to the stairs, probably to go to the attic where he'd slept last night.

Tucker came back through the front door carrying a baseball glove, a softball, and a bat. "Come on, Jackson, let's go out to the backyard and play some ball! This'll get your muscles workin' better."

Jackson appeared skeptical, but they stood up and followed Tucker outside. I went over to Nicky. He'd mastered the remote, and he paused his program—some sort of British detective series.

"Would you like to go outside and watch Tucker and Jackson?"

"Sure." He sat forward and whipped the throw blanket off his legs. I was glad to see his magic core was starting to whirl a little faster. He had a long recovery ahead of him, but he'd make it. Physically at least.

I leaned over to pick him up, and he shrank back, his eyes going wide. I straightened again. "Sorry, I didn't mean to startle you."

He put a hand up and closed his eyes briefly. "Not your fault. It was... a bad memory. Um, can you back up a bit?"

I took two steps back from the sofa. Nicky scooted to the edge of the cushion and put his feet on the floor. Then he looked at me and held his arms up. "Okay, try now."

Instead of looming over him this time, I squatted down and lifted him so we remained face-to-face. Nicky nodded and put his arm around my shoulders to hold on. "Thanks. I want to try standing up after lunch."

"Great! Whenever you feel strong enough." I opened the back door. Tucker was showing Jackson how to throw a softball.

Nicky leaned in and sniffed my neck. "I knew you before, didn't I?"

I set him down in the chair I'd sat in last night. It was only a coincidence that I got to sit in the one Reno had used. I rubbed my jaw and sighed. "Yes, but you were very young when we saw each other last. You were only twelve years old when you were taken, and you'd been in Canada during the war. It won't surprise me if you don't remember much."

"I remember my parents were King and Queen. My mother was pregnant, and she'd gone back home to the other place. But I never lived there. I was born on Earth, and I wasn't happy about having to leave." He stretched his arms out as if trying to soak in the sun.

"I don't blame you."

He gave a cynical laugh. It was the most adult he'd sounded since we'd rescued him. "I guess the vamps didn't want to leave either."

I shook my head. "No, the ones who took you had developed a taste for drinking blood directly from Wonders. It isn't allowed in the Elven dimension."

He traced a bite scar on his forearm with one finger. "Did you stay for the same reason?"

My head jerked back, and I sucked in a breath. "No! I stayed to rescue you and stop the *luchd-òl fola*. That's what I've been calling them."

He silently mouthed the words. "I don't know what that means."

Hell, it'd been so long since he'd even heard the Elven language. Understandable that he'd forget it. "Sorry, it means blood drinkers."

"Oh. Makes sense. How many Guards did my father leave behind to help you find me?"

I leaned forward, my elbows on my knees. I forced myself to meet his eyes. "I'm sorry, Nicky, but when they cut your connections, your father assumed you'd been killed. Even when I found evidence to the contrary, he didn't believe me."

"Oh." His voice was low. Across the yard, Jackson threw the ball overhand toward Tucker, but it landed in the grass halfway between them.

I forced a positive tone. "But he let me stay and search for you." I reached out and touched his wrist. He looked at me with those purple Elven eyes. "I'm sorry I couldn't find you sooner."

He shook his head and smiled. "The way they moved around, I'm shocked you found me at all." He sat up and mimicked the throwing motion Jackson was currently practicing. "So, how long until my parents reopen the portal?"

Fuck. I couldn't lie, but... shit. "Your father, um. He was horrified by World War II." I twisted my fingers together. "He told me he wasn't planning to reopen it. Ever." I glanced at him to gauge his reaction. "We're stuck here."

He pressed his lips together, gazing toward Tucker and Jackson. "So I won't get to see my parents again." He blinked rapidly, and one tear escaped. Jerkily he wiped it away. "It seems silly to feel like they abandoned me when they thought I was dead."

"It's not silly." Frankly I agreed with the sentiment. Even after all these years, I was still angry at King Domhnull for not listening to me about his son being alive.

Nicky sniffled, then he spread out his hands. "At the very least they should reopen it to get you back." He studied me. "Would you have rather returned to the other dimension?"

"At the time, yes." I couldn't stop my eyes from looking toward the back door. "But not now. Reno is my mate. He wouldn't be welcome there, so I'm happy to stay here."

Jackson managed to throw the ball far enough that it landed near Tucker. But when he tossed it back, Jackson slapped it away from themself like it would've harmed them.

Tucker cheered. "We need to work on your catchin' game, but you don't have any trouble with your reflexes."

Nicky chuckled. "I need to make Jackson watch a baseball game."

"Do you remember your *dèideag dìon*?"

He raised his eyebrows. "Yeah?"

I tilted my head toward Jackson. "They have almost completed their Becoming."

Nicky gaped. "That's them? I didn't recognize them. They're.... Wow."

I hoped Jackson stayed with Nicky. They'd be good companions and could help each other learn to navigate life on Earth.

A car door slammed in front of the house. I jumped to my feet. "Stay here." I put on extra speed running through the living room, and I was at the front door in a couple of seconds. Another car door shut. They weren't trying to be stealthy at least.

I yanked the front door open, and Cal and Greg were coming up the walkway.

"Hey, Simon!" Cal lifted the cooler in his right hand. "Good to see you. We're here to help find these assholes."

I stood over Lyall's decapitated corpse, exhausted and heartsick. I'd hoped to follow him back to the others, but the opportunity was gone. Eight years of tracking vanished Wonders, and I'd have to start all over again.

"Go on home now. Tell everyone not to walk anywhere alone for a while. There are more of them, but I can't be sure where they are."

The teenage shifter—some sort of deer—nodded fervently and rushed away down the walking path to the nearest village.

I wiped my short sword off on Lyall's shirt, then put it back in its scabbard. I searched his body for anything to tell me where he'd been or was going, but I only gained some money and a decent knife.

His connections would tell the others he was dead. There was a small possibility they'd come to find out what happened, but it was more likely whoever was here would evacuate and move. I'd learned enough to understand they worked in small teams, taking Wonders captive from different areas to avoid creating a detectable pattern.

I drained the body of as much blood as I could, then I left it where it was and climbed the nearest tree to wait. If dawn came and I hadn't seen any sign of the luchd-òl fola, I'd bury the corpse. I'd start my search all over again, visiting the nearest decent-sized town to see if anyone was talking about strangers who'd left suddenly in the night.

One dead, twenty-eight left alive. No sign of Prince Nicol.

No sign of my mate.

I didn't let myself cry.

CHAPTER 7
RENO

I WAS EXHAUSTED, BUT I COULDN'T SLEEP. PROBABLY BECAUSE I was trying to force myself to. Force myself to sleep and force myself to have a vision. Which of course I wouldn't be able to do until I was bonded.

And Simon thought I was his mate. We were compatible for sure, I couldn't deny it. Both because our magic resonated, and because he was sexy as hell. But compatibility didn't mean we had to bond with each other. I didn't even know him. Not to mention I didn't want a mate at all. No way was I bonding with him.

But that thought spiral made me even more tense, which prevented me from sleeping, etc. When I heard car doors slamming out front, I took it as a sign I should get up and go back downstairs.

Seeing Cal was a relief. He was mated, with all the skill enhancements that came with that. *He* could call a vision.

He was handing a cooler to Simon. "Levi had someone from the blood network bring us this for you."

I didn't need our connection to feel Simon's relief. It was in every line of his body. He'd been running low on blood bags, and he'd have had to feed from one of us pretty soon. I shoved away the complicated feelings generated by *that* thought.

"Hey, guys! Thanks for coming." I held out my hand to Cal and then Greg. I'd met Greg in person before, but not Cal. It was strange to realize he'd only been with the campaign for a few months. He'd had such a big impact on all of us.

Greg and Cal entered the house as Shane came downstairs with his duffel bag.

"Hey, good to see you both." He hugged them. "Sorry to bail, but Pia's super upset about me being around the vampires, and since backup is here now...." He spread his arms out.

"Do what you need to do." Greg clapped him on the back. "Where's Ms. Jackson?"

Shane sucked in a breath, and his eyes sparkled. "You have got to see their new form."

Simon pointed toward the back door. "They're out in the yard. Come on. Plus you need to meet Nicky."

"He was one of the captives?" Cal's concern was palpable.

"Yeah. Try not to react too much to his scars, please."

Shane dropped his duffel bag by the front door and followed us. Simon set the cooler on the kitchen island as we passed it, and we all trooped outside.

Tucker and Jackson turned to see the newcomers, and Jackson threw their arms wide. "Cal! And Greg!" They rushed over, not quite running, and circled their arms around Cal's waist, tucking their head against his chest.

Cal's eyes bugged out of his head. "Ms. Jackson?" He gingerly wrapped his arms around them.

They pushed back from him and grinned. "I go by Jackson now." They reached for Greg and hugged him as well. "It's so good to see you!"

"Uh, when did you start using this form?" Cal ran his hand over his head, not taking his eyes off Jackson.

They shrugged. "Yesterday." They pointed. "Tucker's been teaching me hand-eye coordination!"

Tucker introduced himself, then Simon guided Cal and Greg over to the fire pit, where Nicky was sitting in one of the chairs. He looked like he had some energy, and his magical core was a little more vivid.

"Nicky." Simon's voice was reassuring. "These are some friends of mine, Cal and Greg. Cal's a Seer, and Greg is the District Monitor for Central Texas."

"Hi." Nicky ducked his head shyly. Shit, until yesterday the only new people he'd been able to meet were other captives.

"Crap." Cal knelt down in front of Nicky. "They really fucked with your magic core, didn't they?" I let out a little exhale when he didn't comment on the scars.

Simon moved closer, hovering protectively. I felt a flash of emotion—mine this time—I didn't want to identify. "They had to keep him drained of blood as much as possible so he'd be weak. Nicky's not susceptible to vampire mind control."

"No shit?" He stared at Nicky. "Can I ask what kind of...." Cal slowly stood up, raising one hand to cover his mouth. "No way."

Greg echoed him, no doubt getting the information through their bond. "No way."

Cal dropped his hand. "Nicky, does this mean you've been held by those assholes since... since before the portal was closed?" Not waiting for an answer, Cal whirled to face Simon. "Is that why you went after them in the first place?"

"Yes and yes."

"Oh, my god. Shit. I'm...." He sat in the other chair and turned his body to face Nicky. "It's really impressive that you survived. Most people wouldn't have."

Nicky ducked his head again. "They usually left the TV on. I tried to pretend I was a character in one of the shows."

I couldn't imagine.

Cal turned to me. "Simon said you were taking a nap. Any visions?"

I shook my head. "Couldn't sleep."

He made a face. "Too bad. You'd get a lot more nuance out of a vision than I will. But I'm here to try." He slid more firmly into the chair and leaned his head against the seat back.

"Um, here? You don't want to lay down or anything?" I couldn't imagine getting a vision with six people staring at me.

"Nah. We're in the shade. This works." He relaxed, putting his hands on his thighs and closing his eyes. "Okay, I'm trying to see where the escaped vampires will be later today, right?"

"Yes." Simon stood beside me, close enough I could feel the warmth from his body even though it had to be over ninety degrees out here. My dick was interested, but I eased away from him, not wanting to give our magics more opportunity to mingle.

Everyone went silent, and in seconds, Cal's hands clenched into fists and his eyes moved back and forth behind his closed lids. I'd never actually witnessed another Seer having a vision before. There weren't that many of us around, and it wasn't like I needed lessons in how to have them.

I kept time on my watch, and just after the two-minute mark, Cal opened his eyes. "Fuck." He pressed his fingertips to his forehead.

"What do you need?" Greg was at his side, rubbing his shoulder.

Cal clasped Greg's hand in his. I'd never had anyone to hold onto after a scary vision, I thought wistfully. Not that I needed anyone like that; it just would've been nice.

Beside me, Simon was leaning forward, almost balanced on his toes. His jaw was clenched, and I knew he wanted to shout at Cal to tell us what he saw.

I touched his forearm with two fingers. "Give him a minute. It can be disorienting."

He put his weight back on his heels and gave me a nod.

Nicky, however, wasn't willing to wait. "Did you see them?"

"Yes." Cal scowled. "I think it will happen around noon. There weren't significant shadows. The vampires were chasing a rabbit shifter, but she stayed in her human form. They caught her right as she was running out from under some trees onto a grassy area." He closed his eyes and leaned his head against his and Greg's clasped hands. "They bit her neck." He made a face before taking a deep breath. "They took turns draining her dry, then they left her body out in the open and walked away."

"I'm sorry you had to see that." Simon's voice was gentle. "Were there any landmarks?"

Cal lifted his head again and opened his eyes. "Yes. It was a park. There was a path off to one side and a huge tree that looked like it'd been hit by lightning."

Tucker met my eyes. "Roy Miller Park." I nodded. Back when my cousin Daniel had been alive, he'd hosted several District get-togethers there. Tucker squinted at the sky. "The park entrance is about twenty minutes from here, but that tree is another ten-minute walk at a minimum."

Simon shifted restlessly. "We need to leave now."

I scowled. "Not without having a plan."

He swallowed back whatever he wanted to say, but I could feel his tension and frustration through our connection. Now was not the time for me to start feeling his emotions, dammit.

Cal stood up. "I brought my bat'leth, and Greg's got a sword."

I turned my frown on him. "Okay. So we all walk in there with our weapons? We need to find the Wonder, but then what? The vamps will hear us coming."

"I can go ahead in mist form. If I don't see them, I'll turn back to human and I'll be able to smell them." Simon put his hands on his hips.

Tucker rubbed his jaw. "If they don't want to fight, won't they just turn into mist themselves?"

Simon shook his head. "Not if they haven't eaten recently. My guess is last night they stayed in mist form as long as they could. They won't have the energy to change forms today."

Greg pulled out his car keys. "I can drive."

"I need to get some weapons out of my minivan. I'll meet you out front." Simon took off at lightning speed into the house.

I gritted my teeth. We still didn't have a fucking plan. I waved Greg and Cal toward the back door. "Y'all go on ahead. Tucker and I will be right behind you."

"I'll stay here with Nicky and Jackson."

I looked at Shane in surprise. "Are you sure? Didn't you want to get on the road?"

"Not yet. My grandmother is here. I'm sending her with you." He held out a hand toward... nothing. Luckily I was aware Shane could interact with ghosts. "This is Dimi." He made a face. "She'll let me know if things... go badly, and I'll take Nicky and Jackson with me to Houston."

Fuck. "Ah. Okay. Good plan." At least someone was thinking strategically. I faced the space Shane had gestured toward. "Uh, nice to sort of meet you, Dimi. Thanks for helping us out." I regarded Nicky. "Shane, if you don't have anything else to do while you're waiting, could you go online and order Nicky some more clothes and a phone?"

Nicky's worried expression lightened a little. "I get my own phone? I've never even held one."

Shane nodded. "Yeah, definitely. We'll pick one out together."

That'd be a great distraction for Nicky.

I shifted on my feet. I needed to go. "Get him anything he might need. Toiletries and stuff too. Text me the total and I'll Venmo you."

He grinned. "No need. Rory's almost got the fund set up for District Monitor stipends, and expense reimbursement will be part of it. I'll make him use this as a test run for the system."

"Shit, man. Tell him thanks from me." One of Shane's partners had come into a lot of money recently. When he'd learned about the campaign, he'd been horrified that none of the Texas DMs received any sort of compensation for the work, so he was donating the money to rectify the situation.

I headed inside, needing sturdier shoes and my guns. I didn't know how to use a sword, but I had a knife.

After I was dressed suitably and armed, I met Tucker at his car. He'd gotten a Kevlar vest out of the trunk—the one that didn't say "Police" across the back—and he'd stuck it in the rear seat with his baseball bat. His gun was in a hip holster. He might end up shifting, but he always liked to have options.

"I hope we don't run into any NPCs." He opened the driver's side door and slid inside.

"Fuck, a bunch of humans having a kid's birthday party would be the icing on this shit cake. Let's try to come up with some sort of plan by the time we get to the park." I got into the passenger seat and set my backpack between my feet.

He reversed out of the driveway. "I called my mom, but she's watchin' my niece and nephew, so she can't help." He glanced at me. "But before we get to the vampire plan, do you want to talk about findin' your mate?"

I crossed my arms. I knew I was pouting, but, fuck it, I *felt* like pouting. "It's...." I uncrossed my arms so I could throw my hands in the air. "I wasn't *looking* for a mate. I don't *need* a mate. Mates aren't the be-all, end-all people make them out to be. I know my parents thought so, but I'd rather never have a mate than end up with a relationship like theirs. All I want is for a real District Monitor to show up. Then all the Wonders will stop messaging me all the time, and I can get my life back. Maybe one day there'll even be another opening in the department, and I can work with you again."

He threw me a sympathetic grimace, but I knew what he was thinking. When I'd quit, I'd given up any chance of being a police detective again, at least in this town. They'd promote from within before rehiring someone who'd quit for reasons he wouldn't tell them.

I crossed my arms again and stared out the window. "I agreed to be acting DM because the Wonders needed *somebody*, and I was the best choice. But I didn't expect to still be in the role after two freaking years. I didn't expect to have to quit the job I loved because this volunteer position takes so much of my free time. I haven't had a weekend to myself in over a year, Tucker. My kayak is full of dust in the garage. I'm always helping Wonders, talking to Wonders, worrying about Wonders. It's suffocating me." I slapped my hand over my phone in my pocket. "I responded to all of my messages a few days ago. Zero unread on text or Discord. This morning I had almost a hundred new ones to go through."

I crossed my arms yet again. It was comforting. "It'd be better if I had the abilities of an actual DM. I'm constantly stressed I'm missing something important, letting them down, or making the wrong decision." I huffed. "And now on top of everything else, I'm supposed to mate with some guy I met yesterday? I know it makes me sound like some whiny-ass entitled prick, because most people would kill to have their mate show up, but I didn't ask for one. And Simon thinks our connection is permanent, so if I want to have sex again, *ever*, I have to bond with him." I pressed my lips together and tried to swallow against the lump in my throat. "When do I get to choose the path my life will take? When can I do something for me?" I glared at the sign pointing the way to the ocean as we passed it, going in the opposite direction.

Tucker was silent for a moment. "I'm not denyin' you've been forced to make some sacrifices, and you deserve to make all the decisions in your life. But this mate thing just got sprung on you last night." I felt him looking at me, but I didn't turn my head. "Let it sit for a while before you decide for sure you don't want to be mated. Get to know Simon. Give him a chance. He seems like a good guy, and he's definitely not hard on the eyes."

I heaved a huge sigh. "Fine. Can we talk about something else now? Like how we're going to keep from getting killed when we get to the park?"

THESSALONIKI,
GREECE – JUNE, 1961

"Thanks, friend."

The satyr swayed toward me. "We should take this back to my place."

I smiled and wiped my saliva off his neck with my thumb. I made sure he was looking into my eyes. "The street festival is still going strong. You should find a willing partner." My Greek was flawless —the Elves had gifted us Royal Guards with a language spell so we could blend in anywhere. It was one of the most useful skills I had, both in my search and in getting enough blood to stay alive.

A band was playing "Never on Sunday", and we could hear people laughing and talking over the music. His eyes went a little distant. "Mmmm. A big ship docked this afternoon. I'll bet I can talk a pair of sailors into coming back to my apartment."

"Sounds like a great time. Have fun, but get some food first." I pointed him toward the mouth of the alley and gave him a little prod to get him moving.

After he left, I leaned against the nearest wall and rubbed my face. I'd killed two more luchd-òl fola a couple of weeks ago, but the others had left the area and once again I didn't have any clues. I kept thinking there had to be an easier way to find them, but I hadn't run across any more Seers, and I didn't have any other ideas.

I felt movement in my rucksack, so I swung it off my shoulder and hastily opened the bag. The dèideag dìon *hadn't moved or changed shape in months, even though I spoke to them every night before I went to sleep. But at creation they had imprinted on Prince Nicol, and I worried they would revert to nothingness before the Seer's vision of their future came to pass. This movement was a good sign.*

"Hello, little one. Would you like to take a look around?" I cradled the sleeping cat statue in my arms and slung the bag back over my shoulder. It was heavier than usual because of the camera I'd taken from the luchd-òl fola *I'd killed. I'd hoped to find something useful on the film, but none had been loaded. A few days ago I'd bought some more and had been amusing myself taking photos of the Greek shoreline.*

The dèideag dìon *stretched a little, then their runes sparkled.* **Fly time**.

"You want to fly?" Was it time for the Seer's prediction to come true? Would the dèideag dìon *be leaving for America?*

They didn't respond, so after a moment I put them back in the rucksack. This town was too small to find a plane to America. I needed to go to Athens.

It wasn't like I had anything better to do.

CHAPTER 8
SIMON

"We should wait for Reno and Tucker." Cal's tone was cautious, as if he thought I'd throw a fit or something.

I gritted my teeth and opened the door to exit Greg's SUV. "Fine. Unless we see a rabbit shifter or a vampire." Yes, I did want to throw a fit. Or, better yet, run into the park to find Marcas and Roibeart before they could kill anyone else. Waiting on three magic carriers and a cougar shifter would slow me down.

But five of us would be more effective in a fight than just me, so I would give them a few minutes. I could feel Reno getting closer by the second, so they shouldn't be long.

Standing next to the car, I put my arms through the straps of the modified tennis racquet backpack that held my mek'leth. Cal pulled a large rectangular musical instrument case from the back of the SUV. I wrinkled my nose. Once this was all over, I needed to help him find a better way to carry his bat'leth in public. At least the parking lot was mostly empty, so the park shouldn't be too crowded today. But it only took one person getting spooked by Cal's large bladed weapon to call the police. We couldn't afford the delay.

Finally Tucker pulled into the parking spot next to us. He got out and opened the rear door to pull out a Kevlar vest and a baseball bat. He was wearing a baseball cap, and after he put the vest on, he tucked the bat under his arm. Hopefully people wouldn't look too closely at him.

Shane's grandmother—Dimi if I remembered correctly—popped out of Tucker's SUV. She watched Reno get out of the passenger seat, then she thwacked the back of his head with her hand. I started forward, but she didn't do it again. He must've felt something, because he ducked and rubbed his head.

Dimi zipped to a stop next to me. "That boy's going to drive himself crazy before he gets his head out of his behind about your mating."

I managed a smile. "I'm aware. Thanks for coming." I was glad she was here. Not only could she alert Shane if something went wrong, but one of the Hunters could talk to ghosts, so if the coming fight went badly she could let them know as well. Cal had called them, but it would take them at least another thirty minutes to arrive. I was certainly not waiting that long.

I braced myself as Reno, backpack settled over his shoulders, came over. "Did y'all come up with a plan? Tucker and I tossed around a few ideas." He gazed at me with a neutral expression on his handsome face. Our connection still glowed between us, bright as ever. Once Marcas and Roibeart were dead, I could take my time and win Reno over. I didn't blame him for not wanting me as his mate. We'd barely met. Spending time together would solve that issue.

I leaned against the SUV and folded my arms. "We should expect them to be waiting for us." I'd discussed this with Cal and Greg already, but Reno and Tucker needed to know.

"They wouldn't ordinarily leave a dead or mostly drained victim out in the open."

Reno nodded, his expression grim. "They're planning to do it because they expect you to find a Seer."

"Or at least the discovery of the body would be on the news." I shook my head. "I wouldn't be surprised if there isn't already another victim. With as much time as they'd spent in mist form last night, they would've needed to feed before now."

"Shit." Tucker shifted his grip on the baseball bat as if he were imagining using it.

"It's possible they left that victim alive though."

Reno resettled his backpack on his shoulders. "So how do you recommend we approach this?"

I gazed unhappily at the huge park with its thick stands of trees. "We stick together and start walking. They'll make a move eventually, but I'd prefer to see them first. Let me lead any attacks. You try to keep them from getting away, unless they turn to mist. Then I'll go after them."

They all voiced their agreement, and we walked into the park. I'd looked at a map on the way here. There was a main path winding through the entire park with loops that branched off and rejoined it further along.

Trees filled the centers of the loops and lined the edges of the park. Lots and lots of trees. That's where we'd find Marcas and Roibeart. Hiding and waiting.

Tucker cleared his throat. "If there are crowds, we can scan them for someone with a magical core, but just to be on safe side, what was the rabbit shifter wearing?"

"Oh, good point." Cal gave a nervous chuckle. "I forget some-times that other people don't see my visions with me. She was white with long brown hair up in a ponytail. She was wearing bright pink exercise shorts and a white tank top over a black sports bra."

"Fuck, she must not have gotten the word to avoid being alone." Reno's tone held a heavy measure of guilt.

I couldn't stop myself from trying to make it better. "Hey, you don't even know if she's from around here. Maybe she's only in town for a few days."

He made a sort of *hmmph* sound and kept walking. Our connection glowed, even in the sunlight. It'd be even brighter in the shade of the trees.

"Oh, fuck." Everyone stopped and looked at me. I ran my hand over my face. "Reno, our mate connection will make you a target." He went stiff, and I raised a hand. "I can fix it."

His face lit up, and a surge of excitement came through the connection. "You can cut it! Right, I forgot vampires could do that!"

Ouch.

Reno winced as my emotions hit him. "Sorry."

Tucker punched him in the upper arm. "Not cool, man."

I looked away, swallowing as my throat tightened and putting up a block so he couldn't feel my hurt. Now was not the time for this. When I could speak without my voice trem-bling, I turned to him again. "No. Severing a connection this strong would be debilitating for both of us. We wouldn't be able to fight."

He took a step toward me. "Got it. I really am sorry, Simon, I didn't mean to—"

I held up a hand. "Let's focus on the problem. What I'm going to do is sort of like folding over a garden hose. The connection is still there, so you won't feel anything different, but the energy is temporarily prevented from flowing through it. If I do this at both my end and your end, there won't be anything to see between us."

"Holy shit." Cal stared at me. "Can you only do that to your own connections?"

I shook my head. "It's a high-level skill vampires have to study to master, but I can do it to anyone as long as I can see them." I gestured toward the park. "Marcas and Roibeart could only do basic connection manipulation, like severing them, at least when I knew them before." Though Kinnon had been trained to almost the same level as I was, so if he was still in contact with the others he might have taught them.

"Fuck. I'm gonna have a lot of questions for you once this is all over." Cal shifted his bat'leth case to his other hand.

I glanced at Reno, and he nodded. "Go ahead."

I extended my arm to indicate the path we'd been following. "It's already done." I walked ahead, scanning the trees for signs of mist or corporeal vampires.

Thankfully, with energy no longer flowing between me and Reno, we wouldn't be able to sense each other's emotions. I needed to focus on the coming fight, not on the insult Reno had dealt me.

We reached the first offshoot of the path, and I pointed. "They'll be in the trees somewhere, but we won't know if they're on the right or the left." I glared at everyone. "We are *not* splitting up."

Tucker adjusted his grip on the baseball bat again. "The tree

Cal mentioned is more toward the right, so I vote we start there."

"Agreed."

We waited while Cal removed his bat'leth and tucked the case behind a shrub. I loosened my mek'leth but didn't pull it out. If we ran into that rabbit shifter, I didn't want to frighten her more than necessary.

A woman screamed up ahead. We hadn't gotten here soon enough.

"I'm going. The rest of you, stay together!" I didn't wait for acknowledgement; just ran in the direction the scream had come from. My claws were out, and my eyes changed to their battle mode, enhancing my field of vision and depth perception. I went at my top speed, witnesses be damned, but for some reason I felt faster than usual.

No time to dwell on that. Up ahead I could see the huge tree with a twisting scar down its trunk. In front of it, Roibeart had his fangs in the rabbit shifter's neck. Shit. I couldn't knock him away without him tearing her throat out. And where was Marcas?

I drew my mek'leth and came to a stop right next to Roibeart. I put the tip of the blade next to his eye. "Release her." I felt more than saw movement from my right, and I barely turned and got my blade up in time to block Marcas' knife. I didn't even see his gun until the bullet tore into my side.

"Fuck!" I spun away, mek'leth down to guard the wound. Roibeart dropped the woman and ran toward Reno and the others. I hoped they were ready.

Marcas leveled his gun at my head. "I told Kinnon we should kill you before the portal closed. That bastard never listened to good advice."

I tried for a bored expression and affected a casual tone. "Where *is* Kinnon? I expected to run into him before now." Marcas only had one connection, which had to be to Roibeart, so was Kinnon dead?

Marcas snarled, but it wasn't aimed at me. "Ran off after we set up the first safe house. He was all on board with drinking from Wonders, but he couldn't abide us keeping them. Hypocritical fucker." He gave a harsh laugh. "Hell, we thought he was the one killing us off until Saudi Arabia."

I'd pick that apart later. Shouts came from back along the path. Marcas grinned and aimed the gun again. I changed to mist form, and the transformation happened faster than I was expecting, faster than the bullet Marcas shot at me. In that instant I was even able to expel the first bullet, sectioning off only those molecules and sending it to the ground. I'd never had that ability before, never knew it could be done. I'd worry about how I'd gained these new skills later. I was only slightly surprised to find my bullet wound had healed when I reformed to my human shape, chest-to-chest with Marcas.

Before he could react, I stabbed him in the gut and yanked away his gun with my other hand.

"Cal!" Greg's shout came from the path behind us.

Reno yelled, "No guns! If you miss it could hit civilians!"

Time to end this. Marcas staggered back as I lifted the mek'leth to cut off his head, but he misted and moved swiftly toward where Roibeart was fighting the others.

Dammit. I spun around and raced ahead of him, arriving just in time to slam into Roibeart, who had a short sword and a knife and was easily fighting off Greg, Tucker, and Reno. Each of them had cuts here and there. They were arrayed in a line in front of Cal, who was on the ground, lying still.

I slashed at Roibeart's throat as he recovered from my hit, but he ducked and I only got his shoulder. Marcas' mist form hovered nearby, and Roibeart wasted no time misting himself, and they sped away.

"Fuck!" I spun and drove the mek'leth into the soft soil next to the path, both to clean it off and express my frustration. Then I put it back in the case on my back as I jogged over to the others. "Is Cal okay?"

Greg was kneeling next to Cal's head. "He's unconscious, and he's got a nasty head wound. The vampire blocked his bat'leth and drove the handle into his temple."

Fuck, that could've gone so much worse, but I didn't say it. "Let me go get the rabbit shifter and we'll figure out what to do." I let go of the barrier I'd created in Reno's and my connection, but no emotions came through immediately.

I didn't see any civilians on my way back to the girl, which was fortunate. She was alive, but she'd lost quite a bit of blood. I picked her up, hoping no one would notice the bloodstained grass before it rained, and we were back to the others in seconds.

Cal was awake, blinking but appearing aware of himself. His eyes opened wide when he saw me. "Is she okay?"

"She will be." I hoped.

Reno and Tucker were packing Cal's bat'leth into its case. Reno scowled at me. "Are you injured?" He pointed at my side, where my shirt was coated in blood. Damn, I hadn't thought to try cleaning my shirt while I was in mist form. I could do it, I knew.

"Not anymore." I regarded Cal, then I turned to Tucker. "If you'll carry her, I can carry Cal to the car."

"The hell you can! I'll walk." Cal struggled to sit up as Greg tried to keep him prone.

I gave him an exasperated look. "Cal, I promise you, I can." Sure, he was heavier than the average human male, but Tucker could carry him, though for a shorter distance. With my new abilities, however I had gained them, I was pretty sure I'd be able to lift two of him without an issue.

I set the rabbit shifter down while Tucker removed his Kevlar vest and took off his t-shirt. I helped him dress the woman in it, which hid most of the blood covering her neck and chest.

Shane's grandmother popped into view. I couldn't stop my reflexive snarl as I rushed to put myself between Reno and the perceived threat.

She frowned at Cal and the rabbit shifter as I relaxed and grimaced ruefully at the others, who'd all gone tense at my reaction. "Sorry, Dimi's here." I carefully didn't look at Reno as I walked over to Cal.

Dimi waved a hand at him. "Jackson is willing to try to heal both of them, but they're worried they might not be able to due to the restrictions the Elves put on that ability."

I thanked her and relayed what she'd said to the others.

"What restrictions?" Cal winced as I lifted him into a bridal carry.

I was glad of the distraction answering him gave me. Between the fight and Reno's rejection of our mating, I was not interested in being alone with my thoughts. "Jackson is a *dèideag dìon*, which is a sentient being created by powerful Elves when their children are born. The *dèideag dìon* have their own magic for protection and healing, as long as it is for the benefit of a child. They can heal any child, not just the one they were created for, but for them to heal an adult requires the magic to be convinced it's necessary for a child's well-being."

I began walking back the way we'd come. Greg hovered at my side, glancing anxiously at Cal's head every few steps.

"But Jackson healed Nicky, and he's not a child." Reno scanned the park continuously, probably looking for civilians.

"No, and Jackson says they don't remember this, but Nicky is the child for whom Jackson was created."

This caused some murmurs of surprise. Cal touched his fingers to his temple and grimaced. "So when I gave Jackson my magic a few months ago, did it, like, turn them into some sort of super version of, um, whatever you called it?"

I smiled. "No, you helped them get to where they should've been. As the child they are paired with grows, the *dèideag dìon* slowly absorbs enough of the child's magic to go through what we call 'Becoming', which is basically an evolution from a barely cognizant toy into a being capable of complex thought and body shapes. It is considered a sign an Elf is a great leader if their *dèideag dìon* Becomes capable of taking the form of an adult Elf. Or, in this case, an adult human. Jackson's Becoming was inhibited early on. When I found them after Nicky was kidnapped, they were unusually small for their age, and I believe that was caused by their giving Nicky a majority of their magic to try to fight off the vampires. And then of course later they were stuck in one room for decades."

We reached the cars without any humans coming near us. Reno said he'd call Dominic to update him on the fight. I put Cal across the back seats of Greg's SUV, and Tucker put the rabbit shifter in the back of his car. I would have preferred to ride with Reno, but there wasn't room, and he didn't want me near him anyway.

Cal dozed and Greg was silent on the way back to Reno's house. He kept flexing his hands on the steering wheel, and I could tell he was checking on Cal through their bond every few minutes. Cal's magic looked strong, and he was already healing. He probably wouldn't need Jackson's help, but he'd have to take it easy for a few days. The rabbit shifter wasn't bonded, so she wasn't as resilient.

When we arrived, Cal was able to stand to get out of the car, and he let Greg help him into the house. "I just want to lie down for a little while, and then I want to go home." Greg nodded and kissed him on the forehead. I offered Cal the guest bedroom, and Greg went with him.

Tucker carried the rabbit shifter into the living room and set her down on the couch. Reno waved a cell phone at me as he went toward the backyard to get Jackson. "Her name's Meg. I found this in her pocket, and I was able to get hold of her emergency contact, which is her roommate. They're in town from Colorado for some conference. The roommate's on her way over."

Great. If Jackson could heal her, Meg would be well enough to leave with her roommate. We had enough on our hands looking after Nicky.

Jackson and Shane came inside. Jackson hurried over to Meg, and Shane gestured toward the backyard. "Nicky doesn't want to see another vampire bite." I suppressed a wince, hoping he never had to see me feed.

Jackson perched on the couch cushion next to Meg's head. They frowned. "She needs healing, but my magic won't let me do it."

Reno sat down on the ottoman he had instead of a coffee table. It looked like it might be hollow inside, and I imagined sitting next to Reno on the couch, pulling my knitting out of the ottoman while he watched TV or played a video game. One day.

Reno leaned forward with his elbows on his knees. He still had smears of blood on his arms, but the cuts from the fight with Roibeart were healed. "Jackson, Nicky can't bear to see another vampire bite. He won't be able to come inside until Meg here is healed."

I smiled. My mate was so smart. Then my smile died and I sighed. I wished he was my mate.

Jackson gazed at Meg as they considered this, but they shook their head. "Not enough."

Reno held up Meg's cell phone. "I don't know their relationship, but Meg lives with a very young girl."

Jackson cocked their head. "How young?"

Reno shrugged. "I couldn't tell you exactly, but *very* young. *Very.*" His voice rang with conviction.

Jackson smiled and used one finger to scoop some glittering goo out of their knee. Shane went back outside, and I headed for the kitchen to wash my hands and find some snacks for Jackson to replenish their energy. Everyone else would probably want to eat as well. I needed blood, but I didn't have the same urgent hunger I usually did after misting.

I put together a tray of cheese, fruit, and crackers and gave it to Reno, who had been looking at his phone while he and Jackson waited for Meg to wake up. I took another plate of the same snacks outside, though I doubted Nicky would be very hungry after I told him Marcas and Roibeart were still alive.

ATHENS, GREECE
– JUNE, 1961

Once I was close to the airport, I pulled the dèideag dìon out to see if they had any instructions, but they gave me nothing.

The Seer had mentioned a bar, and it seemed likely that people flying to America would have drinks at their hotel. I drove toward the airport until I saw a couple of Wonders standing in front of a small hotel. Perfect.

After I parked, I pulled the dèideag dìon out again. "Is this the right place?"

They did not respond.

Sighing, I put them back in the rucksack. I was about to get out of the car, but I hesitated. I'd been sleeping rough for several days now, and I looked it. I hadn't bothered shaving, and my shirt was dirty and stained. But the luchd-òl fola I'd killed two weeks ago had been carrying fat wallets. Might as well get a room and take a bath. Maybe the hotel offered laundry service.

I stuffed as many of my clothes as I could into a carryall, then I strode into the lobby, booked a room, and arranged for my things to be laundered as if I did it all the time. The clerk even pointed me at a barber shop across the street. I tipped him well, so hopefully I merely came across as eccentric.

Three more Wonders were sitting in the lobby, and we exchanged nods as I walked to the lift. Most Wonders and magic carriers assumed I was a type of Wonder they'd never encountered before. Which, once I thought about it, was true. Those of us non-Elves who worked around the palace tended to think of ourselves as separate from the Wonders, but we really weren't. I wasn't an Elf, and I wasn't a magic carrier. I was a Wonder.

They were my people now.

Putting on my cleanest clothes, I left the rest stacked on the bed as instructed, ready to be laundered. I took my rucksack with me to the barber, and the dèideag dìon didn't make any movements. Hair trimmed and beard shaved off, I felt more like someone who could talk a stranger into taking an Elven-created being across the ocean with them.

The bar wasn't too crowded, so I took a seat on a stool where I could see the entire place at a glance. No fox shifters were here yet, but it was still early.

I nursed two Sidecars before the bartender, who'd been impressed with my mastery of the Greek language, encouraged me to order some food. The kleftiko *was delicious, and I was scraping the last of the sauce off the plate when someone appeared at my elbow.*

"Man, you can get food here? Seems like you enjoyed it. What was it?"

I looked up, feeling an odd combination of certainty, dread, and anticipation when I locked eyes with a fox shifter. He appeared to be around thirty years old, but he was probably a lot older. He had tousled reddish hair and a roguish grin.

I smiled politely. "I had the kleftiko. *Lamb marinated in garlic and lemon with potatoes." I tilted my head toward the bartender. "He can set you up."*

The bartender, used to tourists, spoke enough English to take the man's food and drink order, so I didn't need to translate. I'd put my rucksack on the floor between my feet, and I nudged it to see if the dèideag dìon was moving, but I didn't feel anything.

The fox shifter leaned on the bar and eyed me up and down. He glanced at the bartender, who was helping a customer several stools away, before turning back to me. "I'm Jimmy."

"Simon."

"Nice to meet you, Simon. Sorry for staring, but your magic looks familiar, though I can't place it."

I twisted to face him more fully. Could he have seen some of the luchd-òl fola? Might as well find out what the truth got me. "Vampire."

He froze, his drink halfway to his mouth. Then he narrowed his eyes. "I thought all of you went... away when the portal closed." This last was said in a whisper.

I blinked. "Most people don't know about us. Only the Earth myths."

He grinned. "I'm a pilot. I flew some Elves back and forth across the Atlantic during the war."

"Interesting. You weren't conscripted to the U.S. Air Force?"

After another quick look around, he held out his hand and began a partial shift. His fingers fused together, but he was able to stop the transformation there. "Sadly I was born with a congenital issue that didn't allow me to serve."

I raised my glass. "Smart."

He sipped his own. "I'm not a joiner, but I did do my part. Which is how the Elves found me. I was transporting some Jewish kids out of France, and they were trying to do the same thing. I met a couple of *vampires on one of my flights. They were talking about going home. Didn't you want to go back too?"*

Time to try some honesty again. "*Right before the portal closed we discovered some Wonders were being kidnapped. I stayed behind to track down the people responsible."*

His eyes went wide. "*Did you find them?"*

The bartender put the guy's dinner down on the bar, so I waited until he left to reply. "*Some of them. I'm still chasing the rest. Have you heard of any Wonders going missing recently?"*

He frowned down at his food, then he pointed his fork at me. "*I was about to say no, but I was just in Patras, and a banshee was complaining that her no-good son had run off."* He shrugged. "*Might be something, might be nothing."*

I nodded. "*I don't have any other leads right now, so it's worth checking out. Thanks."* I sipped my Sidecar and gave him a few minutes to eat in peace. When he slowed down and started picking at his food, I began the conversation I'd come here for. "*What are you doing now that the war's over?"*

He lifted one shoulder. "*Moved on to transporting packages, products for companies and such. All on the up and up of course."* He winked.

I smirked. "*Of course. Are you in Athens long?"*

The bartender came by to refresh our drinks and we thanked him.

The fox shifter clinked his glass with mine. "*To successful journeys."*

"*To successful journeys."*

He sipped and then put his glass down. "*I'm headed home in the morning. New York City."*

"No kidding? I haven't been there yet." The King had kept to Scotland for the most part, which as the head of his Royal Guard, I appreciated. But it meant I hadn't been able to see much of Earth. Until the portal closed, of course. I rubbed my finger along the bar top. "Like I said, I've never been to New York, but I wonder if I could engage your services to take a... friend back with you."

He leaned one elbow on the bar. "It's not cheap."

"I have twenty British pounds."

He smiled. "I'm listening. Tell me about your friend."

I picked up my rucksack and opened it. After giving my own glance around the room, I pulled out the dèideag dìon.

The fox shifter's eyebrows went up. "Not a very talkative friend."

I ran my fingers over the runes on the dèideag dìon's back, and they sparkled.

"Shit!" He looked around, but no one was paying attention.

I put them back in the bag. "They're sentient. The Elves created them. They can take different forms, and if you know Elvish, they can communicate through the runes."

His eyebrows drew together. "You're sending them to someone in New York?"

I shook my head. "They asked to go. No specific destination yet."

He sat back in his chair, running his hand over his stubbled jaw. "Okay, so say I take them with me. Then what?"

I smiled. "Well, they might stay with you, in which case you'll have acquired a hell of a protector for your family. They love children. Or they'll make it known to you that they need to be given over to someone else." I spread my hands out. "It's up to them."

He eyed my rucksack before meeting my gaze, one eyebrow raised in challenge. "What if I sell them?"

I shrugged. "They have some foresight skills. They asked to be brought here and to fly away. Whatever you do with them, they'll already know it'll happen."

He cursed under his breath and leaned back on his stool. After taking a hefty swallow of his drink, he turned back to me and nodded. "I don't have a family of my own yet, but I like the sound of a protector for my loved ones. You've got a deal."

"Thank you." I was relieved the dèideag dìon would be on the path they were meant to take, but I dreaded losing the only companion I'd had for the last fifteen years. I'd have to remember to take a photo of them before they left.

Jimmy gave me another up and down look, but this one was much flirtier. "The vampires I met during the war, they told me if I let them feed from me, it would be... pleasurable."

I gave him a once-over back. "It can be."

He drained his drink. "Prove it."

CHAPTER 9
RENO

TUCKER LEFT TO GO HOME AND GET CLEANED UP. I PROMISED I'D call him if we had any developments. Meg woke up a few minutes later, gasping and shrinking away from me and Jackson.

"Hey, it's okay. You're safe."

She clapped a hand to her now-healed neck, pulling it away again to inspect it, probably for blood.

"You're healed. You lost a lot of blood, though, so you'll want to eat as much as you can and drink a lot of water."

Jackson held out a bottle of water and a piece of cheese. She looked between us frantically. "Who *are* you?" She scooted around so she was sitting upright on the cushions.

I could've slapped myself. "Yeah, sorry. I'm Reno Torres. I'm the acting District Monitor for South Texas." She relaxed slightly. "This is Jackson." They held out the water and cheese again, and she hesitantly took both. "Oh, and your room-mate's on her way over here. I found her number in your phone." I picked it up off the ottoman next to me and offered it to her. Except she didn't have any free hands, so I set it on the couch cushion by her hip.

I explained about the vampires as she ate the cheese and drank the water. "Stay around other people while you're in town, and you'll be fine."

"Um, I think I'll be going home tomorrow. Maybe tonight." She touched her neck.

Jackson looked up, and we heard a car door slam outside. Thank fuck, the roommate was here.

Fortunately Jackson didn't seem disturbed that the roommate was in her mid-twenties, instead of being a small child as I'd been heavily implying to them earlier. In my defense, she did have a pretty high-pitched voice, and compared to me—hell, more compared to Jackson, Nicky, and Simon—she was a baby.

The two women were gone within five minutes, both of them making plans to leave town as soon as they could.

I went back into the living room to relax on the couch for a minute. I wanted to take a shower, but it seemed like too much effort right then. Jackson had moved to the corner of the sectional and was staring toward the back door.

I was debating whether pushing the button to activate the recliner and make the footrest pop up would be a bad idea or not when Greg came out of the guest bedroom.

"Hey, how's Cal?"

"Better. He doesn't have a concussion anymore." He glanced around. "Is Meg gone?"

"Yeah. Her roommate picked her up. She's pretty freaked out."

"I bet." He dropped down onto the ottoman where I'd been sitting earlier, then he gazed at me with a solemn expression.

"I'm taking Cal home. He and I—we're not fighters. I can't risk him again."

I sat up so I could reach out and grasp his shoulder. "I understand. I'm sure he feels the same way about you."

I sat back and he rolled his eyes with a grin. "There may have been some swearing." He ran his hand through his hair. "Cal said tomorrow after he's rested up he'll try to call a vision every couple of hours. He thinks he'll be able to reach this distance because he's directly interacted with the vampires."

I raised my eyebrows. Cal's bonding with Greg meant his Seer abilities were much stronger than mine, but he was talking about over two hundred miles. "Has he had a vision that far away before?"

Greg shook his head. "No, but Delphia and Edgar are out of the country, so he's all we've got unless you have a spontaneous vision."

"Out of the country?" Delphia was Greg's mother, and Edgar was his great uncle. They were the only other Seers in Texas besides me and Cal, and both worked at TWIST, a Wonder rescue organization outside of San Antonio.

He nodded. "Now that they hired someone to manage TWIST, Mom's doing all the fun stuff she missed out on all those years she was running the show. She booked a river cruise in Europe, and Uncle Edgar and Aunt Bettina decided to go with her."

"Good for them."

He leaned forward. "If it turns out Cal can't call visions for you, we'll find out how long it would take Mom and Edgar to come home."

I made a face. "I hate to ask that of them. Let's see what Cal can do when he feels up to it. We'll talk more tomorrow.

Maybe we'll get a clue or something by then. Hell, I'm a fucking private investigator. You'd think I could find a couple of measly vampires."

He snorted. "Find a couple of measly vampires who can turn into fog and fly away? I don't think any detective is that good."

I rubbed my face. "Either way, let's talk tomorrow and see where things stand, okay?"

"Okay." He stood up and turned to Jackson. "Do you and Nicky want to come to Bent Oak with me and Cal?"

They shook their head. "No. We are needed here."

Shane came in from the backyard. "Hey, I talked to the Hunters." He waved his phone in the air. "To no one's surprise, when they finally showed up at the park, they didn't find any evidence of where the vampires had gone."

I refrained from sighing, but Greg was right. Finding the vampires was almost impossible right now.

"Dominic did say they're assigning some Hunters here to stay outside the house around the clock."

I ran my hands over my face but nodded. It made sense. We hadn't even looked to see if we'd been followed by suspicious clouds of fog when we'd left the park, and it was well within the distance Simon had told us the vampires could travel in their mist form.

"Good. I feel better about us abandoning you." Greg crossed his arms over his chest.

I kicked him in the shin. "Don't be a dumbass. You need to get Cal and yourself out of harm's way." I pointed at Shane. "Same goes for you. Don't feel guilty about leaving. Pia is your priority."

He sighed. "Yeah, that's easy to say, but...." He shrugged. "I still feel guilty. I asked Nicky if he wanted to come to Houston with me, and he said no."

"He must stay here." Jackson picked up the last cracker off the tray Simon had made and put it in their mouth.

The back door opened, and Simon carried Nicky inside right as Cal came out of the guest room. We all said our goodbyes, and then it was only me, Simon, Jackson, and Nicky.

"Okay, I have to go take a shower. Anyone need anything right now?" They all shook their heads, so I retreated to my room for some desperately needed alone time.

Fuck, today had been a lot. Simon wanting me to be his mate, Nicky, the fight, Cal getting injured, Meg almost being killed. And now our best hope of finding the vampires was Cal calling a vision from beyond any Seer's range.

Unless by some miracle I had a vision in my sleep. I'd never had one manifest while I was awake.

I let the hot water beat down on my neck and back, loosening the tight muscles. My brain helpfully supplied an image of Simon standing behind me, also naked and rubbing my back. I fought down an erection, because I wasn't sure my attempts at blocking our connection were working. I didn't want him to find out I was attracted to him and then get his hopes up that I might give him a chance.

I wished there was a way for Simon and me to have sex without any strings, because I'd been having a long dry spell. Between the Wonders demanding my attention at all hours and my PI jobs, I didn't have a lot of free time to find a hookup. And when I did make an effort to look on an app, the whole process seemed too time-consuming, and I ended up just jerking off.

But Simon wanted a mate. Hell, if he wasn't already connected to me, he wouldn't have any trouble finding someone else. Someone who wanted to settle down and had time to devote to a partner.

A partner. Wouldn't that be nice? Too bad what I needed a partner for wasn't even close to what Simon had to be picturing. I needed what amounted to a business partner. Someone to share the load of the District Monitor duties. Someone to help me attract clients for my PI business and split the late hours.

It was a pipe dream. The best I could hope for would be that one day a new DM would show up and resonate with this District. Then I'd only have the one job, and at least my late-night stakeouts wouldn't be constantly interrupted with texts and Discord messages.

I continued my pity party of one as I dried off and got dressed, but I put on a pleasant smile when I returned to the living room.

Nicky and Jackson were watching an episode of *Doctor Who*, and Simon was coming through the front door carrying a plastic tub and a duffel bag.

"Hey, do you need help?"

"No, thanks." He nudged the door closed with his hip. He'd changed clothes, and his hair was up in a bun. It was unfairly attractive. "But, FYI, there are two Hunters outside. They're going to be here in shifts in case the *luchd-òl fola* find us."

"Yeah, Greg warned me." I briefly considered following Dominic's request for us to relocate to a hotel, but the thought of those vampires in a building full of NPCs was horrifying.

I got Nicky and Jackson more snacks—caramel popcorn, pretzels, and chips this time. Both of them could use the empty calories. Nicky was acting more than a little withdrawn, but he did nibble on the food when I handed it to him. In addition to being tired, he was probably worried about the escaped vampires. All of us were, but it was a lot more personal and triggering for him.

I needed to write up a report to my client, but doing it in my study seemed antisocial, so I set up my laptop on the kitchen table and began to make notes and go through all the photos I'd taken the night before last. My phone buzzed occasionally, but I ignored it. They all knew to call if it was an emergency.

"May I sit here?" Simon stood at the other end of the table holding the plastic tub he'd brought in from his minivan.

"Sure, of course." Though, to Simon, I could understand why he wouldn't believe there was any *of course* about sitting near me. Shit, I needed to make an effort to be friendlier to him.

He got a glass of water from the kitchen then sat down and opened the tub, pulling out a heavy knitted blanket. The cream-colored yarn appeared soft and cozy. He reached in again and produced a pair of knitting needles.

"You *knit*?" I couldn't keep the incredulity from my tone.

He looked up, his cheeks darkening a bit. Fuck, I'd embarrassed him.

I waved a hand as if to erase what I'd said. "Not that I think there's anything wrong with knitting. It's just... unexpected."

He made a complicated series of expressions I had no hope of deciphering. "I live out of my van most of the time. I get bored."

I'd put my foot in it again. "Understandable." I cleared my throat. "Look, Simon, I wanted to apologize for earlier. I—"

He held a hand up. I was grateful he wasn't pointing his knitting needle at me. "I don't want to talk about any of that tonight. I'm too tired. We can talk if you like, but I'm not discussing our connection or our mating. Okay?"

I grimaced. I wanted to apologize, but this wasn't about me, and I wasn't a big enough asshole to push it when he'd asked me not to. "Okay."

He gave an almost inaudible sigh. "I searched the two laptops we found in the house, and they didn't contain anything useful. Mostly games and movies."

"Got it. Thanks for going through them."

I tabbed through more photos and made notes for my report based on the time stamps. After a few minutes, I couldn't stand the silence between us anymore. I checked the living room to make sure Nicky was occupied with the TV. Jackson had taken their panther form and had their head in Nicky's lap. I cleared my throat. "Can I ask how you tracked down the vampires, um, before? I know you found them here because of the tracking device, but how did you do it when you didn't even have the internet?"

He glanced over at the living room as well before answering. "I found Wonders and magic carriers wherever I could and asked if anyone had gone missing recently. It took years to find them, and then if I killed one of them, the rest would run, and I'd have to start the process all over again."

I sat there with my mouth open, staring at him. "Since World War II? You've been traveling solo, chasing those vampires, this whole time?" And I'd been whining all day about how my two years as acting DM had been so awful. I was a fucking tool.

He nodded, looking down at his knitting. Then he made an odd little shrug. "I did stop for a few months in 1992. A friend helped me learn to use computers and do some hacking." He lifted the blanket. "He's also the one who taught me to knit."

A few months? He'd only stayed in one place for a few *months*? Once? My throat tightened. "Um, he sounds like a good friend." Was that jealousy in my voice? Fuck me. I glared down at my laptop screen.

"He was." He put one of his knitting needles down in his lap and touched the silver pendant he wore around his neck. I'd noticed it earlier, but I hadn't been able to make out what it was.

"He, uh, passed away?"

"Yes." Simon picked up his knitting again.

"I'm sorry to hear that." I went back to my report, feeling like the worst asshole who'd ever lived.

After a few more minutes, Simon put his knitting aside and stood up. He went into the garage and came out with a blood bag. Right, Cal had brought a cooler for him this morning. He held up the bag. "Will it bother you if I drink this in front of you?"

I scowled. "Of course not. You need to eat." I sat up straight. "Wait a minute. Why did you put the blood in the garage fridge? I told you to use the one in the kitchen. There's plenty of room."

He paused in the middle of unplugging the toaster. "Most non-vampires don't want to see bags of blood next to their orange juice."

I stood up, feeling irrationally angry. "You're a guest in this house. In *my* house. Your needs are just as important as anyone else's, and fuck them if it makes them uncomfortable." I threw down my reading glasses and stomped past the kitchen and into the garage. Inside the new refrigerator were neat rows of bags filled with blood, each dated and signed with a name. A couple of them had little messages, like "Enjoy!" or "Hi, Simon!" My chest felt warm, and my eyes prickled.

Blinking rapidly, I filled my arms with the bags and took them into the kitchen.

Simon did a double-take. "What are you doing?"

"Putting these where they belong. Open the fridge, will you?"

He raised his eyebrows but obediently opened the refrigerator door. I put his blood bags on the second shelf, right next to the cans of soda. "There." I nodded in satisfaction and went back to the table.

"Um, thanks?" Simon gently shut the fridge, then he went back to the counter where he'd plugged in an odd-looking white appliance.

"What's that?"

"Oh, it's a bottle warmer."

I could not have heard him correctly. But yes, Simon poured the blood from the bag into a fucking baby bottle. It had a cap instead of a nipple, but the shape was the same. He put the bottle in the warmer and pressed a button to start the machine.

"Uh, you can't just microwave it?"

"No. Microwaving doesn't heat the blood evenly enough, so you can get clotting or the blood cells can burst."

I made a face. "Got it. The bottle warmer is a great solution."

"Thanks. It was easy to use when I had to live in my van." He turned the warmer off and poured the blood from the bottle into a coffee mug.

I worked on my report, pretending not to be hyperaware of him as he rinsed out the bottle and then sat down at the table with his mug. Soon the clicking of his knitting needles started up again.

I cleared my throat. "Um, what hobbies did you have back in the Elven dimension?"

He blinked then smiled wryly. "Mostly training with the other Guards. Fighting, running, climbing, that sort of thing. None of us had much time for leisure activities like this."

"Hah. I know what that's like these days. Did you have to leave any family or, uh, loved ones behind?"

He stopped knitting and looked at me. "My parents, their siblings, and a few cousins. I sent letters back with the king." He frowned down at his blanket. "Two of my cousins are in the Royal Guard, and I worry for their safety. The *luchd-òl fola* who stayed on Earth could not have been the only ones."

"The... what you said, those are the rogue vampires?"

"Yes. It's what I call them at least. It means *blood drinkers*. The king's Royal Guards are entirely made up of vampires, as we have the best fighting skills of any of the species. I did not know until Nicky was kidnapped that some had developed a taste for blood from the source." He lifted his head, and his eyes were dark and sad. "I never expected any of the Royal Guard would betray us. I was complacent."

I cocked my head. "Why do you sound like it was your responsibility?"

His lips twisted into an awful smile. "I was the captain of the Royal Guards."

"Oh." Oh, fuck. No wonder he'd felt he had to stay to rescue Nicky. "I'm sorry. That must've been very difficult to find out. That you'd been betrayed like that I mean."

"Thank you. What of your family? You said your cousin passed away. Do you have anyone else besides your aunt?"

"No, not anymore. My parents are both gone, and Daniel was my only cousin. It's just Tia and me." I snorted. "Well, and Tucker and Shirley. Tucker and I met in kindergarten. We were the only kids in the school who were part of the campaign, so we bonded pretty quickly. I spent almost as much time at Shirley and Tucker's house growing up as I did at my own."

He smiled. "They seem like good people. I'm glad you have them in your life." He looked down at his knitting. "Do you have any hobbies?"

"Mostly video games for indoor activities, but my favorite thing is to go kayaking." I was about to complain about how long it had been since I'd been able to go, but I kept my mouth shut. My problems were incredibly trivial compared to what Simon had gone through. Not to mention what Nicky had endured.

Simon's eyes were bright with interest. "I've never been kayaking. What do you like about it?"

It took me a moment to respond. No one had ever asked me that before. "Uh, I like to go out on the bay where there aren't many waves. It's quiet. It's a great way to be alone in nature without disturbing anything. I see birds and fish and dolphins all the time."

He smiled. "It sounds peaceful."

"Exactly." And that's when my mouth decided to keep talking. "You know, we should take Nicky when he's got his strength up a bit. I bet he'd like it, and if his arms got too tired to paddle, we could just tie his kayak to mine." Fuck, fuck, fuck. Making plans with Simon was a stupendously bad idea. What the fuck was my brain doing?

Simon's smile stretched across his entire face. "I think Nicky and I would both enjoy that very much."

"Okay." My face was burning with how red it was.

We went back to our respective tasks, but at least the tension between us had cleared. I snuck glances at Simon every few minutes. I had no reason to study him, but it was harder *not* to look. His auburn hair, even though it was caught up in the bun, gleamed in the light from the overhead fixture, and I had a strong urge to touch it to see how soft it was.

I jerked my eyes back to the laptop. I would've liked to have blamed that little fantasy on the mating connection, but that pull hadn't come from my magical core. It'd come from my dick. Or at least that's what I was going with. No emotions involved. At all. Nothing to do with my learning about Simon's heroic decision to stay on Earth and his decades-long journey to find Nicky. Or finding out what a fucking nice guy he was. Shit, if we'd met under any other circumstances, I'd have been desperate to get him to notice me.

Determinedly, I got back to work. I still had bills to pay after all. When I finished the written part of my report, I went through my stakeout photos again to decide which to send to my client. I was tabbing through them, trying to find the one where my client's wife entered her lover's apartment building, when my eye caught on something.

"What the fuck?" I clicked on one of the photos. I'd been across the street, taking pictures of all the windows on the second floor to figure out which one was the lover's bedroom. The duo had solved that mystery for me by turning on the bedside lamp, but this shot was taken a few seconds earlier. It showed the next-door neighbor's bedroom window, lights on and blinds open to the room inside.

The soothing sound of clicking needles stopped. "What's the matter?"

"I...." I squinted at the photo. "I'm not sure anything's the *matter*, but it's weird."

I spun my laptop around and pushed it toward him. Instead of leaning over the table, he set his knitting in the plastic tub and stood up, coming around to stand next to my chair. The faint odor of blood mixed oddly pleasantly with the honeysuckle scent of the body wash I kept in the guest bathroom.

I repositioned the laptop so he could see the screen. "I was on a stakeout the other night. Cheating spouse, nothing unusual. This is the next-door neighbor of her lover." I tapped the window in question.

He leaned over. "What's that? A costume?" The silver pendant swung away from his chest. It was a jaguar head with green gemstone eyes. I forced my gaze back to the screen.

The costume was either fabric or leather. A body and a detached head were hanging separately on the closet door.

I zoomed in as much as I could without losing the resolution. Simon leaned closer. "That's a remarkably good likeness of a gargoyle."

Grimly, I touched the screen, pointing at the green markings on the head and shoulders. "This coloring is only found in post-adolescent gargoyles, those who are around twenty to thirty years old."

Simon sank into the chair next to mine. "Do you have any gargoyles in this District?"

"A family of three. The daughter is in her twenties." We both stared at the screen. "I can't think of a benign reason for someone to have a costume this detailed and accurate."

"You're thinking about the Wonder trafficking."

"Yep. Have someone stand in a shadow wearing this, and she might go investigate? Or any Wonder would, really." I ran my hands through my hair and blew out a breath. "I don't want to alarm anyone unnecessarily, especially with everything else going on. I'll find out who lives in that apartment and make a plan from there."

"A reminder not to go anywhere alone wouldn't be a bad idea."

I nodded and clicked on my web browser to bring up Discord. I winced at all the unread posts in both the District server and my private messages. "I'll deal with these later." I didn't bother scrolling through them. I posted asking everybody to remember to always have someone with them when in public, and I promised to read all their messages and get back to them as soon as I could.

It was a relief to close the browser.

"That was a lot of messages. They've been texting your phone as well?"

I groaned. "Yeah. I responded to most of the texts earlier, but I haven't touched Discord for a day or so." I sighed. "It's not their fault. Having a connection to a DM, who has DM abilities and can tell when they're in trouble, is a lot more reassuring than having me as merely a kind of point of contact for relaying any important information."

Simon studied me. "You're holding yourself to the same standards as someone who was born with the magic to do the job?"

I rubbed my forehead and peered at him from underneath my hand. "No. Well, not intellectually. But my gut doesn't like letting them down. And now this." I sat up and waved at the laptop. "How the hell can I figure this out when we have two vampires running around putting all the Wonders in danger?"

Simon looked at me like I was missing something obvious.

"What?"

"You don't have to do everything yourself. I'm here. I can hack into most systems. If we need to go somewhere in person, we can either leave Nicky and Jackson with the Hunters or we can take them with us." He put his hand on my arm and our magics danced together in happiness. "Reno, you're not alone."

Oh, shit. I could *not* get a crush on Simon.

FIVE MILES OUTSIDE ZALIM, SAUDI ARABIA – MAY, 1964

I braked sharply, unable to believe my luck. In town, the locals had exclaimed over how I'd just missed two men who'd "looked like me", and I'd raced to catch up to them. A car was stopped on the side of the road, both doors open. Several yards into the desert, an abandoned pack, walking stick, and a trail of clothes told me they'd spotted a shifter and had given chase.

I put the car in Park, then grabbed my knife and gun and jumped out. The trail was easy to follow. The shifter had been making for some rock formations up ahead, and the luchd-òl fola *following them weren't being quiet about it.*

"Here, puppy!" They made laughing noises. "We're not going to hurt you. We only want to talk to you!"

Yeah, no one ever believed that.

Not wanting them to hear my footsteps, I misted to the top of the tallest rock and reformed, crouching down to peer over the side.

Ruari and Murdo were trying to capture a hyena shifter who'd backed into a divot between two rocks. Ruari, the one who'd been taunting them, darted forward, causing the shifter to lunge and swipe with their claws. He danced back, staying to the shifter's right side. Murdo stood off to the left, hiding behind the rocks. The shifter would either tire itself out defending against Ruari, or they would bolt for what appeared to be an opening to the left, and Murdo would take them down.

Ruari made the weird laughing sounds again, and I realized he'd been trying to mimic a hyena. Badly. I aimed my gun at his head and fired. He dropped. The shifter backed further into the crevice, and Murdo flattened himself against the side of the rock.

I jumped to the ground, firing immediately at Murdo when he looked around the corner.

"Sìomon? What the hell are you doing here?"

I didn't answer, misting over the rock and reforming in the air above him. His instincts had him ducking away, and the knife I'd been aiming at the back of his neck as I fell hit his hip instead.

He collapsed beneath me but then misted before I could stab him anywhere else. Cursing, I got to my feet as he flew toward the car. If I chased him, there was no guarantee I'd catch him, and Ruari might wake up before I could return here.

"Fuck!" But better one died than neither.

I trudged around the rock, startling when I came face-to-face with the hyena shifter, who I'd stupidly forgotten about in my eagerness to kill Murdo. They were bigger than they'd seemed from above, with impressive claws and teeth. Their growl echoed against the rocks.

"Hey, I'm not here for you. You're free to leave." I forced down my battle mode, causing my claws to retract and my eyes to return to their normal color. Holding my hands out to the side, I leaned down and carefully placed my knife and gun on the ground. Then I backed up against the rock and gestured at them to return the way they'd come. "Go on now. Maybe stay around people for the next few days, though. I don't know where the rest of them are."

They edged past me, watching me warily, and with one last contemptuous lip curl they ran for their belongings and the road.

Sighing, I picked up my knife and gun and went to make sure Ruari never woke up.

CHAPTER 10
SIMON

"YOU DON'T HAVE TO HELP ME." HE GLANCED DOWN AT MY hand on his arm, so I let go and went back to my chair at the other end of the table.

I held in my exasperated sigh. *Prickly* didn't even begin to describe my mate. And then he went and did things like move my blood to the kitchen refrigerator while ranting about how I was an equal member of the household. Good thing I could handle a challenge, because the more time I spent with him, the more I wanted him, mate bond or not. "I can't search for Marcas and Roibeart until we get a clue to their location. And I don't want any Wonders trafficked, so if I can help, I will."

He looked like he might object again, but he focused back on the laptop instead. "Okay, thanks. I'm going to finish my report so I can get it off my to-do list. Do you... you said you can hack?" He blinked at me over the top of his reading glasses, which was cuter than it probably should have been.

I smiled. "I can. And I'm pretty good at research. Would you like me to find out the name of the person who lives in the apartment?"

"Yeah, that'd be really helpful." He picked up his phone and texted me the address before he started typing again. I had been assigned my task and dismissed.

It wasn't a rule that your mate would be as excited about you as you were about them, I reminded myself for the thousandth time since last night. I was trying to avoid remembering how elated Reno had been at the park when he thought I could sever our mating connection, but the memory bled through every so often.

I put my knitting in its storage box and carried it into the guest bedroom, where I retrieved my laptop and brought it back to the kitchen table. We worked together for several minutes, and then I heard, under the sound of the television, Nicky saying something to Jackson in an insistent tone of voice. I turned around, and he was on his feet and walking, sort of. He was facing away from us, leaning half his weight on the back of the sectional sofa, and mostly sliding his feet along the floor. But he was doing it on his own. Jackson, hovering a few feet away, saw me looking and put their finger over their lips, so I didn't say anything. I did lean toward Reno and tap my finger on the table to get his attention. When he glanced up, I mimicked Jackson's finger over the lips and pointed.

Seeing Nicky, Reno grinned and silently raised both fists in the air. Fuck, he was beautiful when he smiled.

We both went back to our respective laptops. For all of Reno's defensiveness and rejection of our mating, I enjoyed working alongside him. Companionship wasn't something I'd had much of since the portal closed. I'd only been with Davi for a few months, and my memories of working with the other Guards were tainted by how evil so many of them had turned out to be.

I'd already determined who owned the apartment building, and now I was identifying their corporate server so I could hack into it to get the tenant information. By the time Reno sent off his report and closed his laptop, I had what we needed.

"Emiliano Duran, age twenty-six. Works as a machine operator at a steel pipe manufacturer. He has an Instagram account, but he hasn't posted anything in a couple of months. Before that it was occasional pictures of himself at rock concerts."

Reno pulled off his reading glasses and rubbed the bridge of his nose. "Doesn't sound like someone who'd know how to make a gargoyle costume."

"No. Which means it was given to him, or he paid to have it made. I'm not quite good enough to hack into his bank accounts, but tomorrow I can break into his apartment while he's at work."

He opened his mouth, then closed it. "Let's discuss it in the morning." He raised his voice loud enough to be heard over the television. "Nicky and Jackson? Are you ready for dinner?"

Both were sitting on the sofa again, and they replied in the affirmative.

Reno and I stood up. I took my laptop back to the guest room before returning to the kitchen. "What can I do to help?"

Grudgingly, he allowed me to make a salad while he heated up the remainder of the food Esperanza had left for us.

When dinner was ready, Nicky demanded to be allowed to walk to the table. "I won't get any better unless I keep moving my muscles!" Jackson and I put our arms around his back for support. Since Nicky was a good foot shorter than I was, that meant he was mostly leaning on my forearm, but we made it work.

After he reached the table, everyone heaped a ton of praise on him. Even better, he was able to eat a little more than he had last night. After dinner we all settled on the sofa to watch a movie. Reno had arranged us so he and I flanked Nicky and Jackson. He was still blocking our connection, so I couldn't tell what his mood was.

About an hour into the movie, which honestly I wasn't paying attention to at all, Nicky and Reno were both asleep, their seats reclined back with their feet up. Jackson had changed to their panther form, but their eyes were still on the TV. During a quiet scene, I heard Reno's phone buzz on the kitchen table. It was almost 10pm. How late did the Wonders think it was appropriate to text him?

I got up and collected the phone so it wouldn't disturb him. I'd exchanged numbers with Tucker earlier, so I sent him a text.

ME:

What's the passcode to Reno's phone?

TUCKER:

I feel like that's something you should be asking him

ME:

He's asleep and he probably wouldn't agree. I want to respond to all the Wonders who keep texting him.

TUCKER:

Well, if it's for a good cause. 2345

ME:

[eye roll emoji] I'll get him to change it to something more secure.

TUCKER:

Yeah, good luck with that

Reno had fifty-four text messages, so I dealt with those first. I did tell everyone I responded to who I was, so Reno would know I wasn't pretending to be him. The messages were mostly wanting reassurances regarding the escaped vampires, but there were a few others. One person's child needed to learn to drive but they didn't own a car, one woman wanted to tell her boyfriend about the campaign, and a wolverine shifter couple were planning to move to Corpus Christi and wanted to know where the Wonder-friendly neighborhoods were. For each of those I created a group chat with my own phone, muted the notifications for it on Reno's, and responded that I would ask Reno and get back to them as soon as the danger from the escaped vampires had passed.

Once that was done, I opened his Discord app. From my own phone I requested to join the South Texas District server, and on Reno's app I gave myself admin rights. Then I started with his direct messages. He had well over a hundred. This would take a while.

———

When the movie was over, I carried Nicky to the bathroom and then settled him on the sofa again with a pillow and a blanket. Jackson curled up next to him in their panther form. Reno had woken up during this process, so I didn't have an excuse to touch him and see his sleepy eyes open. On his way to bed he picked his phone up off the kitchen table where I'd left it.

The next morning I was awake before everyone else. I did a brief yoga session in the backyard, pretending I didn't see the Hunter camouflaged in the corner. They'd been switching teams out every four hours or so, which, if they had the people to do it, was an optimal amount of time to make sure everyone was fresh and alert.

Nicky was awake when I went back inside. He held onto me as I helped him to the bathroom, but he was able to lift his feet off the floor as he walked. His magic was replenishing itself and healing his body a tiny bit at a time.

When we came back out, Reno was standing next to the coffee maker. He glared at me as I got Nicky to the table. Would he yell at me in front of Nicky or not?

I was calculating the odds when he spoke. His tone was stiff but calm. "Simon, you went into my phone last night without permission."

"Yep." I threw him a wink. "Nicky, do you want coffee?" Jackson's furry head popped up from the sofa. They loved coffee.

Nicky, tired from his trek from the sofa to the bathroom and then the table, brightened. "Yes, please. I've never had it before, but everyone on TV is always drinking it."

This had the intended effect. "What? You can't—coffee isn't nutritious, Nicky. It's not good for you while you're still recovering." Reno waved his mug around while he sputtered.

I patted his shoulder as I nudged him aside to get a mug for Nicky and a bowl for Jackson. "I'll put a lot of milk and sugar in it. It'll be fine. If he doesn't like it, I'll make hot chocolate."

Nicky beamed. "I like almost anything, but hot chocolate is the best."

Grumbling, Reno bent down to get a pan from a lower cabinet. I stopped with my hand on the handle of the coffee pot. How had I not remembered to admire Reno's ass until now? This was a tragedy I needed to spend the next hundred years rectifying. He was wearing shiny black basketball shorts, and they draped lovingly over his buttocks. I couldn't see any outline of briefs, so he was either wearing something like boxer briefs, or he was commando. *That* was not an image I needed in my mind while I was standing in the middle of the kitchen. I got my eyes back under control and finished making the coffee.

Reno made pancakes, which Nicky adored, particularly because he'd seen characters on TV eating them. He liked the bacon but wasn't sold on scrambled eggs. "When I was a child we had them all in one piece? Can I have them that way?" Reno promised to try that tomorrow.

When everyone was done eating, Reno cleared his throat. "I didn't have a vision last night. Cal's feeling better, and he'll try to call a vision today, but with him so far away I'm not confident he'll see anything."

Nicky set his coffee cup down and pushed it away. "So, what? If Cal doesn't have a vision, we just wait for the vampires to find us?" His voice rose with each word.

Reno pressed his lips together, then gave a half-shrug. "I'm sorry, Nicky. We don't have a lot of options until we get a clue as to their whereabouts."

Nicky's face went even paler. "You mean until they attack someone else."

Reno made a face but shrugged. "I hope it doesn't come to that, but it might." He rubbed his forehead. "Okay, since we can't do anything to find the escaped vampires this morning, I do have something Simon and I need to work on." He explained about the gargoyle costume. "We need to go check out this guy's apartment and see if we can find anything to tell us what he's using that costume for."

"You mean like Grace Kelly going into the apartment across the courtyard to look for evidence in *Rear Window*?" Nicky's worried expression wasn't much of an improvement over the frightened one he'd worn a few minutes ago. "Are you sure you won't get caught?"

I was about to respond when Jackson cut in. "I will go. No one will see us."

I smiled. "Thank you. That'll be very helpful." With Jackson there, we could take our time.

"Hold it." Uh oh. Reno was mad again. "Somebody needs to stay with Nicky, and I'm the one with the private investigator license."

I raised my eyebrows at Nicky. "Wanna break into an apartment? I'll carry you on my back and you can help search for clues." And it might distract him from thinking about Marcas and Roibeart.

He seemed intrigued. "Like on *The Rockford Files* and *Moonlighting*?"

"Exactly like that." But hopefully without the villain of the week pointing a gun at us.

————

I texted the Hunters that we were going out on an errand for Reno's PI business, and Dominic said they'd follow us but wouldn't interfere unless Marcas and Roibeart appeared.

Nicky didn't have enough magic yet to cast a glamour, so Reno lent him a baseball cap to put over his ears and help hide his eyes. Shane had had some of Nicky's new clothes delivered same-day yesterday, and while the joggers and hoodie he was wearing were still a little baggy, they didn't look like they'd fall off if he moved too fast.

Nicky had tried to get us to let Jackson wear his Castiel-style trench coat, "so he'll be like Peter Falk in *Columbo*," but Reno said it would draw too much attention in June.

The apartment complex Emiliano Duran lived in had four buildings of twenty units each, and Emiliano's was in the building closest to the street. Tenants had assigned parking in the row next to the building, and the rest of the lot was for visitors.

"He drives a 2017 Dodge Ram pickup. It's got front and rear seats, and it's dark gray." Reno parked and we all scanned the lot. Emiliano wasn't home. From here we could see his apartment windows, but all of the blinds were closed.

We got out of Reno's SUV, and he helped Nicky get situated on my back. Nicky didn't weigh much, and his legs were awfully thin beneath my hands. Even though he was small for an Elf, he was too large to pass for a human child. Jackson would make sure no one saw us.

The stairs and hallways were open to the air, and there weren't any security cameras. When we got to the apartment door, Reno handed us some nitrile gloves. Once we were ready, I held his camera as he produced a set of lockpicks and got to work.

"*Oooh*, there was an episode in season five of *Castle* with lockpicks exactly like that!" At least Nicky kept his voice to a loud whisper. "Will you teach me how to use them?" The way Jackson was staring at the lockpicks, I wondered if they wanted to learn as well. Might be a good way to work on their fine motor skills.

"Sure, Nicky." Reno was sexy as fuck, leaning over and focused on his task. Would he look like that during sex? I wouldn't mind having all that concentration turned my way.

Shit, not the time. I shifted Nicky's weight and turned to keep watch down the hallway.

After only a minute or two, Reno had the door open, and we hurried inside.

"Wait here." Reno unholstered his gun and did a quick sweep of the apartment. Damn, him in cop mode was sexy too.

The place was a one-bedroom furnished with inexpensive pieces typical of a twenty-something male, with a huge TV and elaborate gaming system setup. No art on the walls but lots of framed photos on the bookshelves.

"Clear." Reno had holstered his gun when he got back to us. "I didn't see the costume, but I could've missed it in the closet."

We all followed him into the bedroom. The closet door was open, and the space was about four feet deep. There was no gargoyle costume, just jeans, casual shirts, one suit, and a couple of winter coats. Shoes were on the floor, and on the shelf above the clothes were board games and a couple of blankets.

"Well, shit." Reno put his hands on his hips, which drew his shirt tight against his muscles. I put the camera down on top of the bureau and started going through the drawers so I wouldn't ogle him.

Nicky patted me on the shoulder. "Why don't you put me down? I won't be much help like this, and I've got to be getting heavy."

I stifled my response that I wished he were heavier. His arms might be getting tired from gripping my shoulders. "Okay." I gazed around, but in here the only place to put him was the unmade bed, and one glance told me the sheets hadn't been changed in way too long.

Reno went to the doorway of the bedroom and looked into the living room before waving us forward. "Nicky, why don't you sit in that chair by the window? You can keep an eye out for Emiliano's car."

Reno had the best ideas. I took Nicky into the living room and over to the chair, making sure he could see out through the blinds and had a decent view of the tenant parking area. Jackson was going through the kitchen cabinets, so I returned to the bedroom. Reno was on his back under the bed with his phone's flashlight on.

"Do you need help? I can lift the bed."

"Nah, I don't see anything under here." He slid out, and when he stood up I helped him brush the dust bunnies off his back and return them to their home beneath the bed. I did *not* touch any part of him below his waist, even though I was dying to. "You can help me lift the mattress off the box spring if you like."

"Sure." Emiliano didn't keep any secrets under his bed. His nightstand had a few sex toys and some lube, but that was it. The bureau revealed t-shirts, underwear, a few pajama bottoms, some cufflinks, a watch, and socks.

"Hey, guys? I think he's home."

Reno and I rushed into the living room to look out the window. A dark grey Dodge Ram pickup was parked in one of the tenant spots closest to this building, and a man was walking around the front of the truck on his way to the stairwell.

"Fuck." Reno turned to Jackson. "Can we get out the door before he gets up the stairs?"

Jackson shook his head. "No. I can't prevent him from seeing us if he's already there."

I bent down so Nicky could climb on my back. "I could mesmerize him." I didn't love doing it, but we couldn't get caught.

"No." Jackson pointed at the bedroom. "The closet is the best option."

"Okay, everyone in the closet. No jokes." Reno spread his arms out and essentially herded us into the bedroom closet. I made sure to grab the camera on the way. "When we got here the door was slightly open." He pulled it until it was only a couple of inches from closing. I was glad for the light and the air circulation.

We'd barely stopped moving when we heard the apartment door unlock, then open and shut again. Keys hit the kitchen counter, and the refrigerator door was opened. He was home for lunch. I glanced at Reno, and he showed me his phone's lock screen. 11:43 a.m. Hopefully Emiliano's lunch break was only thirty minutes. Plates clinked, and what was probably a bag of potato chips rustled. The sink ran, and then we heard the TV turn on. ESPN. At least he wouldn't hear us if somebody made a noise.

As soon as the thought crossed my mind, the sound of a fart tore through the closet. A loooong fart. It must've been a good five seconds before it stopped.

"Sorry." Nicky whispered, putting his forehead down on my shoulder. I tried to keep my chuckles silent, but then the smell hit, putrid and heavy.

"Fuck, Nicky!" Reno covered his nose with one arm and pushed the closet door open a little more with the other.

"I'm sorry!" He shrank into me like he was trying to hide.

Shit. I didn't have a free hand to pat his hand with. "You're eating regularly for the first time in decades. None of our digestive systems would react well."

Reno must've caught Nicky's mortification. "Yeah, don't worry about it, Nicky. Sooner or later Tia Esperanza will make her charro beans and we'll all be farting for days."

Nicky snickered, and I sent a wave of gratefulness through the connection to Reno, even though he might not feel it. Nicky'd been outgoing and confident as a child, and I hoped that part of his personality would reemerge someday. Hopefully he'd feel more and more himself as time went on and his body healed.

The TV turned off, and dishes were placed into the sink. The keys scraped the counter as they were picked up. We all held our breaths. Well, for multiple reasons.

"What the fuck?" We heard Emiliano sniffing the air. Oh, shit. I glanced at Jackson and their eyes were closed. Footsteps came into the bedroom. "Shit, better do laundry tonight."

We relaxed as the footsteps went out of the room, and the front door opened and closed. "He's gone." Jackson reached over Reno's shoulder and pushed the closet door open. They'd been right behind Nicky, so they'd borne the brunt of the stench.

None of us wanted to stay in the bedroom. "What's left to do? Take some pictures?" I pointed at the shelves of framed photos.

Reno wiped his forehead with the back of his gloved hand and looked around the living room. "Yeah, thanks. I'll get that stack of mail. Jackson, did you finish in the kitchen?"

"Yes. Nothing unexpected."

"Okay, can you make sure Emiliano doesn't come back for some reason while Simon and I finish up?"

"On it." They stood next to the chair where Nicky had been sitting earlier.

I turned Reno's camera on and went over to the photos. Emiliano was a cute guy, with dark hair and a fantastic smile. "I think he has a girlfriend." She was in four or five of the photos, almost as tall as Emiliano, with black hair, pale skin, and a sturdy build. He held onto her like he didn't want to let go.

I took a few shots of each of the rooms in the apartment in case we thought of something later, but then we were done. Jackson gave us the go-ahead to leave, and we wasted no time exiting the apartment. Reno used the lockpicks again to turn the deadbolt, and it was as if we'd never been there.

We got back in the car and grinned at each other. Reno even smiled at *me*.

TABORA, TANZANIA
– DECEMBER, 1979

They were getting complacent. It'd been four years since I'd last been able to find any evidence of the luchd-òl fola. In this area, such a large group of pale-skinned people stood out and was commented on. They were forgetting their training, which I was grateful for.

I approached the house in the darkness, stopping in the shadow of a shed on the neighboring property. My only goal was to get Prince Nicol out. Once he was safe, I'd hunt down the luchd-òl fola, one at a time if I had to.

I stayed in place for over thirty minutes. There were no patrols, and I didn't see anyone at the windows. When I felt confident enough to get closer, I crept around the outside of the building, listening for voices. I could hear a television, but no one moving around or talking. I smelled four or five of the luchd-òl fola, but no Wonders.

This wasn't their safe house. It was a trap.

The exterior lights turned on as I moved to leave. Five of them came at me, and I was gratified that I'd been right about one thing at least. They hadn't been keeping up with their training.

Only one of the bastards got away alive.

CHAPTER 11
RENO

WE STOPPED ON THE WAY HOME, AND JACKSON AND SIMON stayed in the car with Nicky while I bought some groceries. I was glad for the excuse to get away from Simon for a bit. The man was too attractive for my well-being.

Intellectually, I was still opposed to being mated—to Simon or anyone. As soon as a new District Monitor showed up, I was taking as long a vacation as I could afford. By myself. If I could get rid of this damn connection with Simon, there'd be plenty of guys to fuck wherever I ended up, and I wouldn't have to talk to them or spend time worrying if they were happy.

Of course, the part of my hind brain that wanted to be mated to Simon—merely because of the connection we had—told me bonding meant you always knew whether your partner was happy without having to ask. It also reminded me of the rumors I'd heard about how good sex was once you were mated. And I'd certainly noticed how attractive Simon was and the fluid way he moved. He'd be good in bed without a doubt, but I was not ruled by my libido.

We got home, and I made lunch, making sure Nicky ate a salad with his turkey sandwich. His new phone had arrived, so while he took a nap, Jackson set it up for him. I could've used the time to respond to messages from the Wonders, but Simon had taken care of those already.

Which I definitely had mixed feelings about. I'd meant to yell at him this morning for breaking into my phone without my permission, but he'd been so matter of fact about it, I hadn't been able to. And, honestly, did I *want* to have been the one to respond to all those messages? No.

I had a few inquiries for PI services via my website form, so I replied with my rates and let them know I couldn't take on any new clients until next week at the earliest.

Around 2:00 p.m., Cal called. I took the phone outside so we wouldn't disturb Nicky. Simon and Jackson came with me, so I put it on speaker. "Go ahead, Cal. Wait, how are you feeling?"

"I'm fine today. This bonded healing shit is the best." He blew out a big breath into the phone. "I tried calling a vision about the vampire who attacked me. I figured I'd have a better chance at it since I'd seen him in person." I had a sinking feeling I knew what he was going to say. "But I couldn't get anything. I tried again a little later, but same result."

Fuck. Simon's expression was blank, so I couldn't tell what he was feeling. No way was I unblocking the connection. I tried to keep my tone upbeat when I replied. "Okay, well, thanks for trying, and thanks for letting us know. I'll tell the Hunters."

"I'm sorry, Reno. Do you want me to ask Delphia and Edgar to come back from Europe?"

I considered that. Best case scenario, even if they somehow got on a plane within the next couple of hours, it would take them ten to twelve hours in the air to reach Houston, then another two to three hours to get through customs and catch a plane here. They wouldn't be close enough to call a vision until tomorrow evening at the earliest.

I had a bad feeling I already knew what needed to be done. "Let us think about it. I'll call you if we decide we need them."

"Okay. I'll get their itinerary so we have it in case we need it. Be careful and keep us posted on how things are going."

After we hung up, I walked over and sat down in one of the chairs next to the fire pit. I needed to make a decision. And before I discussed it with Simon, I wanted to get there on my own first.

"Can I sit here with you?"

Or not. I gazed up into Simon's beautiful tawny eyes and found myself nodding even though I'd intended to ask for some time alone. I couldn't turn away, not even when the back door shut as Jackson went inside.

"I think—" My phone rang. Automatically I looked down at it. Amelia Mishra, a naga who lived north of town. "Excuse me, but if they're calling it's urgent." I answered. "Hi, Amelia, what's up?"

"Reno!" She was crying.

I sat forward in my chair. "What is it?"

"Bennie and I, we...." She gasped out a sob. "We went out for our usual evening walk before dinner."

"Okay. What happened?" I met Simon's eyes. I didn't have to put the call on speaker for him to hear her. His hands gripped his knees so tightly his fingers were white.

"We stopped at the pond to look at the ducks, and it seemed to both of us that we'd lost track of time, so we started walking again. But... but then I noticed Bennie had a cut on his neck." She took a ragged breath. "And I have one too."

Fuck, they'd been left alive. A message perhaps?

"Shit, Amelia, I'm so sorry that happened. Are you safe now?"

"Yes. We're home, and we locked all the doors."

"Good. That's good. Um, hang on. I'm going to put you on speaker so you can talk to Simon too. He's the vampire who's been helping us."

"Wait!" She practically shrieked the word.

"What's the matter?"

Her voice went into a whisper. "Are you sure he's not working with the others?"

I let my head fall forward and shut my eyes. "Yes, I'm sure. I've seen him fight them, and I would trust him with my life." Beside me, Simon inhaled sharply. I opened my eyes to frown at him. This was a surprise?

"Okay, I guess that's fine then. I'm sorry, I'm... spooked."

"Completely understandable." I switched the call to speakerphone. "Okay, Simon's here. Simon, this is Amelia Mishra. She and her husband Bennie were out walking and lost time. They have bite wounds on their necks."

"Hi, Amelia. That must have been very scary. Reno says you're home now and safe?"

"Yes. We're just so frightened."

"Of course you are." Simon stared down at the phone, his voice warm and comforting. "Do you have any injuries other than the bites?"

"No."

"Good. And you'll be relieved to hear that vampire saliva has antibiotic properties, and it should heal quickly. However, you might have a small scar."

She started to cry again. "Thank you for telling me."

"Before you do anything else, I want both of you to eat something and drink at least a full glass of water. Can you do that?"

"Yes. Yes, we can."

"Good. I don't think you're in any more danger from them, but you might feel better if you stayed with a friend or at a hotel tonight."

"Oh, that does sound like a good idea. Thank you so much."

While Simon wrapped up the call, I had a hard talk with myself. It was time to face facts. If we were going to find these fucking vampires before they hurt or killed someone else, I had to be able to call visions.

I had to bond with Simon. Mate with him. Now.

Fuck.

I stood up and went inside, not waiting to get my phone from Simon. Nicky and Jackson were watching *My Hero Academia.* "Hey, are y'all ready for dinner?"

Both of them were enthusiastic. Despite being stocked with groceries, I wasn't in the mood to cook. We were out of tamales, and pretty low on soup, so delivery it was. Nicky had a list of things he wanted to try, but I didn't want to upset his stomach, so we compromised on Chinese food. I didn't order anything spicy or fried, and I got extra rice.

Simon had come inside, and he was sitting at the kitchen table going back and forth between my phone and his. I felt a niggle of guilt, but I was mostly grateful he had taken on some of the messages from the Wonders.

Cal and Greg needed to be alerted about what had happened to the Mishras, but instead I went into my bedroom. I wanted a few minutes to myself so I could make sure of my decision.

I sat down on the bed, then I thought, *fuck it*, and got fully prone with my head on a pillow.

Okay, we had to find the escaped vampires. The Mishras lived on the north side of town, but the vampires could be anywhere. They could've stolen a car, or maybe they were flying around in their fog forms.

I could only think of two options to find them. First, I could have a vision that would tell us where they were or would be. Second, we could set up a trap and use Nicky as bait.

No way was the second one happening, which meant I needed to have a vision. I'd tried to call one this morning, but I hadn't been able to. Of course I'd had my mating connection to Simon blocked, so that might've prevented me from getting as much upside to my abilities as I could have had.

Okay, so step one would be to unblock the connection and try to call a vision. No pressure or anything. Just laying all of my emotions bare for Simon to feel, and knowing if I couldn't call this vision, I'd have to complete the mating.

I let myself have a one-minute primal scream as close to a whisper as I could make it. Then I relaxed my muscles one by one and focused on my breathing. When I was nearing a meditative state, I released the block I had on the mating connection. I had to ride out the surge of emotions coming from his end—worry, stress, desire, and sadness—before I was ready to try.

I wasn't sure exactly what would work for me, so I went with the first thing I thought of. I visualized my hands raised in a classic framing pose: forefingers and thumbs in an "L", and each hand creating a corner of a rectangle. Into the frame I pictured the question, *Where are the escaped vampires?* I added their names, Marcas and Roibeart, in case it would help. Not that I knew which was which.

I waited, making sure my mind felt open to receive the vision. Nothing. After about two minutes, I gave up.

"Fuck."

I rolled off the bed and got to my feet, unable to keep still anymore. I'd only paced one length of the bedroom when the doorbell rang. Dinner was here.

Grateful for the distraction, I went downstairs into the living room. Simon had retrieved the food and was taking it to the kitchen. He gave me a long look, but he didn't say anything. Fuck, the connection was still open. I was too tired to bother blocking it, and if we got mated later, he'd be all up in my business anyway, so I just let it be.

The table was already set. Jackson and I helped Nicky walk over to it. He was doing a little better every time he tried. His magical core was slightly brighter too.

Nicky was a big fan of the beef with broccoli and the garlic eggplant, but he wasn't sold on the beef lo mein. Simon updated me on some of the messages from the Wonders in the District, but neither of us mentioned the vampire attack on the Mishras. Nicky would only worry.

When dinner was over, Nicky and Jackson went back to the couch. I got out my Switch and put it in the dock so they could play *Mario Kart 8*. Jackson had only played video games a few times, but they were familiar enough with the Switch to help Nicky figure it out.

My chest heavy with the weight of what I had to do, I jerked my head at Simon and went outside to sit in the chairs again.

He shut the back door softly, then came to sit beside me. "You tried calling a vision?"

I nodded, leaning forward to put my elbows on my knees and staring down at my hands. "I didn't get anything."

He sighed. "I thought about getting Jackson to make themselves look like Nicky, but their magic is completely different, and Marcas and Roibeart wouldn't take the bait."

"We can't risk Nicky." I laced my fingers together so I wouldn't clench my fists. "And we can't wait for Delphia and Edgar to get back from Europe, but we need to be able to call a vision."

He went still. "What exactly are you suggesting?"

I forced myself to meet his eyes. "We have to bond. Once I'm mated to you, my Seer skills will be enhanced, and I can call visions."

A complicated set of emotions came through the connection. Hope, determination, and resignation overrode the rest.

He put his hand over mine. "No. We'll figure out something else."

"There isn't anything else, and you know it. This is the only way."

His fingers tightened. Our magics sparkled and wrapped around each other, making their opinion on my proposal clear. But Simon was not sold. "Not when all I'm getting from you through the connection is dread."

I glared at him. "I'll do it, okay? I won't back out."

He let go of my hand and sat back in the chair with a sigh, running his palm over his gorgeous hair. The light was fading, but I could still make out the reddish tint to it. "Reno, the magic won't complete the bond unless you consent to it."

"I'm consenting."

He pressed his lips together and looked to the side. A wave of sadness came through our connection, and I felt like a complete jerk. He turned back to me, his eyes glistening. "Can you please explain to me why having a mate would be so awful? I promise you, I know what I'm doing in bed." He tried to smile, but his lips trembled.

I couldn't stop myself from reaching out and grabbing his hand. "It's not you, Simon. I've told you. And, hell, if I have to be mated to someone, I'm glad it'll be you."

All that got me was a mess of frustration coming through the connection. I tried again. "I want to be single. I don't want any obligations." I winced. "Every time the phone vibrates or rings, my blood pressure goes up. It's like I can't breathe sometimes. I don't want to let the Wonders down, but I've about reached the end of my rope with this acting DM role. And I know my issues seem like nothing compared to what you, or especially Nicky, have gone through, but all I want—all I need—is time to myself. I can't have that with a mate."

He cocked his head at me, his eyebrows scrunched together. "Why would having a mate keep you from getting time to yourself?" He waved a hand. "Outside of the initial bonding period where there's a distance limit of course. After that, there's nothing stopping you from taking time on your own."

I huffed. "You say that now, but I watched my parents. They couldn't be out of each other's sight for more than a few minutes without practically having a panic attack. Neither of them had their own friends, only couples they would see together. I don't want to live like that."

Simon frowned. "It's not that way for every mating. You saw Shane. He was fine while he was here without his mates. Our bond will be the same."

I rubbed my face. "I'm not sure it's something we can control. But you're right. Maybe we'll be lucky." I slashed my hand through the air. "And either way, we need to bond. I want to do it. I'm ready."

He disengaged his fingers from mine, then crossed his arms over his chest and gazed out into the yard. "I've been looking forward to meeting my mate since that Seer told me her vision in 1949." He gave me a sad smile. "I was so happy when I met you. And I want more than anything to give you what you want right now, the time alone you crave. Because I can be patient, and I know one day you'd come back to me, refreshed and ready to be together."

I blinked at him. Was he right? Would I one day start thinking about the mate who was waiting for me and be ready for that life? Hell, anything was possible.

He grimaced, uncrossing his arms and looking down at his hands. "But I don't think the Seer meant I could complete my mission just being in the same room with you, without us being mated. I think you're right. We have to complete the bond in order to finish the mission, to take out Marcas and Roibeart."

The perfect solution came to me, and I smiled. Simon must've felt my excitement, because he whipped his head toward me. I grabbed his hand again. "Then we'll bond. We'll complete the mating. And once those two are dead, and Nicky's safe, you'll sever it." He sucked in a breath, and I felt his horror at the thought. I held up a hand. "And after I go do my solo thing, maybe you're right. Maybe I'll be ready for a mate. For a permanent bond."

I was too late. After I'd tortured this location out of Kier, I'd raced here as fast as I could, but they'd felt him die, and they'd taken precautions

I stared down at the smoking rubble of the house the luchd-òl fola had been staying in. Metal bars stood in one corner, and I hoped they'd killed any Wonders they'd been keeping captive before they set the place on fire.

Fuck.

This was the closest I'd gotten to Prince Nicol, if he was still alive. But there were still nineteen luchd-òl fola to guard him.

They'd either leave town by car or by boat. Flying was too public, especially if they still had the prince. But the port was huge. They could hire a captain to take them anywhere. I got back in the car. Time to use my vampire abilities to get some information.

———

The harbor master's office was tiny and full of papers, but it boasted a huge set of windows overlooking the port. And, luckily for me, it also held an ancient security camera system. When I'd asked about a large group of people needing a boat at the last minute, the man's eyes had narrowed, and he'd eagerly started hinting at how large a bribe he'd need to tell me which ship they'd taken.

I didn't have time to negotiate, so I put him in thrall right away. I'd tuck some money in his pocket when I left.

On my instructions, he fast-forwarded through one of the security camera tapes and showed me a dock. The time stamp was ten hours ago. I'd been so fucking close.

I wrote down the ship's name and identification number. The harbor master told me it was taking a load of petroleum to Rio de Janeiro. On the screen we watched the luchd-òl fola walk aboard. Fraser was carrying someone wrapped in blankets as if they were ill. The person was human-sized, too short to be an Elf or another of the luchd-òl fola, but it couldn't be anyone other than Prince Nicol. I was relieved to know he was still alive, even if I was also horrified at what he had to have gone through all these years.

When the tape showed the ship casting off from the dock, I made the harbor master go back and slowly play the part where my former colleagues walked onto the ship. I wrote down everyone I saw so I could compare it to the list I'd been keeping.

But Kinnon wasn't there. He hadn't gotten on the ship.

I hadn't killed him, and there was no way he hadn't been involved in the initial kidnapping of Prince Nicol.

Had he had a falling out with the others? Had he died from some other cause? Had he stayed behind to hunt me down?

Now I had yet another reason to catch up to the luchd-òl fola. Good thing I could take a plane to Rio and get ahead of that ship.

CHAPTER 12
SIMON

I DON'T KNOW WHY I WAS SHOCKED. I WAS OVER TWO HUNDRED years old. I shouldn't have been shocked. But for Reno to suggest—to be *happy* to suggest—that we bond and then sever it? Like it would be nothing?

I shut my mouth, which had dropped open in my astonishment. "Um." How best to approach this? I certainly didn't want to put myself through that. But was it possible he didn't know what he was asking? "Reno, have you ever felt a connection get cut? Someone you cared about pass away, maybe?"

He shrugged. "Yeah, of course. My parents and my cousin."

"And were any of those deaths sudden?"

"Nooo? My dad had cancer, and my mom had a lung infection. My cousin had congestive heart failure."

Fuck. I rubbed my forehead. "Okay, so in those cases the connections start to become thinner as death approaches. There's no wrenching pain when it happens. Cutting a connection without warning, or even worse, cutting a bond, is painful and debilitating." I frowned. "Didn't Shane tell you what it was like when the *luchd-òl fola* cut his bond with

Ellis?" Before they'd bonded with their third, Shane and Ellis had been mates. Ellis had been briefly captured and had all of his connections and his mate bond severed by the *luchd-òl fola.*

"No. I only heard what happened from Greg and Cal."

I sighed. "Reno, I want nothing more than to be mated with you. And you're right that we need you to be able to call a vision. But completing the bond when you're not willing to keep it permanently? You're asking me to essentially tear a hole in my soul. And yours."

He glanced down at the ground, then back up at me. "Would that be worse than you staying mated to a guy who doesn't want to *be* mated?"

Fuck, it was a fair question. "I don't know." Neither of us looked at the other for a while. "Alright, what about this? You call Shane and ask him to tell you how it felt to have his bond severed. And we both sleep on it tonight. Maybe you'll have a vision spontaneously. If not, we'll talk in the morning and decide."

He nodded slowly. "That's a good plan. Thanks for not just rejecting the idea."

I didn't know how to tell him I'd have a hard time denying him anything, even if it meant going through something as painful as getting a brief taste of our bond before I had to destroy it.

———

Reno went up to his bedroom to call Shane. I alternated between working on my knitting and monitoring the South Texas District Discord chat. I'd posted a message earlier to let everyone know the vampires were still out there and that they'd attacked two Wonders but not hurt them seriously. Most of the comments seemed concerned but not panicking.

Nicky walked the length of the couch a few times, only holding on with one hand. He was making tremendous progress, but his magic wasn't built back up to even a quarter of the way to where it needed to be.

Eventually Reno came out and handed his phone to Nicky, saying it was Arlo calling to check on him. I got a "Good night," before he went back into his bedroom. He'd blocked our mating connection again, so I guessed Shane had explained how difficult severing our bond would be.

When Nicky was done with Reno's phone—Arlo's contact info now stored in Nicky's—I went through the new text messages and his Discord private messages. I responded to a few and told the others we'd get back to them next week. Reno hadn't been kidding about how often the Wonders contacted him. Was it like this for every District Monitor, or was it only because these Wonders felt unsettled without a true DM connection?

I went to bed late, but I couldn't sleep. How long would Reno allow us to keep our bond after Marcas and Roibeart were dead? Would he want to have sex when we completed the bond? I wanted to make love to Reno more than anything, but it might not be the best idea. I'd know what I was missing after the bond was gone.

Part of me wanted to rage at the universe for only giving me a taste of what happiness could be like, especially after I'd given up everything to stay on Earth and track the *luchd-òl fola* for almost half my life. But Reno had needs too, and they weren't conducive to a proper mating.

I didn't fall asleep for hours.

I woke up to the clink of dishes in the kitchen. Slowly, both from being tired and from halfway dreading hearing Reno's decision, I took a shower and put on some jeans and a t-shirt. When I couldn't delay any longer, I went out into the living room. "Good morning, everyone." They were all in the kitchen, so I made my way over to the coffee maker. I met Reno's eyes, and he gave me a grim head shake. No vision then. Fuck.

My hand trembled as I set the coffee mug down on the table. What had he decided?

I managed to choke down some eggs and toast. After breakfast, Jackson took Nicky outside. They set him up on one of the Adirondack chairs in the middle of the backyard, and Nicky threw Tucker's softball in Jackson's general direction while Jackson swung the bat at it.

Reno finished putting the dishes in the dishwasher and sat down next to me at the table. "I didn't have a vision."

I nodded and clenched my fingers around the coffee mug. "What did you decide?"

He gazed out into the backyard. "Hunter security guards or not, Nicky's in danger every second those vampires are out there."

"So you want to complete the bond?" My stomach was clenched tight.

Reno's eyes were serious, resolved. But he was still blocking our connection. "I think we have to."

"And you want it to be temporary." I didn't make it a question.

His eyes skittered away, looking first at the kitchen, then down at the tabletop. He took a breath and met my gaze. "I don't want to give you false hope. I want to go into this with the intention of it being temporary. But Shane—" He ran one hand up and down over the opposite forearm. "Shane said once we were mated, I might not be able to go through with severing the bond."

I felt like I was getting thrown around on an amusement park ride, but I wasn't having any fun. "And you're okay with possibly being permanently mated?"

He cringed a little. "I'm open to the possibility that my feelings on the topic might change." He grimaced. "Which I know isn't fair to you at all."

Reno's phone buzzed with an incoming text, and he flinched. The Wonders wanted answers. And then there was Nicky, who'd be in danger until Marcas and Roibeart were dead.

I pressed my palms against the tabletop and closed my eyes. I could sit on this for a few minutes, but I already knew I was going to do it. I was going to bond with Reno even though he might ask me to sever it later. And if he stayed mated with me, I'd always wonder if he regretted it.

I must've been a fucking masochist.

Or I was in love with my mate.

I opened my eyes. "Let's do it." I glanced outside at Jackson and Nicky. "Can Tucker come over and hang out with them while we're, uh, busy?"

Reno's cheeks flushed. We hadn't discussed sex yet. I wouldn't pressure him, but my cock was highly aware it might happen.

"Yeah, I'll call him." He picked up his phone and I went out to the backyard to wait.

———

Tucker breezed in forty-five minutes later, bringing donuts and coffee. "I figured Nicky's probably never had a donut." He carefully didn't comment on what Reno and I were about to do, just went out to the backyard. Nicky was basking in the sun with his eyes closed while Jackson attempted to kick a soccer ball.

Reno cleared his throat. "Uh, my bedroom?"

I gestured for him to lead the way. My heart was pounding. I hadn't been in his bedroom yet. The walls were painted a dusty blue that gave the whole room a feeling of being safe in a romantic cocoon. When I shut the door behind us, I managed to ask the big question. "Did you want to have sex, or you know we can bond without it, right?"

His cheeks went even ruddier than they'd been earlier. "I kind of assumed we would? Have sex, I mean. But if you don't want to, that's fine, I—"

I put my hand on his cheek. Our magics sparkled together. "If I only get to have you for a short time, I want it all. But I need to warn you that vampires bite during mating. I'll take a little of your blood."

His eyes dilated, and his heartbeat sped up. "Will it hurt?"

"Only for a second. Then it'll feel amazing." I eased closer, not wanting to spook him. "Can you unblock the connection?"

"Oh, shit. Sorry." He released his block, and I felt a surge of stress, terror, lust, and hope.

I stopped moving. "Reno...."

"It's fine. *I'm* fine. I want you." He sent over a wave of determination, then he slid his hands under my t-shirt.

I clamped my hands over his. "You're not very aroused."

He glared. "There's a lot of pressure happening here. I was hoping we could make out a little and things would, you know, heat up."

I huffed an aggravated breath. "Okay, but if you're not feeling it within a few minutes, we're doing it the other way."

He copied my huff. "Fine."

I smiled. Reno's prickliness came out when he was feeling defensive or stressed, so my job was to relax him as much as possible. He'd leave this bed knowing how good sex between mates could be. One more thing to make him think twice about severing our bond. "Can I kiss you?"

He nodded, not taking his eyes off mine.

I kept the first kiss soft, delicate even. Just a taste. But our magics surged together, and when I eased my head back, Reno chased my lips with his. I let him take the lead for a moment, and he pressed against me, his erection grinding into mine through our clothes as he thrust his tongue into my mouth.

I rumbled a groan into our kiss before tearing my mouth away. "Naked."

"Right." He was panting, and our mating connection was sun-bright between us.

I yanked my t-shirt over my head and unbuttoned my jeans. Reno's body was even more sinful than I'd pictured it. His broad chest was flushed under the soft, thick hair. He didn't have defined abs, but I couldn't wait to cuddle into his belly. And his cock was a thing of beauty, nicely wide and thick. I didn't like thinking about how long it'd been since I had anything inside me but a toy. Too bad we didn't have time for penetration right now.

I guided him down onto the bed. The first touch of his naked skin against mine, our magics flaring high and twining together, felt like the reward I'd earned after all the years of loneliness. I tucked my face into his neck, smelling the blood so close under his skin. "I'm not going to last long. Can we...?" I wrapped my hand around his cock and moved so I could bring mine into the circle of my fingers.

He sucked in a breath. "Yes. God, yes." He made an abortive thrust with his hips. "Lube. I have lube." But his hands were gripping my shoulder and ass, and he didn't move them.

I was salivating over the scent of his blood, so I released our cocks and took a second to spit into my hand. He moaned, his legs moving restlessly as he thrust against me. His now-slick cock slid along mine. The sensation was so good, I didn't even notice my fangs descending until they were hovering over Reno's neck. "Can I bite you?"

"Uh-huh." He pushed into my fist again, hauling my body into his as if he were trying to make us one.

Right. Our mating.

I reached for our mating connection, now a bright river between our whirling magical cores. "I consent to this bond." I closed my eyes and saw our cores start to spin in sync with each other.

Reno stiffened in my arms, but before I could ask him if he wanted to stop, I felt that determination coming from him again. "I consent to this bond." He took his hand off my ass and joined it with mine around our cocks instead. The additional pressure doubled in intensity as it echoed through the connection between us.

Gently I used my fangs to make a small slice in his neck, just below the line of his beard stubble, then I sucked. Reno's blood was delicious, better than anything I'd ever tasted. Rich, sweet, and fizzing with his magic. He moaned, and his cock swelled as he thrust into our hands. My pleasure chased his, and I could feel what he felt, the friction of our cocks moving together and the heat of my mouth on his neck. I sucked harder, and the sensations whirled through us like a tornado. We both came, and the double shockwave of our orgasms had my whole body clenching, clinging to Reno for what seemed like forever.

At last we shuddered to completion, our muscles lax. I licked Reno's neck to heal the cut, and he shivered. "The wound will be gone in a minute or two, now that we're mated."

"*Mmmm.* I forgot about that benefit."

He'd also get a longer lifespan if we stayed mated, but we had time to discuss that later. Right now, Reno's face was more peaceful than I'd ever seen it, the stress lines temporarily gone and a small smile on his lips. I closed my eyes to admire our joined magical cores.

Except the joining was... off. Our cores were not bonded into one. It was more like they were *attached*, with multiple strands of magic trying desperately to tie the two cores together. They spun side by side, but mine turned a tiny bit faster than Reno's, making the magic strands twist and stretch as they tried to accommodate the difference. I felt nauseated just looking at it.

How fucked up was our mating? Could we even speak mind-to-mind?

Reno.

His entire body jolted, so I guessed I had my answer. He slapped my chest and scowled. "Warn a person!"

I caught his hand with mine. "Sorry. But you need to look at our cores." I tried to control my panic. The bond had taken at least enough to allow mind-speak, but would it be enough for Reno to call a vision? For him to want to stay bonded with me? Right now we might be able to undo the bond by unraveling the magic that was tying our cores together. Should I ask Reno if he wanted to?

He closed his eyes for an instant, then jackknifed up into a sitting position. He squeezed my fingers with one hand and patted his chest frantically with the other. "It didn't take? It was me, wasn't it? I screwed it up." He stared at me with pleading eyes. "Can I even call a vision like this?"

My heart hurt to see my mate in distress. I could feel his worry and fright, and it helped me push my own panic aside. I sat up and put my arms around him. "*Shhh*. We'll figure it out." I synced my breathing with his until he calmed a little. I kissed his cheek. "The bond took at least a little bit, or I wouldn't have been able to communicate mind-to-mind."

He relaxed a bit more. "Okay. True." I didn't point out that we were touching, and even unbonded partners with strong connections could mind-speak while skin-to-skin. No need to worry him until I tested it.

"We should probably clean up. And, um, we can see how far from each other the bond will let us get." Most partners had about a five- to ten-foot radius from each other for the first few days after bonding. Reno and I hadn't remembered to discuss how we'd navigate that, but if the bond wasn't complete, it might not be an issue.

He must've had the same thought, because he swallowed. "Okay. Let's head for the bathroom. I'll go first." His body was stiff as he slid to the edge of the bed.

I dropped his hand, and—"Ow!" I leaned forward, clutching as much of Reno's body as I could. I'd never heard of bonded partners who couldn't even let go of each other.

Our bond was majorly fucked up.

RIO DE JANEIRO, BRAZIL – APRIL, 1992

I'd lost the trail. I'd flown here to arrive ahead of them, but they'd paid the captain to dock in Santos, three hundred miles to the south. The first mate had told me all about the "tour group" of nineteen people, one of whom was very ill with cancer and had to be carried to shore.

I'd been so angry I'd left the docks on foot and walked for hours. The luchd-òl fola could be anywhere by now. I'd have to start from scratch. Again. Talk to Wonders and listen for rumors of disappearances. It'd be years before I caught up with them. Fuck.

But right now, I needed to feed. Rio had small pockets of Wonders here and there, usually family groups. Magic carriers were more likely to be out and about on their own, like the one walking into the mercado down the block.

I sped up, planning to linger around the entrance so I could intercept him as he left. But he hadn't been inside more than a few minutes when he exited, walking backwards with his arms raised defensively. A tiny woman in a green apron yelled at him in Portuguese, something about not wanting his kind in the store. She didn't have any magic, so that couldn't be what she was referring to.

The man walked stiffly away, heading in the same direction I was going. He turned right at the first corner, and when I followed, I found him leaning against the building, his face in his hands.

"Are you alright, friend?" I addressed him in English in hopes he might be my mate.

He dropped his hands and barked a laugh. "No. I—" He blinked at me. I'd stopped a few feet away so I wouldn't be a threat. He examined my magic core. I didn't resonate with him, so even though he spoke English, he wasn't my mate. Which was too bad, because he was attractive, a little thin, but with thick black curls, copper skin, and ink-dark eyes. "What are *you?" He held his hands up. "Sorry, that was rude of me."*

I smiled. "I don't mind." I looked around to make sure we were alone. "I'm a vampire." When I'd first set out on my mission, I'd avoided telling anyone what I was. Most Wonders had never met any of the Royal Guard, and their only reference points for vampires was the novel Dracula *and silly myths. But over time I'd cared less, and I'd had some success getting Wonders and magic carriers to voluntarily let me feed from them for the sheer novelty of it. Most of the time, though, I still wiped their memory afterward.*

He gaped for a few seconds, then laughed. "No shit?"

"It's true. Do you mind if I ask what happened at the mercado?"

He hesitated, and I could tell he was considering brushing me off or lying, but in the end he turned his head and pointed at the right side of his neck, where he had an ulcerous lesion.

"You have AIDS." Now that I was close enough, I could smell the sickness in him, but his magic was still strong.

He nodded. His shoulders slumped and his head drooped so he was staring at the ground. "I was on AZT, but it stopped working." He only had a few connections, and they were faint, childhood friendships that had faded over time.

"I'm sorry. That's rough." The woman at the mercado no doubt thought she or her customers could catch it just by being in the same room. Ignorant and bigoted.

He lifted his head. "Now you know, you can leave. It won't hurt my feelings. You're a tourist, right? Do you need directions back to your hotel?"

Shit, he'd been treated horribly by more people than not, I'd have bet. I shrugged and switched to Portuguese. "I'm not leaving. Even if I could catch it, I know it's not transmissible through the air, unlike some assholes." I hiked my thumb back toward the mercado. "And I'm not exactly a tourist. I'm here on business, I guess you could say."

He blinked a couple of times, then changed to Portuguese as well. "Your accent is impressive. But, really, I'm fine."

I gave him an overdone rakish grin. "You are." I wiggled my eyebrows. He looked at me like I had a screw loose, but he did smile. "It might interest you to know that vampires can't catch human diseases at all."

His eyebrows went up. "You can't? You can't catch HIV?"

I shook my head and moved closer, reaching out to run my finger along the neck of his shirt. "Not even if you let me suck your blood."

His mouth dropped open, and his face brightened. "You... you don't mind being around me?"

"Not at all." I thought back to his attempt to go to the mercado. "In fact, would you like to join me for dinner? I do eat regular food too."

He smiled. "Could we pick something up and eat at my place?"

I grinned back. "Sounds great, but I'm not from around here, so you'll have to choose."

He swept an arm out. "This way. There's a place that doesn't mind serving me as long as I get my food through the takeout window."

He must've seen my scowl because he made an aborted gesture as if he were about to pat my arm, but he didn't end up touching me. "It's better than the people who scream like I'm going to spit on them or whatever they imagine." He rolled his eyes.

We walked for a few minutes, dodging other pedestrians. "Oh, shit." I squeezed his arm, ignoring his gasp. Did no one touch him anymore? "I'm so rude. My name is Simon."

He grinned wide, his teeth white against the inflamed redness of his gums. "Hi, Simon. I'm Davi. It's nice to meet you."

CHAPTER 13
RENO

"UH, WHAT THE FUCK?" THIS WAS BAD, VERY BAD.

Simon scooted over so he was more sitting next to me than hugging me around my middle. He rubbed his sternum. "I think the bond is trying to fix itself, and it needs us to keep the skin-to-skin contact."

"Fucking hell." I examined our magical cores again. They were still trying to hogtie themselves to each other with tendrils of magic. "I'm so sorry. This is my fault." I'd gone into this thinking the bond was something I *had* to do, not something I wanted.

Simon shook his head as he looked down, and his hair fell over his face like a curtain between us. "I feel like I pressured you into it." Guilt came through the bond, loud and clear.

Oh, hell, no. Simon was the last person to blame for this fiasco. I put my arm around him. "It wasn't you. It was the situation." Hopefully he could feel my sincerity. "Do you think... do you think you should cut the bond now? Would it be easier?" I was strangely reluctant to suggest that, but it was only logical.

He hesitated. "Maybe? But I think you should try calling a vision before I do anything with the bond."

I scrunched up my face. I didn't have much hope that it'd work, but Simon was right. We'd gotten this far, so I might as well give it a shot. "Okay. But I want to get cleaned up first."

We held hands as we got out of bed and shuffled into the bathroom. "The shower will be easiest." I turned it on to heat up, then I froze. "Um, I need to...." I waved in the direction of the toilet.

"Ah." The bond helpfully informed me that Simon was experiencing sympathy, mild embarrassment, amusement, and awkwardness. His face, however, didn't convey any of those things. He just smiled and gestured for me to lead the way.

The toilet was in one of those little tiny rooms with a door on it, which I'd always imagined would be convenient if you had to take a shit while your significant other was getting ready for their day. I was beyond grateful all I had to do was piss right then. At least I could stand with my back to Simon while he hung out in the doorway with his hand on my shoulder.

As I released my bladder, I tried to picture the best way for Simon to stand if I had to sit on the toilet sometime in the next several hours. I'd decided the best pose would be where he put his hand on the top of my head and turned to face the rest of the bathroom when he started laughing.

"Oh, shit. Could you see that?" I flushed the toilet and, red-faced, shoved him out into the area in front of the sinks, making sure to keep hold of his wrist.

His grin was huge, and his eyes were sparkling. My embarrassment vanished as I took in his gorgeousness. He wiped his eyes. "I'm sorry. I was trying to remember what I'd learned about imperfect bonds, when my mind was suddenly filled with this image of you on the toilet, and my hand on your head." He started laughing again, doubling over and putting his free hand on his knee.

"Fuck off. I was trying to solve a future problem."

Still smiling, he pulled me into a hug and kissed my lips. Something fluttered in my chest, and I was just starting to sink into it when he stiffened, and his eyes went wide. "Is this okay?"

I hugged him back. "It's fine. I like it. You can kiss me anytime." Because I was a fucking hypocrite, wanting Simon to kiss me while asking him to sever our bond.

We got in the shower, and while I thought I could've talked Simon into some naked shenanigans, both of us felt the clock ticking. I needed to call a vision.

Showers had always helped me think through problems. Simon was washing my hair while I lathered up his chest when I came up with a possible solution to the have-to-be-touching-all-the-time issue. "Hey, you know that thing you did in the park, where you put a kink in our connection so it wasn't visible to the other vampires?"

"Yeah?" He guided me under the spray to rinse my hair.

"What if you did that to our bond? Would it let us be apart from each other?"

He frowned as I helped him rinse himself off. "It would, but I don't think I could hold it for very long; it would take a lot of energy. And I'm not sure what effect it would have on a bond like ours, since it's already kind of twisted up."

Well, crap. "Okay, just a thought."

We got out and dried off, then we put our clothes back on, which required some gymnastics so we could maintain physical contact. We did figure out that the bond didn't mind a layer of fabric between us, which would make things easier.

I checked the clock. Fuck, it was only a little after 10:00 a.m. It felt like a lifetime had passed since I'd woken up this morning. "Okay. I want to lay down. I'm going to meditate for a few minutes, then call the vision."

"Where do you want me?" Simon, who'd been holding onto my wrist, rubbed his thumb along the inside of my forearm. I shivered.

"Um, how about sitting or lying next to me? I think it'd be less distracting if I was touching you with my shoulder or leg instead of our hands."

"Got it." He shifted his grip to my upper arm as I got onto the bed. I hadn't bothered to pull the quilt up after we'd had sex earlier, so I just kicked it out of the way of my feet for now. I shuffled my body to the far side of the bed, and Simon tossed his phone onto the mattress then climbed in after me. Soon I was lying on my back with my head on a pillow while Simon sat propped up against the headboard. My shoulder and upper arm were pressed into Simon's thigh. It was oddly comforting, knowing he was there. He was trying to focus on his phone, but his worry and concern for me were coming through the bond.

I was worried too. Worried I couldn't call a vision. Worried those two vampires were out there attacking more Wonders. Worried I'd made Simon bond with me for nothing.

His hand landed on my arm, and I jolted, my eyes flying open. He stared down at me. "You're supposed to be meditating, not stewing over things you can't control."

I put my hand over my eyes. "Sorry."

"Here." I looked to see him put his phone on the nightstand. Then he scooted himself down on the bed so he was lying next to me, our shoulders and arms pressed together. "Okay, we'll both meditate. Match my breathing. In." He sucked a breath in for longer than I usually did. "And out." That also pushed my lungs' comfort zone. Which was of course the point. I had to pay attention to my breathing to sync it with his. After a few minutes I relaxed and felt centered enough to try for a vision.

Where were Roibeart and Marcas? I pictured their snarling faces and opened myself up to receiving a vision of their whereabouts.

But I got nothing.

It only took a minute or two of trying before I gave up. I opened my eyes. "It's not happening."

Simon rolled up onto one elbow. "It's okay. We can work on healing our bond, then you can try again."

I rubbed my face. "What if it doesn't happen? I don't want to have to use Nicky as bait, but I don't see any other option."

He blew out a breath. "Let's ask Cal to get Delphia and Edgar to come back from their trip. That'll give us a couple of days to work on the bond, and if we haven't fixed it enough by then, we'll have two other Seers who can call visions."

"Okay."

Simon grabbed his phone and dialed Cal. He put the call on speaker and held it between us.

When Cal answered, we explained the situation with our bond and that I couldn't call a vision.

"Fuck. I'm sorry, y'all. Let me look at the river cruise itinerary and see when they'll dock next." We heard clicking. "Uh, this isn't good. They won't dock again until tomorrow afternoon their time, which will be around 8:00 a.m. here."

"Shit. Can you think of anything else we can try in the meantime?" When had I taken hold of Simon's hand? I dismissed the question as unimportant and laced my fingers through his.

He made a humming noise. "Okay, I couldn't see anything when I tried to call a vision from here, but my head's fully healed now and I'm good to drive again. I'll try again to call one here, and if that doesn't work, I'll drive to, say, Cuero. Then I'll be within a hundred miles of you, which is well within my usual range. Even Greg won't be able to bitch about me putting myself in danger at that distance."

I sagged against Simon. "Thank you, Cal. Really. That would be amazing."

"Anytime."

We hung up and sat there in silence for a moment or two before Simon spoke. "Do you still want me to see if the bond can be broken?" His voice was neutral, but I could feel his reluctance.

Still, I felt bad keeping him bonded to me when I obviously wasn't as committed as he was. Even the magic could tell. "Yeah, I think it would be for the best."

He nodded. "Okay, but only if it can be done easily. If it will be debilitating, we need to wait, because I can't risk impairing my fighting abilities."

Raising my eyebrows, I pointed a finger at our arms, which were smashed together as we sat on the bed.

He rolled his eyes. "For the duration of a fight, I can suppress the bond like I did our connection at the park. Now let me concentrate." I grinned at his snark. At least he didn't hate me for putting him through all this.

RIO DE JANEIRO,
BRAZIL – APRIL, 1992

"This is home." Davi unlocked the door to his apartment and waved me inside. The building was modest, but he'd done a nice job decorating his place in aquas and beiges suitable for a seaside city.

"Wow, what's all this?" Half of his living room was taken up with a row of desks, each with a computer and multiple monitors. There was even a camcorder on a tripod. One desk chair on wheels, with what looked to my untrained eye like a hand-knitted throw blanket draped over it, was positioned in the center of it all.

He took the food bags from me and carried them into the kitchen. "I do freelance computer programming. Some of it's even legal."

I laughed. I hadn't made time to learn to use a computer. The luchd-òl fola certainly didn't own one, so I hadn't seen the need.

We ate in front of the TV. Davi made me watch Vamp, a telenovela he'd recorded on his VCR. It was a musical comedy about a rock star who'd been turned into a vampire. I didn't find it as amusing as he did, but I thoroughly enjoyed the novelty of sharing an evening with someone just for fun.

When we finished eating, Davi seemed tired, so I took the plates to the kitchen and washed them. He was asleep on the couch by the time I was done. I considered putting him to bed and going to find a *hotel, but I didn't want him to think I'd left for good. I let him sleep and I watched the next episode of* Vamp, *which was equally as dreadful as the first, but I couldn't be bothered to figure out how to watch something else.*

Davi stirred a couple of hours later. "You're still here."

"I am. I didn't want to wake you."

He looked at his watch. "Fuck, it's not even that late. I get so goddamn exhausted all the time." He got up and shuffled into the bathroom. When he came out, he sat next to me on the couch again. "Um." He fiddled with the buttons on his shirt. He glanced at me, then down at his lap. "Were you serious about the blood thing? Do you need to, like, feed?"

"I do, but I won't if you're not comfortable with it, or if you aren't feeling well. I can find someone else."

He glanced up again but kept meeting my eyes this time. "If I say yes, can you... would you fuck me? Too?" Before I could respond, he held up a hand. "Only if you want to. It's not a requirement. You can have the blood anyway. I—"

I grasped his hand, then I leaned in and kissed him, hard. He whimpered as I pulled back. "I'd love to fuck you."

His eyes glistened, and his lips trembled. "Yeah?"

"Yeah. But you don't need to let me feed from you. I'll have sex with you either way."

A tear spilled, and he brushed it impatiently away. "Sorry, I—it's been so long, and I thought I'd never get to be with another person like that before I died." His face crumpled and I pulled him into a hug.

"Trust me, it'll be my pleasure."

He took one shaky breath, then sat back and smiled. "So, uh, are the stories about vampires drinking your blood true?" He popped his eyebrows up and down a couple of times.

I grinned. "If you mean, will you find it arousing? Yes, if you want it to be."

"Hell, yes. But let's move to the bed, okay?"

When we got to the bedroom, Davi was shy about getting undressed, so I took over, peeling off his clothes. Under his shirt he was wearing a silver necklace with a pendant carved into a snarling jaguar head. The eyes appeared to be emeralds. I left that alone and bent to licking him and scraping my fangs gently over his skin. He was dotted with other lesions, and the smell of the illnesses wracking his body was noticeable. He probably only had a few months left to live, if that. I pushed those thoughts away. I couldn't heal him. Hell, without the Portal open, no one could. All I could do was distract him and give him what he needed.

When he was a panting mess, I pulled off my own clothes. "How do you want it?"

"Um." He looked away and toyed with his necklace. "Whatever you like is fine."

Oh, no. That wouldn't do. I leaned up on one elbow. "Nuh uh. You've got something in mind, I can tell. What is it?" I held up a hand. "If I don't want to do it, I won't."

His face did that complicated almost-crying expression again, then he closed his eyes. "I want to be held. I want gentle, tender. I want to be able to pretend that you care about me."

My heart twisted, but I put on a smile in case he opened his eyes. "I can do that." I kissed him softly but insistently, and when he finally relaxed and responded, I did my best to give him the experience of making love, not just fucking. When he was close to orgasm, he groaned my name and said, "Bite me." He tilted his head so I could get to his neck. I made sure to choose a spot as low as I could, so he could cover the mark with a collar if he wanted to.

He tensed when I made the cut, but as I started to suck, I flooded him with all the arousal I was feeling. He gasped and came, and I was right behind him. When he collapsed to the mattress, I retracted my fangs and licked the wound so it would close. I hoped my tiny bit of healing magic wouldn't be affected by his immune system being offline.

I rolled to my side and pulled him against me. "Can I stay the night?"

He chuckled. "If you keep that up, you can stay as long as you like."

I didn't sleep much. My thoughts were full of Davi, and how little time he had left. How he couldn't easily buy groceries, and who would take care of him when he couldn't take care of himself anymore. I knew there were clinics and hospices, but when I pictured Davi there all alone, it tore me up inside.

But then there were the Wonders who were getting kidnapped and fed on by the luchd-òl fola. As much as I wanted to stay with Davi, could I really justify putting his needs over all the Wonders in danger?

When I woke in the morning, he was already up, working at one of the computers in the living room. The knitted blanket, which had a wavy blue and green pattern, was draped over his lap. He pointed at the kitchen. "There's coffee and bread for toast, but not much else. I'll have to try again to buy groceries today." His voice was carefully neutral.

Damn it.

I fixed my coffee and brought it into the living room, where I leaned against the corner of his desk. He appeared to be reading a series of short messages. "What's that?"

He grinned. "It's a chat room for the campaign in one of the states to the north of us. The District Monitor is having trouble with some of the Wonder children revealing their true forms to the locals. It's hilarious."

"The... campaign? And what's a District Monitor?"

He looked at me with shock. "You don't know about the campaign?"

"No?"

"Oh, honey. Here, pull that chair over here. Have you at least been on the World Wide Web before?"

In minutes I was educated about Dungeons & Dragons, and how the terms from the game were being used to allow Wonders and magic carriers to communicate more openly, particularly online.

"I'm not officially part of any of these chat rooms, but I like to keep an eye on them." He shrugged, turning a little red. "It doesn't make me any money, but it's my way of helping the community. Every once in a while, something happening in one place will happen elsewhere, and I can put people in touch with each other."

I sat there with my mouth open. The possibilities were endless. This could make my mission so much easier. I would bet my last coin that the luchd-òl fola didn't have access to a computer or the understanding of how to use one. I could get ahead of them. Finally.

I turned to Davi. "Will you teach me?"

CHAPTER 14
SIMON

RENO WAS GLAD I DIDN'T HATE HIM. IT HAD COME THROUGH loud and clear. My bonded mate was glad I didn't hate him.

I'd never been one to wallow in self-pity, but the only reason I wanted to get rid of this bond with Reno was so I could feel sorry for myself without him knowing.

He was glad his mate didn't hate him, and I wished my mate would love me.

Gritting my teeth, I closed my eyes and examined the bond. It looked slightly better than it had right after we'd mated. Some of the magical tendrils tying the cores together were going through them instead of around them. The disparity between the speeds at which our cores were spinning seemed to be smaller too. It appeared that our magics wanted this bond to take, which didn't bode well for me undoing it right now.

Tentatively I tugged at one of the tendrils of my magic tied around Reno's core. My core threw out a new tendril to effectively slap me back. "Shit!"

I opened my eyes and gave Reno a rueful look that I hoped

didn't convey any of the relief I felt. "It's fighting me. Our magics want to stay bonded."

His eyebrows went up. "Huh." Then he frowned. "I guess that makes sense. Our cores sent out the original mating connection after all." He squeezed my hand. "Thanks for trying."

"Of course." Anything for you.

He stared at me for a beat, his cheeks turning pink. Shit, did he hear that thought through our connection? "Um." He glanced around the room. "I must've left my phone in the kitchen. I'd like to research that Emiliano guy some more while we wait to hear from Cal. Are you ready to tell the others what happened? Or didn't happen?"

I squeezed his hand back. "I'm ready."

When we went downstairs, Jackson was in the kitchen getting snacks out of the pantry, and Tucker was helping Nicky get settled on a chair at the kitchen table.

"Whoa." Reno, who'd been walking ahead of me, stopped in his tracks.

"What is it?" I could see over his shoulder, and I didn't note anything concerning.

He pointed at Tucker. "His connections. I can tell which ones are friends and which ones are family."

"You can? Fantastic. The bond is sharing some of my abilities with you."

He turned slowly to blink at me. "That's not the way it works."

"What do you mean?"

Reno made an impatient gesture. "Bonding enhances the abilities people already have. Like once he got bonded, Cal could call visions and his geographic range is bigger. That's what should be happening to me. I've never heard of anyone gaining their partner's abilities."

Vaguely I remembered reading about that in the compendium Cal had written. "For vampires, each partner's abilities get combined with the other's skills. Like, if one of the partners has more experience at manipulating connection magic, on bonding the other partner realizes the same level of skill." I shrugged. "In the Elven dimension it wasn't that noticeable, because vampires only mated with vampires. I'm pretty sure the Elves don't know."

He raised his eyebrows at me, and I got a combination of astonishment and worry through our bond. "Does this mean you'll start getting visions now?"

Well, shit. I hadn't considered that. "I don't know. As far as I'm aware, I'm the only vampire who's ever mated outside our species." Wait a minute. I sucked in a breath. "That's why!" I grabbed Reno's shoulders. "When we were fighting Marcas and Roibeart at the park, I was faster than usual, and I healed my wound when I misted. I'd never been able to do that before. I'm getting my abilities enhanced, like any other magic carrier's mate would, and you're getting some of my abilities, like a vampire's mate would."

That means I'll never be able to call a vision. I was counting on our bond acting like any other magic carrier or Wonder's bond. Reno's realization echoed between us like a death knell. Our bond delivered the thought he hadn't voluntarily sent to me: *What use am I?* and then a horrified, *I made Simon mate me for nothing!*

I hugged him, drawing him as close as I could. I'm so sorry I didn't realize earlier. And your calling a vision might have

been why we decided to bond today, but it was never any part of why I want you to be my mate.

He didn't respond, but I got a swirl of gratefulness, guilt, and a feeling of inadequacy. Working through Reno's feelings would take longer than we had right now.

We held each other for a beat until Tucker interrupted. "So, you're mated? Is that typical for how a vampire mating bond looks?" He pointed at us.

Sighing, Reno broke away from our hug and tugged me to the table. "Yes, we're mated. No, it didn't take completely, because I'm an asshole and subconsciously I wasn't all in. And the whole thing was for nothing because I can't call a vision." He gestured at me. "And it doesn't seem like I'll ever be able to."

My knee-jerk reaction was to object to him calling himself an asshole, but he squeezed my hand so I let it be.

Tucker cocked his head. "Your scents have mingled, and you're holding hands, so it can't be all bad."

Reno shook his head and pulled out one of the chairs. "No, we have to stay touching each other."

Jackson and Nicky hadn't commented. They were both too busy staring at the ramshackle bond Reno and I had created.

I saw Reno's phone on the kitchen counter, so I grabbed it. His aunt had messaged him, but otherwise he only had a few new texts from Wonders. They'd all reacted positively to my responses, and many of them had started contacting me instead of Reno. I handed him the phone as I sat down next to him. He was explaining Cal's plan to get closer if he couldn't call a vision now.

Speaking of Cal, my phone rang. I answered. "Hey, Cal. You're on speaker with me, Reno, Jackson, Nicky, and Tucker.

"Hi, everybody. So, same result. No vision. I'm in the car on the way to get closer to you. It'll take me about two hours. I have a good success rate with calling visions within a smaller range, so I'm hopeful this will work. If it doesn't, I'll contact Delphia and get them to come home."

But we all knew Roibeart and Marcas wouldn't wait that long to feed again.

After wishing him good luck, we hung up. Tucker glanced at his watch. "I've got to be at work in a bit, so I need to get goin'. Do you want me to see if my mom can come over this afternoon, in case Cal finds out where the vamps are?"

Reno gave me a questioning look, and I shook my head. "If you can have her on standby, we'll call if we find out anything."

"Okay. Good luck with the, uh, bond. Reno, I'll text for an update when I'm on break."

He left, and Jackson filled the table with chips, crackers, cheese, deli meats, and fruit. We didn't get plates, but we got napkins. I'd had worse lunches.

After we ate, I loaded the photos from Reno's camera onto my laptop and tried to use image search to figure out who Emiliano's girlfriend was. Using a photo of another photo, especially one behind glass, made it challenging, and I had to spend quite a bit of time cleaning up the pictures before I could get any search results at all. Reno worked next to me, going through his messages while we maintained physical contact by pressing our knees together under the table.

"Hey." I nudged him. "Here, let me add your fingerprint so you can access my computer." I turned my laptop toward him and pointed at the power button.

He held his hands up and leaned back. "What? Why? That's your private stuff."

I lifted an eyebrow. "At this point I don't think we have any secrets from each other. Besides, this way you can get to my Discord account and texts in case you need to find a message from a Wonder."

He considered this for a minute, then he made a huffing noise and put his finger on the button on my laptop. I got him added to the facial recognition on my phone as well, and I felt a little thrill that my mate was even more integrated into my life. Reno eyed me a little curiously at that point, so he must've felt something through the bond, but I pretended not to notice.

He hadn't tried to block the bond yet, or at least not that I was aware of. The magic might not even let him do it right now, but either way I hoped he didn't try.

We worked together well into mid-afternoon. I finally identified Emiliano's girlfriend—or at least her Instagram username. She didn't have any personally identifying information in her bio, but the face was the same as the one in Emiliano's photos. I started a list of the accounts she'd tagged so I could investigate those.

I knew Reno didn't love his job as a private investigator, but other than the low-key tension he'd had since he hadn't been able to call the vision this morning, he seemed content enough. Maybe he'd just needed a partner. I loved that I could do that for him.

That thought definitely made it through the bond to Reno. He didn't look at me, but his cheeks flushed, and he stopped typing the email he'd been composing, his fingers poised above the keyboard for a few seconds before he carried on.

I refused to be ashamed of my feelings. Besides, how could he make an informed decision about whether to keep the bond after all this was over if he didn't know how I felt?

Reno cleared his throat. "I think it's time we alert the local gargoyle family about Emiliano Duran. I meant to do it yesterday, but...." He rubbed the back of his neck.

"We got distracted."

"Yeah." He took his reading glasses off and fiddled with them.

"Sure. Do you want to call them, or—" My phone rang. "Hold that thought. It's Cal." Nicky and Jackson were watching TV, but they paused it as I put the phone on speaker. "Hey, Cal, how did it go?"

His voice was urgent. "Get Nicky, and all of you stay together. I think they're in the house." Reno and I jumped to our feet as Cal kept talking. "The Hunters in the backyard are dead. The rest of the Hunter team will know, but I don't have any idea how long it will take them to get there. My vision was for right now, I'm sure of it."

Reno and I both looked out the window to the backyard, but nothing was visible except the grass and shrubs. He took hold of my arm, and I grabbed the phone. "Cal, can you call Tucker? No, he's at work. Shirley then. She might be able to get here faster than the Hunters." We ran over to the sofa and stood next to the outside corner of the sectional. Nicky was wide-eyed with fear, and Jackson crouched over him on the cushions in their panther form.

I cast around. My mek'leth was in the guest bedroom. Too far, especially if Reno had to come with me. "Weapons?"

"Here." Reno pulled me over to the side table nearest the front door. I held onto him while he opened the cabinet and took out a gun case. He unlocked it and proceeded to load the handgun. "This is all I've got."

"No." From beneath Jackson's stomach, Nicky stretched out his hand so he could reach over the back of the couch. The baseball bat Tucker had left by the back door flew into it, and he held it out to me.

"Thank you, but your magic is still weak. Don't waste it." But I accepted the bat as Reno and I took position again at the corner of the sectional. "Reno, I'm going to do the thing with the bond."

A pause, then he nodded. "Do it."

I didn't dare close my eyes, but I reached inside and did the best I could to twist the bond so it didn't flare between me and Reno like a beacon. Tentatively I took a step away from him, sighing with relief when there was no pain.

"Should we take this outside?" Reno answered his own question. "No, we're more defensible here. Alright! Let's take these fuckers down." Reno kept the gun down at his side as he swept the room with his gaze.

We didn't have to wait long before Roibeart and Marcas misted into the living room from the guest bedroom hallway. My claws came out and I could feel my fangs elongating. I stood between the intruders and Nicky and Jackson, holding the baseball bat at the ready. "You won't win here. The Hunters are on their way."

They reformed, Marcas coming at me with a sword, and Roibeart darting around us to get to Reno. I blocked Marcas' blade, trying to shove him away from the sofa and into the open space next to the kitchen table. The gun fired, and Roibeart grunted. I laughed into Marcas' face. Vampires should be too fast for a magic carrier to shoot, but the mate bond must have gifted Reno with some of my speed.

I deflected Marcas' swing again and reached under him to swipe at his belly with my claws just as Reno shouted, "No!"

My head filled with a roaring pain, and I fell.

GUATEMALA CITY, GUATEMALA – AUGUST, 1992

I pulled out my ear plugs and left the target range, heading for my van in the parking lot. The submachine gun was probably my favorite of my new purchases. It was astonishing what kind of weapons you could buy if you had enough cash.

I reloaded all of the weapons before putting them in a carryall in the passenger side footwell so I could reach them on the fly.

Getting into the driver's seat, I slipped on my sunglasses then tugged on Davi's jaguar pendant before letting it fall to my chest. I gritted my teeth against the familiar wave of grief and put the van in gear.

The one friend I'd made in the last fifty years was dead. And he'd left me a legacy of so much more than a necklace.

Davi's gift from the Elves had turned out to be an intuitive understanding of strategy, which made computer hacking and financial investments simple for him. As a result, he hadn't had to think very hard to know what I'd be like after he was gone. "Promise me you won't be alone. I know you have to travel around, but you can talk to people online. Get to know them. Let them get to know you. Let them care about you."

I might not make any online friends, but the chat rooms dedicated to "the campaign" were a good way to find local magic carriers. In my downtime from searching for the luchd-òl fola, I planned to meet as many as possible. One of them could be my mate. It'd been long enough since that Seer's vision. Surely my mate was out there by now. If I had a mate, I wouldn't be alone, and I could complete my mission.

In addition to teaching me about computers and how to sneak around online undetected, Davi had helped me rethink how I'd been hunting the luchd-òl fola. Before, my goal had been to recover Prince Nicol first, then take out as many of the luchd-òl fola as I could. Davi pointed out that I should be focused on reducing the number of luchd-òl fola so it would be easier to rescue the prince. And it wasn't like I wanted to leave any of them alive to kill more Wonders.

That afternoon, as I drove through some nameless little town roughly an hour from where the gossip in the chat rooms said the latest Wonder had gone missing, I idly turned my head and saw Barabal walking along the sidewalk, bold as you please. "Well, fuck. Thank you, Davi."

I pulled over on the opposite side of the street and watched as she turned into a parking lot and got into the passenger side of a rusty Ford sedan. As the car circled the lot to exit, I caught sight of the driver. Tavish.

I followed the car until we were outside of town on a rural two-lane dirt road. No one else was around for miles. They might already suspect I was following them, but if they made a turn, I wouldn't be able to pretend anymore. No way would they lead me to where they were hiding the Wonders and the prince. Time to implement Davi's plan.

I reached into the carryall and pulled out what I needed. I waited until the road was as smooth as it was going to get, then I rolled down the window. Bracing my knees against the steering wheel, I propped the barrel of the grenade launcher on the side mirror.

I bared my fangs at the car ahead. "Davi, this is for you."

CHAPTER 15
RENO

THE VAMPIRE WAS FAST. I DIDN'T KNOW HOW I'D BEEN ABLE TO hit his chest with my first shot, but at least it made him wary of me. I retreated toward the front door to give myself room to maneuver, but now the asshole was darting back and forth, no doubt to make it harder for me to aim. He was succeeding.

Then he snarled and turned to run toward Simon. He reached behind his back and pulled out a gun of his own. Fuck! Jackson flattened themself over Nicky as the vampire passed them. I ran after him, but I couldn't shoot without risking hitting Simon as he fought the other one by the back door.

In an instant, the one I'd been fighting had his gun pointed at Simon's head only a few feet away.

"No!" I fired without even analyzing my aim, somehow hitting my target in the back of his head. But I was too late; he'd done the same to Simon. Both of them went down at once. "Simon!"

Our bond snapped back into view, brilliant and glittering. He was still alive, thank fuck. The bond wanted me closer to him, but it wasn't painful, so it could wait. I pointed my gun at the vampire who'd been fighting Simon.

He raised his eyebrows and smirked. I couldn't hear well since my ears were ringing because of the gunfire, but I thought he said, "Simon is bonded? How cute." Then he lifted his sword and swung it down toward Simon's neck. I emptied my gun into him, chest, arms, shoulder. I should've gone for the head, but I was too focused on preventing him from swinging the sword to think of it. He staggered back, the tip of his sword hitting Simon with a glancing blow near his temple. I winced in sympathy, but our bond didn't even flicker. He was okay.

I darted forward, snatching up the baseball bat Simon had dropped when he fell. It wasn't much, but it was something. Except the vampire ignored me and, despite the bullet wounds covering his body, lunged sword-first at Jackson instead. Jackson reared up to meet him, claws out and fangs bared. They jumped at the vampire, making him step back. Jackson ripped at the vampire with their claws, too close for him to swing the sword. The vampire gouged Jackson with the claws on his other hand, and Nicky screamed. But the vampire couldn't get any purchase, his claws sliced through Jackson but didn't catch on any muscle or skin. A few drops of glittering goo hit the floor, but Jackson didn't seem injured otherwise.

As Jackson and the vampire grappled, I ran over to the sofa and pulled Nicky over the back, setting him on his feet right behind me. He put one arm over my shoulder, and I nudged him to walk backwards towards the front door. I held the bat up, just in case the vampire came at us.

The vampire shrieked as Jackson dug their claws into his sides, but then he got his sword in between them against Jackson's neck. Jackson let go, so their neck must've been more vulnerable than the rest of them. They retreated a few steps, as if to regroup, but they tripped over Simon, and their back legs went out from under them. The vampire leapt forward and swung the sword across Jackson's neck, separating their head. I gasped in horror as glittery magical goo fountained out of the wound.

"No!" Nicky tried to go to Jackson, but his legs collapsed beneath him. Fuck.

"Nicky! Stand up!" I couldn't lean over to pick him up, because the vampire was strolling casually toward us with a gloating expression, swinging his sword idly.

Nicky hauled himself to his feet, using my free arm and the waistband of my jeans for leverage. He put his arms around my belly, and I supported him with my hand on his waist. He leaned toward the vampire, his face contorted with hatred. "No more killing!" His hands glowed, sparkling with magic and pressing into my stomach. I could feel his energy pouring into my core.

"Nicky!" I was torn between watching the vampire and trying to see whatever Nicky was doing.

The vampire froze in place, still several feet away, and he held up his free hand. "Wait. We can talk about this."

My eyesight sharpened, and everyone's connections and magical cores became the brightest things in the room. Was this what it was like for Simon? The mating bond between us, imperfect as it was, glowed in a magnificent rainbow river. Nicky's friend connections glinted gold. The vampire's only connection was to the other one on the floor. It wasn't even a friend connection; it was more like one you'd have to a teammate or colleague. Sad.

The vampire started to rush forward, raising his sword to attack, but everything seemed to slow down. I knew exactly what to do. It was as if I'd always known, but I'd needed the mate bond with Simon and the magical boost from Nicky to unlock the ability.

As if I had all the time in the world, I sent my magic out to surround the vampire's magical core. And then, smiling as I met his eyes, I used my magic to squish his out of existence.

Time sped up again, and he fell on his face with a thump, his sword clattering on the floor next to him. The other vampire was still alive, so I did the same to him, squeezing his core until it popped.

Nicky, panting with effort, was still flooding me with his magic. I dropped the baseball bat and put both of my arms around him. "Nicky, stop. We're safe now. Keep your magic. You did good, thank you."

The energy flow into me stopped, and he gasped out a sob. "You did it. I wasn't strong enough to do it myself."

"That was smart of you to combine our magic." My view of his connections and mine were fading back to normal.

I half-carried, half-dragged Nicky past the dead vampire. He'd probably set his recovery back quite a bit, but at least he was alive, and the danger was over. When we got to Jackson's body, Nicky let out another sob and reached out for them, so I set him down on the floor. I knelt next to Simon, trying not to look at the bullet entry wound on the back of his head. The sword tip had caught him just above and behind his ear. He'd lost a little hair, but the wound had stopped bleeding.

I turned to Nicky to see if he knew whether I should try to feed Simon, but he'd crawled over to Jackson's head and was pushing it back toward their body. Both, er, pieces were still in panther form, and my heart ached to see the dullness in their eyes, the runes in their fur no longer visible. Their connections were gone. They didn't exactly have a magical core—it was more like they were made of magic—but that glow had faded to nothing. As Nicky pushed Jackson's head along the floor, it dug a path through the glittering goo.

"What are you *doing*?" I wasn't proud of how scandalized I sounded.

"This." He'd gotten over to Jackson's body, and he put one hand on their shoulder and the other on the top of their head, then he shoved the two, er, parts together. The glittering goo glowed at the seam. I sucked in a breath and gripped Simon's hand. Was Jackson still alive? Nicky didn't comment, just heaved a relieved sigh and patted Jackson's shoulder. Then he folded his arms on their back and leaned his head down onto them, closing his eyes.

I looked down at Simon. I wanted to cry, but I held it in. Nicky didn't need to see that right now. I wished Simon would open his eyes. I'd give a lot to see him smile at me again. I knew he'd heal from the bullet in his head eventually, but how long would it take? The bond was super happy to feel us touching, but it didn't give me any hints as to what to do. "I bet I need to feed you." But how?

"Hello? Reno? Simon? Can someone hear me?"

Shit. "Cal?" Was he still on the line? I stood up, the mating bond protesting my leaving Simon, but it still wasn't doing the pain thing it'd done this morning. "Can you hear me?"

"Reno! Thank fuck. Are you okay?"

I found Simon's phone still on the couch cushion where he'd left it. "Yeah. The vampires are dead. Nicky's okay, but he used a lot of his magic. Simon took a bullet to the head, so he's unconscious, but he'll be fine, I think. Jackson, um, got their head cut off." Cal made a distressed noise. "Uh, but Nicky put it back on? I'm not sure...."

"Shit, Reno. I hope they'll be okay. I'm on 183 and I should be there in about an hour and twenty. Have the Hunters gotten there yet?"

"No. Haven't seen them."

"Well, my phone says it's only been around twelve minutes since I called y'all, but they should get there soon. I messaged both Shirley and Tucker, so they'll probably show up too."

"Hold up. It's only been twelve minutes?" It had felt like a lifetime. I sank back down to the ground next to Simon. "Hey, Cal. Do you know how to get Simon to feed from me while he's unconscious?"

"Noooo? Maybe make a cut on your wrist and put it in his mouth?"

"Yeah, I guess."

A key turned in the front door lock, and the door cracked open. "Holy shit!" Tucker pushed it wide. "Reno?"

"Over here." I waved. "It's Tucker," I said to Cal.

"Okay, now that he's there, I'm going to end the call so I can focus on driving. I'll be there as soon as I can."

"Thanks, Cal. If you hadn't have warned us, it would've been a lot worse." I wouldn't have had my gun, Simon wouldn't have had the baseball bat, and neither of us would've been near Nicky and Jackson. "We owe you our lives."

"All in a day's work, Reno. You know how it is."

"Still. If you ever need anything. We're here for you."

Shirley followed Tucker inside, and they both stepped around the dead vampire to get to us. "Oh, hell. Jackson!" Tucker crouched down next to Nicky, who raised his head blearily before letting it fall to his forearms again.

As Shirley bent over to hug me, I wished I could lay my head down too. "Jackson might heal. The, uh, stuff around their neck was glowing a minute ago."

"Damn, I hope so." Tucker stroked their fur. "Simon'll be okay?"

I sighed, and there was definitely a hint of a sob in it. "I think so. His magic is still bright. But I don't know how long it'll take, and I feel like I should give him some blood, but I don't know how when he's unconscious."

He frowned. "There's bagged blood in the fridge. That might be easier to pour down his throat."

I shook my head almost instantly. "Not for this. It needs to be mine. I can't say why. Maybe it's a mate thing."

"Okay, okay. It was just an idea."

Shirley leaned over to peer at Nicky. "When was the last time either of you had some water?"

"Uh... I don't remember?"

She shook her head. "I'll be right back." She straightened up and started toward the kitchen right as the back door slammed open and three Hunters came in, guns and knives aimed everywhere. Four more came in the front door, also armed to the teeth.

Shirley, Tucker, and I raised our hands. "Don't shoot! The fight's over."

"Stand down, everyone. I repeat, stand down!" Dominic took off his helmet and came over. "Y'all okay?" He grimaced at Jackson and Simon. "I guess not. Sorry. We were following up on a possible sighting across town."

"Cal said the Hunters guarding us were killed?"

He took a deep breath and glanced out the back door. "Yeah. Carter and Franklin."

"I'm sorry."

He nodded in short jerky movements. "Thanks. Can you tell me what happened from your perspective? After that I promise we'll get the dead vamps out of here. Um, shit, we need to take their heads off, don't we?" He started gazing around, possibly to find a sword. Tucker looked alarmed as well.

"No." I held my hand up. "Normally, yes, But it's not necessary for these guys. Their magical cores are gone." Not to mention I'd really rather not have more blood to clean off the floor.

Dominic eyed me with disbelief, but he didn't comment, just went to get a chair from the kitchen table to sit on.

Shirley came over and shoved a bottle of water into my hand, then she sat next to Nicky and made Tucker prop him up against his shoulder so they could get some water into him.

I kept one hand on Simon as I told Dominic and the others about the fight. Shirley glared at me to remind me to drink my water, and she brought me another bottle when the first one was empty. Dominic kept his face expressionless the entire time I spoke, but when I finished, he rubbed his jaw and shook his head. "Y'all were fucking lucky."

"Trust me, I'm aware."

One of the Hunters took photos of everything before they wrapped the dead vampires in some tarps and took them away. Dominic told me they'd be doing a reconstruction of the fight for training purposes. I shuddered. I didn't want to know.

"Okay, if you're done with me, I want to move Simon to my bedroom so I can give him some blood and get him cleaned up a bit."

"I'll help carry him." Tucker started to stand, but Shirley put a hand on his shoulder.

"Stay with Nicky. He needs a familiar face if he wakes up. I'll carry Simon."

Dominic got up from his chair. "Do you want me to leave some Hunters here overnight?" He examined the blood and goo on my floor and the bullet holes in my walls. "Or we can take y'all to a hotel."

"No. We'll be fine. The danger's over and tomorrow's soon enough to clean up." I needed to be in my own space with Simon. No, I needed Simon to be in my space.

Dominic followed the rest of the Hunters out the door, and the house was quiet again. I stood, wishing I were strong enough to carry Simon myself. I gestured at Jackson and Nicky. "Do you think we should move them too?"

Tucker gave me a horrified look. He pointed at Jackson's neck. "We don't know if that's even... together!"

I shut my eyes. "Okay, yeah. Sorry, I'm tired."

"I'll order some pizza or something."

I swallowed. If Tucker could think about eating right after discussing what might happen if we moved Jackson, more power to him. Maybe I'd be hungry by the time the food actually arrived.

Shirley carried Simon up the stairs to my bedroom. I put a towel over the pillows until I could clean his poor head, and she helped me get his shoes and jeans off. His shirt was covered in blood, so she just shredded it with her claws to remove it.

I got a couple of damp washcloths from the bathroom, and Shirley and I wiped the worst of the blood from Simon's face and neck. His hair would be a problem for later, after he'd fed. At least the hole in his skull wasn't as large as it had been earlier. I hoped the bullet would come out on its own, because I really didn't want to figure out how to go in after it.

Once I'd removed my own blood-spattered jeans and shoes, I climbed onto the bed and positioned myself next to Simon's head. "Okay, here goes." Then I looked at my wrist. "Ugh. I forgot to bring a knife or something. Um, Shirley, would you mind using one of your claws to make a cut?"

She leaned over Simon and lifted his upper lip. "No need. His fangs are still mostly descended. If you use those, maybe it'll trigger some of his feedin' instincts."

Huh. "Good idea." She snorted and rolled her eyes. "Hey! I'm sorry I'm not a vampire expert after only knowing Simon for a few days!" Grumbling, I stuck my right thumb into the corner of Simon's mouth and eased his jaw open. "Don't bite down, now. I need my fingers." I carefully scraped the inside of my left wrist against one of his fangs. The skin parted almost painlessly, and blood welled up. I pressed my wrist to his mouth, hoping Simon's subconscious would take care of the rest.

After about thirty seconds of nothing happening, I stroked his throat. I wasn't sure exactly what I was doing, but I'd seen a vet do something similar to a puppy he was trying to feed a milk bottle to on one of those animal rescue reality shows.

It worked! Well, something did. Simon started sucking on my wrist. I grinned up at Shirley. "He's drinking." And each pull seemed directly connected to my dick, but I wasn't going to mention that to her. I dropped my free arm over my lap, hoping she wouldn't be able to smell my arousal.

She smiled back. "Don't let him take too much. I'll get you

some cookies or somethin' to keep your blood sugar up until the pizza comes."

"Thanks." I wasn't sure I had any cookies. Jackson had eaten quite a few last night before bed. Indeed, when Shirley reappeared, she was carrying a plate of butter crackers with jam on them, along with a large glass of ice water.

"This was the best I could do."

"This is perfect, thank you. Any change in Jackson?"

"Not yet. Tucker cleaned the floor, though, and we put Nicky on some couch cushions right next to Jackson so he could lie down."

I exhaled loudly. "That's great. I was worried he'd get a crick in his neck."

"Same. I'm gonna run downstairs, but when I get back, you'd better be done lettin' him feed on you." She raised an eyebrow at me. The same one she'd been raising at me for over forty years when I did something she didn't quite approve of.

"Yes, Shirley."

She sniffed and turned on her heel to leave the room.

Keeping an eye on my watch, I let Simon suck on my wrist for another five minutes. The blood in my throbbing dick counted off the seconds for me. When I pulled my wrist away, his lips and tongue tried to reach for more, but he quieted almost immediately.

I jumped out of bed and hurried into the shower to get cleaned up. I didn't want to give Shirley an eyeful of my erection. Fuck, Simon needed to get better quickly, because I wanted to sex him up like now.

But was that even fair to him, if I was still planning on asking him to sever our bond? A piercing pain went through my chest as my magical core expressed its opinion of the idea.

But my magical core wasn't in charge. I was still planning to ask him to sever it.

Right?

I didn't have an answer I was happy with by the time I'd showered and put on clean clothes. I mean, I wasn't enough of a dumbass that I didn't know Simon was a complete catch. Why he thought I was the guy of his dreams, I didn't understand. But if I were to be mated to anyone, he was the one I wanted. I was just having a hard time letting go of my desire to carve out some time to just be *me*. To be selfish for once.

And then there was the fact that we'd bonded so I could call a vision, which had turned out to be impossible. I still felt horrible about putting Simon through all this for no reason. Although, if I hadn't been bonded to Simon, I wouldn't have been able to see connections like vampires did, and Nicky might not have been able to help me kill the rogue vampires.

So in the end I guessed I could justify our temporary bonding. But if we were going to sever it, we'd need to do it now, before we got even more emotionally entangled.

The bond and my magical core vehemently let me know they did not approve of that idea, and this time the pain lasted even longer than before.

FT. LAUDERDALE,
FLORIDA –
DECEMBER 31, 1999

I followed Dermid and Hendry through the crowds around the clubhouse of some fancy golf resort. It was closing in on midnight, and the humans were drunk, attempting to dance to "Livin' La Vida Loca" by Ricky Martin while holding glasses of champagne. The celebration would provide good cover for kidnapping a Wonder.

The luchd-òl fola had never taken a magic carrier, probably because Wonders were naturally more resilient and longer-lived. A magic carrier wouldn't last being fed from every few days.

Yesterday I'd seen some online chatter about a dryad going missing ten miles or so from here. I'd developed a technique of scanning my surroundings for teammate-type connections, and tonight I'd been lucky enough to pass Dermid and Hendry on the highway. It'd been ridiculously easy to make a U-turn and follow them. They'd parked on the street in a residential area near the resort and just walked between two houses and onto the golf course, easy as you please.

Which meant they'd planned this. They were hunting a specific person.

I saw her right as they did. An alligator shifter. Long-lived and tough as hell. No wonder they wanted her. She was standing at the edge of the crowd, talking to three or four humans. She was dressed in golf clothes, as if she'd been playing a round this afternoon and hadn't bothered to go home and change.

Dermid and Hendry went up to the bar, apparently trying to blend in so they could approach her. I scanned the area. The golf course was shrouded in darkness, and there were several stands of trees they could drag their victim into. The question was how they intended to get her away from the human witnesses.

Hendry faded from view, melting into the shadows around the side of the building. Dermid chatted with a group of humans to their target's left. There. He bumped into her, spilling his drink all over himself—nice touch, not as suspicious as spilling it on her. She apologized, and, as midnight came and the humans nearby lost interest, he mesmerized her before drawing her away from the others.

I'd lost sight of Hendry, so I kept to the crowd as Dermid walked with the woman, his hands gesturing as if they were talking. Once they were around the corner, I sped up until I could peek after them. Yes, now Hendry had joined them. They'd thrown a dark cloth over the woman and were carrying her at high speed to the closest stand of trees. No human would catch a glimpse of them.

I waited to give them time to be far enough in the trees so they wouldn't see me coming after them, then I went into battle form. Claws and fangs at ready, I ran in a blur across the short grass.

They'd gained a significant amount of distance, so I misted to get ahead of them. I reformed where they could see me, and both of them came to a dead stop. Dermid was carrying the woman, and Hendry told him, "Get her to the van!"

I grinned as Dermid ran off through the trees. I'd put a tracking device on their van. They'd almost caught me doing it in Mexico, but I'd managed to get away in time. That tracking device had led to *four* luchd-òl fola *dying, and I hoped this one would do the same. But first, Hendry.*

The fight was over quickly. More and more I was noticing poor techniques and form among them. They weren't keeping up with their training, even though they all knew I was after them. Whoever was in charge—if anyone—wasn't doing them any favors, not that I was going to complain.

After beheading Hendry, I left his body where it was. No one would find it in the trees for a few hours at least. I ran for my car, which I'd parked half a block from Dermid and Hendry's van, but their van was still in place. I jogged more slowly back onto the golf course, and then I could hear it. Thrashing amid the trees near the ninth hole.

Dermid hadn't been able to maintain his control over the alligator shifter while she was wrapped up and being carried. When I found them, she'd shifted into her alligator form, a 10-foot beast with wicked teeth and claws. Dermid was bleeding from his arm, and he hadn't been smart enough to give up and leave. His connection would've told him Hendry was dead.

I crunched twigs and leaves so the shifter would hear me approach, but I didn't give Dermid time to react. I didn't want him shifting to mist form, and even someone who made poor choices like he'd done would know he couldn't win against me plus an alligator shifter.

I was on him, tearing his throat out with one swipe of my claws. The shifter went quiet, watching me carefully to see if I would attack. "Hello, there. My name's Simon." I put my foot on Dermid's upper spine and tore his head from his body. "I'm no threat to you. I was after these guys. The other one's dead too." I sighed as I looked down at my blood-covered hands and clothes. "I don't suppose you know which of the golf course ponds are free of alligators, so I can wash off?" I grimaced. "After I bury the bodies, of course."

She turned back into her human form. "I'm Roberta. I can dig holes for you, if you'll help me find what's left of my clothes so I can get my car keys." She glanced down at herself and sighed. "And I might need to borrow your shirt."

I grinned. "I've got clean clothes in my van, no worries."

We found her clothes, and as she helped me bury the bodies, I explained about vampires and that she should stay with friends for a few days, but the luchd-òl fola had probably already left the area.

We rinsed ourselves off in one of the alligator-free ponds, and then we went to my car where I gave Roberta a pair of my sweatpants and a t-shirt. I put on clean clothes as well.

It was almost dawn when we cut back across the golf course to Roberta's car in the resort's parking lot. I made sure no one was hanging around, and she gave me a hug before driving away.

I was exhausted, and I still needed to search Dermid and Hendry's van. I'd scored the key plus around five hundred dollars from their pockets, but nothing else. I didn't have high hopes for the van, but I had to look.

I trudged across the parking lot as the first rays of sun came over the horizon.

"Okay, everyone, get ready. We'll do a sun salutation sequence as the day breaks on the new year." The voice came from over by the clubhouse. A group of about fifteen people were standing on mats facing a man with long blond hair and a serene expression on his face. He saw me and grinned, waving me over. "You're just in time. Hurry!"

I spread my hands out. "Thanks, but I don't know how to do yoga."

He waved harder. "You don't have to. Come on and follow along as best you can. There are spare mats right over here. You'll feel amazing afterwards, I promise."

When was the last time I'd felt "amazing"?

What the hell. If I didn't like it, I'd leave. I grabbed a mat, unrolled it, and kicked my shoes off before bemusedly following the man's instructions to put my feet together and breathe in as the sun rose fully over the horizon.

CHAPTER 16
RENO

I WAS WORKING ON CLEANING SIMON'S HAIR WITH A DAMP TOWEL when Shirley came in, carrying a plate with three slices of pizza, followed by Cal, who had Simon and my phones and laptops. "Thought you might want these."

"Thanks. And thanks for coming." I tossed the wet towel into the bathroom, then took the plate from Shirley. Cal set the electronics down on the bed on Simon's other side.

Shirley paused on her way out of the room. "I'll be downstairs, but yell if you need anythin'."

"Thanks, Shirley."

She opened her mouth, shut it, then apparently decided to tell me what was on her mind. "That's a good man you have there. A good mate. You may not be aware, but those are hard to find. I know you were worried about getting' bonded, but don't forget you and Simon are not your mother and father." I opened my mouth, but she held up a hand. "I'll only say this once, and then I won't bring it up again. Your parents might have been joined at the hip for their entire matin', but that was their choice. Either of them could've asked for boundaries but they didn't. They set a piss-poor example for you, if you'll pardon me speakin' ill of the dead."

She pointed at me. "You may be afraid of repeatin' the past, but it's your and Simon's choice how your matin' looks." She gave me a sharp nod and left the room.

I focused on scarfing down pizza instead of looking at Cal.

He must've decided to ignore the elephant Shirley had dumped in the room. "Both of your phones have been going off, but I can post an update on Discord if you like."

"Thanks, I'd appreciate it. I'm not really in a good mindset to deal with everyone right now."

"Hah. Understandable."

I pretended he was only referring to Simon being injured. "The guest room's all yours if you want to stay the night. There are clean sheets in the hall closet."

"Thanks, I'd like to see what happens with Jackson." He rubbed his chest, right where his connection to Jackson had once emerged.

"You're welcome here as long as you'd like to stay."

"Thanks. I'm gonna head downstairs and write that post. You need anything?"

I lifted the plate. "I'm good, thanks."

I was exhausted when I finished the pizza, so I laid down next to Simon and pulled the sheet over both of us. I was out before I had a chance to stew over what Shirley had said to me.

I woke a few hours later, my phone buzzing with a text. It was a little after midnight. I checked on Simon, but there wasn't any change that I could see. Getting up and stumbling to the bathroom and back took enough time I knew I didn't want to be alone with my thoughts about Simon and our mating. Taking a deep breath, I put on my big boy pants and unlocked my phone.

I waded through the texts and Discord private messages. Most of them were from before Cal had posted the update, so I didn't bother to respond. A few were newer, and a couple of those were only well wishes for Simon to get better.

When I was done with my messages, I looked at Simon's phone and laptop. I really shouldn't... should I? He'd given me access to the devices after all, and he'd specifically said it was so I could check his texts and Discord.

His phone was dead, and I didn't have a charger for it. He'd probably left his in the guest bedroom, but it was past the time when Cal would've gone to sleep. I'd just use his laptop.

I logged in without a problem, but before I opened his Discord app, my eye caught on the icon for his photos. Simon had known how to use my camera when we'd been at Emiliano Duran's apartment. Did he have a camera of his own? What did he take pictures of? Before I could debate with myself about whether anything on Simon's laptop not related to the campaign was off limits, I clicked on the icon.

The first thing that came up was a series of pictures of a bald eagle flying. The file names were labeled, "Eagle, New Braunfels, Texas". I dug a little deeper. All of the photos he'd taken this year—mostly landscapes or birds and animals—were in the main folder, but he'd created folders by year, going back to—holy crap!—1961.

I clicked on that folder. The first and oldest photos were taken in Greece. The coastline and houses were unmistakable, even if the file names hadn't been as carefully labeled as his more recent pictures. But the old cars and the way people dressed and wore their hair were definitely from that era. Too bad Simon hadn't known about selfies back then, because he wasn't in any of the photos. I stopped on one of the early ones, named "Jimmy in Athens". A slim, sharp-faced man was holding a small sculpture of a sleeping cat. Weird.

The rest of the photos from that year chronicled Simon's journey from Greece to Bulgaria, then to Istanbul. I poked around and looked at a few of the photos from each year. I'd known intellectually that Simon had had a long, lonely life tracking the rogue vampires, but these pictures really drove home how alone he'd been and how much he'd gone through to get here now.

I took a minute to stroke his hair. "Finding your mate must've been like the ultimate goal for you. Finally, you'd have someone to share your life with. But you got stuck with me instead, and the first thing I did was tell you I didn't want to be mated to you."

My eyes burned with tears, but I blinked them back. Crying over how guilty I felt wouldn't solve anything. Before Simon woke up, I'd better decide once and for all whether I was in or out of our mating. It was only fair to him.

"Okay, Simon. I have two options. First is my original plan, ask you to sever the bond." I breathed through the pain the bond sent my way as punishment for bringing that up again. "In this scenario, let's say the new District Monitor shows up in a few months. I go off and sit on a remote beach somewhere by myself. It's heavenly." I smiled, imagining putting my toes in the warm sand and watching the sun set over the waves. No phones, no texts, no Discord messages.

"But while I'm doing that, what are you doing, Simon? I can't ask you to wait around Corpus Christi for me." I looked down at his face, still beautiful even with matted hair and a slack mouth. "Wonders and magic carriers will be throwing themselves at you." I pictured some random guy with his hands on Simon's bare chest, and my vision turned red. Was I baring my teeth? Shit, I hoped this mating bond didn't give me fangs. "Right. Okay, so what have we learned here? We've learned that, as much as I want to go on a tropical vacation by myself, I am not willing to risk you finding someone else while I'm away." I blinked. Wow, that was easier than I'd expected.

I sighed and laid my fingers against his cheek. "Looks like you're stuck with me. I hope you like the beach, because we're going on vacation as soon as the new DM appears. But you can stay in the cabana while I sit in the sand. No pressure to join me." In fact, it might be pretty romantic to spend some of the days apart, meeting back up in the evening for dinner and lovemaking. "We'll figure it out, Simon."

Tucking his hand in mine, our bond purring with happiness, I went back to the folders of photos and clicked through the years. In the late 1970s and the 1980s he'd wandered through Egypt, Sudan, Tanzania, and Nigeria. He'd gotten some great shots of animals and birds, but there weren't many photos of people. 1990 and 1991 were pretty sparse, but 1992 had a subfolder in it. I leaned forward. None of the other years had had subfolder. It was called "Davi", and there were a bunch of photos in it, along with a video and another subfolder called "Davi's Photos". This must've been the friend Simon had said he'd stayed with for a few months. The one who'd passed away.

I started with "Davi's Photos". These were typical family and friend pics. Davi had lived somewhere in South America, I guessed based on the houses and beaches. He'd grown from a gangly kid into a handsome young man with curly black hair and laughing eyes. There weren't any photos after he was about twenty years old. Had he been that young when he'd passed away?

I went back to the main "Davi" folder and clicked on some of those photos. For once, Simon appeared in a few. His hair had been a little longer than he was wearing it now, and he had a tan, but otherwise he looked exactly the same. Davi, however, was older, maybe around thirty. And he was obviously ill. He still sported a sassy grin in most of the pictures, but as time went on he got thinner and paler. I could see what had to be a couple of Karposi sarcoma lesions on his arm and neck. AIDS. Fuck.

I rubbed my chest, then I lifted Simon's hand and kissed his fingers. "You stayed with him until he died, didn't you?" How wonderful of Simon to pause his journey chasing the vampires to take care of his friend. But also, how awful for him. He'd been alone for decades, and his one friend had died after what the photos indicated was only a few months.

And then there was the video. It was called, "With Love from Davi" and I knew I probably shouldn't watch it. It was for Simon, obviously, and it'd be rude to snoop.

I glanced between the laptop screen and Simon. His head wound was about the same, but he had some color in his face. I should feed him again. I didn't feel the same antipathy to feeding him from a bag anymore, so I put the laptop aside and went downstairs.

The door to the guest room was shut, so Cal must've been asleep. Shirley and Tucker were sleeping on a couple of the sectional's recliners, and Nicky was sacked out next to Jackson, whose neck actually seemed to be attached to their body now. The goo had dried in a ring where the cut had been, but they were breathing and they glimmered with magic. Thank fuck.

I looked at Simon's bottle warmer, but it was too much bother to figure out how to use it at that hour of the night. The blood bag had a little tab on one end I could cut off for Simon to drink from, so I decided to warm up the entire bag. I grabbed a couple of kitchen towels, got them wet, then heated them in the microwave, making sure to stop it before the timer went off. Then I wrapped the hot towels around the blood bag. Hey, it worked for tortillas in a pinch, so it would work for blood. I managed to sneak back upstairs without waking anyone.

I snipped off the end of the blood bag with my cuticle scissors —I washed them first!—and Simon immediately started sucking the blood down as soon as I got it into his mouth. He drained the bag in minutes, but he didn't seem to want more, so I decided to wait a few hours before getting him another.

I tried to sleep, but I couldn't stop thinking about the video on Simon's computer. I really shouldn't watch it. It was private. But, on the other hand, if I was planning on staying mated to Simon, wouldn't it be important for me to know more about him as a person? Who better to tell me than his only friend?

Decision made, I sat up and put a couple of pillows behind me so I could lean against the headboard. I put on my reading glasses and opened the laptop back up. After glancing at Simon one more time to make sure he was still unconscious, I clicked on the video. Davi appeared, wearing a red t-shirt and huddled under a blue and green knitted throw blanket. Simon had mentioned Davi had taught him to knit.

"Hey, Simon." His grin lit up his thin, ashen face. "I know you told me to stop thanking you for everything you're doing for me but, too bad! I hid this video well enough that you won't find it until after I'm gone. You'll just have to sit there and take it!" He chortled, swinging from side to side in what must be a desk chair. He was wearing the jaguar head pendant. "You may have noticed I'm speaking English instead of Portuguese. That's because I want you to show this video to your mate when you find him."

I eyed Simon guiltily. I'd taken that choice from him.

Davi pointed his finger at the camera. "You have to, or I'll haunt you. You won't be able to hide from me!"

He had to have completely passed on, though. Simon would be able to see his ghost if he hadn't.

"Okay, first the thank yous. Not that I can ever thank you enough for everything you've done for me. Before I met you, I was mostly wishing this disease would hurry up and kill me. None of my family or friends would speak to me, and I was about to resign myself to living out my days at the hospice clinic."

He turned his head and wiped his eye with the back of his hand. "Fuck, I should have brought some tissues." He cleared his throat. "Sorry. Anyway, thank you, from the bottom of my heart. You are the best friend a person could have, and my only regret in this life is that I can't go with you to find those fuckers who kidnapped your prince. I'd do anything to help you and ease your burden. Be your family." He spun around in his chair and craned his neck as he looked to the side, then he spun back with a cheeky grin. "False alarm. I thought you'd come back early, and I'm not done yet.

"I can't be there for you, but that Seer told you about your mate, so at least I know you'll find him before your mission is completed." He pressed his palms to his chest. "Hi, Simon's mate. I'm Davi, and I wanted to make sure you know you won the mate lottery. Simon is the best person in the entire world. He's kind and thoughtful, and he'll do anything for the people he loves. And you know he's fucking handsome as sin." He cupped a hand over one side of his mouth and leaned toward the camera. "And don't be jealous, but I can tell you from personal experience, he's got skills in bed." He sat back, grinning and waggling his eyebrows while he fanned himself. "You are one lucky bastard."

I paused the video, swallowing against the lump in my throat. I really was lucky, wasn't I? And I'd been a selfish jackass, whining about my two years of helping Wonders, when the worst thing that'd happened to me was having to quit my job and losing my weekends. What had Simon lost? His family, his home. He'd spent decades with no way to make friends or put down roots. And when he'd wanted to be my mate I'd essentially shitted on him.

And he hadn't even been mad. He'd been hurt, sure. But instead of throwing a tantrum like I'd done, he'd... helped me. He'd responded to the Wonders, even transferring some of the conversations to his own phone. He'd helped me investigate Emiliano Duran. He'd taken on some of my burdens.

Like a mate would.

I couldn't believe I'd been planning to throw him away. To cut this bond. I felt dizzy at the thought of what I'd almost done.

I squeezed Simon's lax hand. A rush of affection, maybe more, ran through me, and I sent it through the bond to Simon's unconscious mind. He deserved to know. "I'm sorry, Simon. Everyone told me what a fucking dumbass I was being, but I was stuck on the idea of what I thought I wanted. I promise I'll do better. I want to be your mate." I lifted his fingers to my cheek, then I held his hand against my chest as I hit *Play*.

Davi looked to the side again. "Shit, I think you're coming up the stairs. Simon, I would give my life for you if I could. But since I won't have it to give much longer, I'm leaving you all my possessions instead. Use this computer equipment to find those fucking vampires and save the Elf prince. I love you, and I hope you find your mate soon. You deserve all the happiness in the world."

He blew a kiss at the camera, and the video ended.

I gave in and cried.

WICHITA, KANSAS – OCTOBER, 2017

I hummed "Feel It Still" by Portugal the Man as I finished digging the hole. Isla and Wallace hadn't had much information to share, and by now I'd learned how to know if they were holding something back.

Torture methods had been discussed in a theoretical way during my Royal Guard training, but back then I'd never had occasion to use them. Things had certainly changed. I even carried around tools for that specific purpose.

As of tonight, only nine luchd-òl fola were left. I'd forgotten to ask Isla and Wallace about Kinnon, but they'd each only had nine connections that weren't with each other, and by my count that meant he wasn't with the group anymore. Kinnon was either dead or he'd left them a long time ago. The uncertainty itched in the back of my brain, but I couldn't do anything about it. The remaining nine luchd-òl fola were still kidnapping Wonders, and that's what I had to focus on.

I was having a hard time reining in my impatience. I was ready to finish this. Finish them. But there'd been no sign of my mate, and finding him had to come first, according to the Seer all those years ago.

When I'd tracked the luchd-òl fola to the United States, I'd been so happy. Surely my English-speaking mate lived here somewhere. But this country was huge, and there was all of Canada to consider as well. I shook my head. No, my mate would be here in the U.S. I had to believe that.

I heaved Isla and Wallace into the pit and shoveled the dirt on top of them. By the time anyone found the grave, vampire decay rates meant the skeletons would appear to be over a century old. The discovery wouldn't even make the local news.

Nine left.

Nine luchd-òl fola, one Elf Prince, and a mate.

I was beyond ready.

CHAPTER 17
SIMON

I VAGUELY REGISTERED THE TASTE OF BLOOD AS RENO STROKED MY hair and said something about taking me kayaking. It was weird, but it was better than a lot of dreams I'd had, so I didn't fight going back under.

I became fully aware all at once, jerking awake and trying to roll to my feet to fight off Marcas. I got tangled in the bedsheets, though, resulting in me only getting to my knees while knocking Reno off the mattress and scattering laptops and cell phones with him.

"Shit, Reno! Are you okay?" I lunged to the side of the bed, reaching over to touch his head, looking for injuries.

He blinked at me as he sat up. "You're awake!" He smiled, and I felt happiness and relief through our bond. He took my hand and let me help him to his feet. "How are you feeling? Are you hungry or thirsty?"

I sat back on the mattress, tired again. "Um, a little of both, and I have to pee. But tell me what happened with Marcas and Roibeart." I touched my head where it throbbed. "I guess Roibeart shot me. How long was I out?"

Reno smiled and got to his feet. "About twenty hours." He gently put his hands on my head and moved my hair to look at my wound. "Marcas and Roibeart are both dead. Nicky boosted my magic, and I sort of crushed their magical cores."

I leaned back so I could stare at him. "Holy shit! That's not something even I know how to do."

He scrunched up his face, confusion coming through our bond loud and clear. "Um, it wasn't that hard." He waved this away. "Nicky's fine. Jackson had their head cut off but it seems to be almost healed up."

I nodded. "The *dèideagan dìon* can repair themselves from grievous injury." I frowned down at my lap. I really needed to pee, and probably shower, but I felt like my brain wasn't processing at full speed. Marcas and Roibeart were dead. Marcas and Roibeart were dead. I gasped, looking up at Reno. "They're dead! They were the last of the *luchd-òl fola*!" I smiled into his beautiful eyes. "It's finally over."

"It's finally over." He hugged me. I had no idea what kind of emotions I was sending through our bond. My brain was bouncing around with a thousand thoughts. I closed my eyes and tried to focus on the wonderful sensation of his arms around me, and the affection and happiness coming through from him. Our bond was—

My eyes flew wide, and I put a hand on his chest. "The bond! It's whole! How?"

His mouth fell open, and he also looked down. "Wow. It must've happened overnight. I—" Then his face turned red, and a wave of guilt and embarrassment came through the bond.

My eyebrows went up. "You...?"

He sat down on the mattress next to me and lifted his chin. "I decided I want to stay mated to you. I don't want to sever the bond."

My fuzzy brain tried to process this. "Are you sure? What changed your mind?" I couldn't bear it if he didn't actually want to be mated.

He exhaled loudly and gazed to the side. "A bunch of different things, but mostly... it was you." He gave me a small smile. "I didn't react well when you said we were mates." He rolled his eyes. "Understatement. And I'm sorry." He cupped the side of my face. "But you didn't try to change my mind. You... let me be me. And you showed me who you were, every minute. You helped me with all my shit, even though you had your own crap to worry about. You were supportive and wonderful, and—" He choked back a sob and put his arms around my waist and his head on my shoulder. I gathered him close, exulting in the feeling. He squeezed me tight. "When you were shot, the only thing that kept me going was our bond. It was still shining bright, so I knew you were alive."

He gave a small laugh. "I'm not gonna lie, it still took me a while to let go of what I thought I wanted and see what I'd already been given." He peered up at me. "I'm sorry, Simon. You didn't deserve me rejecting you like that."

I smiled down into his stunning brown eyes. "My mate, I was never going to give up on you. You needed time to get to know me and get used to the idea of being mates. My plan was to seduce you slowly, get you to see what it could be like to be mated." I grinned. "Once you'd had a taste of me, I knew you wouldn't be able to give me up."

Amusement came through the bond. "Oh, yeah? Well, why don't we get you showered and fed, and then you can show me?"

I kissed him. It wasn't the all-consuming seduction I wanted and he deserved, but I'd been unconscious, and I could smell the dried blood in my hair. Seducing Reno would have to wait.

He helped me out of bed as I was a little unsteady yet. As we walked to the bathroom, he cleared his throat. "Soooo."

"Yes?"

"I snooped through the photos on your computer."

Oh. "You found Davi's video." I didn't care about him looking through my files. I didn't have any secrets from my mate. But Davi's video was an emotional punch he might not have been ready for.

He nodded and stopped walking to put his arms around me. "I'm glad you were able to be there for him, and I'm glad he could be there for you."

My throat tightened as I leaned into him. "I wish you could've met him. He would've loved you."

Neither of us were dry-eyed as we continued to the bathroom.

Reno had to support me in the shower. I wished I could've taken advantage of our nakedness, but I didn't have the energy. I did make sure to send frequent bursts of happiness and love through the bond, and Reno didn't stop smiling.

When I was clean and wrapped in a towel, I examined my head wound in the mirror. It was behind my ear, so I could mostly cover it with my hair, but there was a definite hole. "It's waiting for the bullet to come out."

Reno made a face. "Um, will the bullet just sort of, pop out?"

I grinned. "Pretty much."

"Great." He helped me sit on the side of the bed, then he went to the closet and produced one of the plastic bins I kept my clothes in. "Sorry, I didn't have time to hang anything up."

I beamed at him. My mate was so wonderful. He'd gotten that bin from the guest room and brought it in here. He wanted me to stay. He'd said so, but actions were important too.

Reno offered to bring me food from downstairs, but I wanted to see Nicky and Jackson with my own eyes. Plus, even though he'd assured me the bond was allowing us to separate now, I didn't want to let him out of my sight.

He insisted I keep one hand on his arm as we went down the stairs. Nicky and Tucker were sitting on the floor next to Jackson, who was unconscious in their panther form. Cal was at the kitchen table with his laptop. "Hey, everyone." I waved.

No one commented on our bond, so Reno must've already told them he was keeping me. I squeezed his arm and sent over how warm and fuzzy that made me feel.

I checked on Jackson first. Their magic was severely depleted, but it wasn't gone. "They'll wake up soon."

"I hope so." Nicky stroked their fur. "They were protecting me, and all I can think of is how Hooch died protecting Tom Hanks in *Turner and Hooch*."

I decided telling him Jackson had been created to protect him wouldn't be a comfort right then.

Tucker must've seen my inability to form a response, because he jumped in. "Um, well, it's a good thing instead it's really like how, in *The Fresh Prince of Bel Air*, Will got shot protectin' Carlton and lived."

Nicky's face brightened, and he relaxed. "You're right. Thank you."

I sat at the kitchen table with Cal while Reno made breakfast. I didn't feel any need for blood, so my dreams of tasting it must've been true.

Cal grinned at me. "Everyone on Discord is excited to hear you're feeling better. Levi's having trouble keeping track of all the volunteers to donate blood for you."

"Oh, shit." I grimaced. "I should probably call him."

Reno turned around and pointed his spatula at me. "Please. He's been texting me every couple of hours."

I ended up calling him then and there. I had a feeling I'd be sleeping for a while after we ate, and I didn't want to forget. Levi alternated between yelling at me for risking my life and telling me how glad he was that I was okay. "You bring your mate up for a visit, you hear? Because if you don't, I'm gonna show up on your doorstep."

After breakfast, or it might've been lunch, Reno helped me back upstairs. My eyes were heavy and I was half asleep by the time he got me in bed. As he was trying to pull the covers up over me, I gripped his t-shirt "When I wake up, I'll seduce you, I promise."

He cocked his head and smiled at me like I was adorable. "I'll look forward to it."

However, I did *not* get to seduce Reno until much later.

When I woke up, he was sitting in bed beside me with his reading glasses on, glancing between his phone and my laptop. I rolled over and threw my arm over his legs. "So sexy." He ran his fingers through my hair, and I made a purring noise.

"You think you're up to going out to dinner tonight?"

I lifted my head to stare at him. Wouldn't he rather stay in bed and celebrate our bond becoming whole? "Like in a restaurant? Um, when?" I blinked and looked around for a clock.

"At 7:30. It's a little after 3:00 p.m. now."

I pushed myself up to a sitting position and shoved my hair out of my face. "I guess so." I took inventory of my body. My energy was up, and my head wound itched more than ached. "I'm feeling pretty good, so we can go out if you want. But you don't have to wine and dine me."

He smiled and leaned over to kiss me. But before I could take it where I wanted it to go, he pulled back. "Unfortunately, it's not that kind of dinner. We're meeting some people."

I raised an eyebrow. This was getting more and more disappointing. "Okay?"

He pointed at the laptop. "Remember how you responded to Alyssa Laurent, who wanted to tell her boyfriend about the campaign?"

"Yeah? I told her we'd get back to her after we'd dealt with the *luchd-òl fola*. But she didn't make it sound like it was urgent." Couldn't we just stay home and make sweet, sweet love?

Reno leaned forward, his eyes alight with excitement. "Alyssa Laurent and her parents are gargoyles."

———

We met the Laurents at a slightly upscale Mexican restaurant near the bayfront. I'd had a bag of blood before we left to make sure I didn't get too tired. I would've felt even better with some of Reno's blood, but that would've led to things we didn't have time for.

It was cute how revved up he was for tonight. Alyssa Laurent had told us her boyfriend's name was Milo—"he pronounces it mee-low"—Duran. We were about to confront the guy with the gargoyle costume.

On the way over we debated how to bring up the topic of the costume, but in the end we'd had to agree to wing it.

Aimee and Bernard Laurent appeared to be in their early forties but were probably closer to a millennium than not. Alyssa passed for being in her mid-twenties, but she also could've been any age. Emiliano, or Milo, was twenty-six according to his DMV records. Like in his photos, he was tall, dark-haired, and slender but with a nice set of shoulders. He appeared relaxed and friendly, and all three Laurents seemed happy with him.

Reno and I shook hands with everyone.

"Thank you so much for joining us." Bernard gestured to the empty seats at the table, and Reno and I sat down. My wound was itching again, but I figured scratching my head at the table would be uncouth, and I didn't want to embarrass Reno.

When was the last time I'd sat down to dinner in a restaurant with multiple people? Hell, I couldn't remember dining out with anyone since Davi. Every time I thought about not having to chase down the *luchd-òl fola* anymore, I felt almost lightheaded. The future was unknown, but I had Reno to share it with. Reno, who'd chosen me, exactly like I'd hoped he would.

He returned my sappy smile, then he addressed Alyssa. "I'm sorry we've never met in person before."

Her face lit up. "Me too. But now you get to meet Milo at the same time." She hugged his arm, and he seemed content to just be next to her.

"How long have y'all been dating?"

She and Milo exchanged glances, and he was the one to respond. "Almost eighteen months now."

Her parents were at ease and smiling. No worries about him from their end.

We placed our orders, and Milo looked between me and Reno, probably trying to figure out our relationship. "What do y'all do for work?"

Trying to flex my jaw to see if it helped with my wound itching, I picked up Reno's hand and kissed it. Then I grinned. "We're private investigators."

Milo didn't react to the implication that Reno and I were involved romantically. Instead his eyebrows went up and his face creased into a delighted smile. "Really? That's so cool!"

After our food arrived, Milo asked several questions about being a private investigator. Alyssa, however, was eyeing us suspiciously. She'd no doubt guessed that we'd investigated Milo.

Throughout the meal, my head wound continued to itch. I imagined it was trying to close but the bullet wasn't out yet, so it couldn't. Finally, after I took my last bite of enchiladas and set my utensils across my plate, I couldn't take it anymore. Using only my forefinger, I pretended I was tucking my hair behind my ear and rubbed gently down the side of my head. Unfortunately, the bullet was on its way out, and my finger dislodged it. It fell, bouncing off my chest and clattering onto my plate, misshapen and a little bloody. Too bad the lighting in the room was fairly bright.

Everyone turned to stare at my plate. Reno looked down at the bullet, then up at me. His face crinkled up like he was trying not to laugh.

"Rude." I stuck my tongue out at him and threw my napkin over my plate. I turned to the others. Bernard and Aimee, at the very least, knew what had happened with my injury. It'd been all over Discord, and their wide eyes said they didn't know how to explain the bullet to Milo. I bumped shoulders with Reno. "This one's always tying crap in my hair."

He didn't even pause to think. He just chuckled and put his arm around my shoulders as he kissed my temple. "Because it gives me an excuse to play with it."

"Was that a *bullet*?" Milo leaned across the table as if he could see through the napkin on my plate.

"Yes." I made sure to sound aggravated as I lifted the edge of the napkin and swiped up the bullet before putting it in my pocket. I hoped Reno had some stain remover at home. "We do target practice a couple of times a month." It could happen.

"Huh. Have you ever had to shoot anyone?"

Before Reno and I had to make up some bullshit answer, Alyssa slapped Milo on the bicep.

He rubbed his arm. "What was that for?"

"Because it was a disrespectful question. What if they did have to shoot someone? It'd be incredibly personal, and I can't imagine it would make for pleasant dinner conversation."

I grinned. I liked Alyssa. Milo wasn't getting out of this dinner looking good though.

He slouched in his seat and sighed. "You're right. Sorry." That last was tossed in our general direction.

Reno chuckled. "No problem. It's fine to be curious, but Alyssa's right, it's not a topic most people want to discuss. Um, but we did have a real interesting case recently."

Everyone perked up. The server came by to clear our plates, and we all asked for coffee, except Milo who asked for hot chocolate.

Reno picked up my hand. "We'd been hired by a guy who thought his wife was cheating on him." He rolled his eyes. "Spoiler—she was." Everyone grimaced. "I took pictures of the apartment building she went to with her lover, and when I reviewed the pictures later, I saw something weird. It wasn't in the woman's lover's apartment, though. It was in the neighbor's apartment next door." The entire table was on the edge of their seats. "It was a costume. Hanging on the closet door. Would you like to see a picture of it?"

They all eagerly nodded. Reno unlocked his phone and found the photo. Then he handed it to Aimee, who was sitting next to him. She gasped, covering her mouth and staring at Reno with horrified eyes. Bernard took the phone and had a similar reaction.

"What? What is it?" Alyssa practically snatched the phone out of her father's hand. She peered at the photo and slowly paled. "Milo.... Milo, this is *your* apartment." She shoved the phone at him.

He frowned down at it. "Yeah, yeah it is." He looked at Reno, and I could've sworn his confusion was real. "Why'd you take pictures of my apartment?"

Reno was faking his calm. He was tense, coiled and ready to react depending on what Milo did next. "I was trying to figure out which apartment belonged to your neighbor."

"Milo." Alyssa wasn't touching him now. "Why do you have that costume?" You could've cut glass with her tone.

Milo rubbed his face. "It was supposed to be a surprise. I was waiting for your birthday."

We all took a beat to process his statement.

"What?" Now it was Alyssa and the rest of us who were confused.

He gave an exaggerated sigh. "I came over one night, but it was late, so I peeked in your window to see if you were still up." He shrugged. "You were wearing a costume just like that, so I figured you were either into cosplay and were embarrassed to tell me, or, uh...." He glanced at Alyssa's parents. "You just liked wearing stuff like that. I took a picture and got a cosplay designer to make one exactly like it." He shifted in his seat. "So you'd know I accept you and love you just the way you are."

Alyssa gasped. "Milo...." Her face crumpled and she threw her arms around him. Bernard and Aimee were holding onto each other with their heads together.

"Awww." I pressed my hands to my heart. "Reno, you're going to let her tell him, right?"

He smiled, not taking his eyes off the couple. "You bet." He pushed his chair back and stood. "Aimee and Bernard, thanks for dinner. Milo, sorry about the confusion with the costume. Alyssa, don't forget to show him the campaign compendium, and let me know if there are any questions you can't answer."

She nodded tearily and mouthed, *Thank you*.

Reno didn't let go of my hand until it was time to get in the car. When we were on the road headed for home, I sighed dramatically. "That was wonderful. I can't wait to do something like it again."

TEXARKANA, TEXAS – MARCH 22 OF THIS YEAR

I gritted my teeth as I opened my laptop. I'd lost the fucking trail. Again. I'd been so close in Arkansas, but now I was back to combing the campaign chat rooms for rumors of Wonders disappearing.

If I were the luchd-òl fola, I'd have headed to Louisiana. Plenty of places to hide there, and no one, civilian or Wonder, would blink at somebody who looked like a vampire. But my gut was telling me to check out Texas first.

The campaign chat rooms for Texas were all on Discord, thank fuck. Facebook was the worst. I missed the days of AOL. Those chat rooms had been so easy to hack into.

The Texas campaign's main server was helpfully called Texas Adventurers. And, look there. Someone named Delphia Shaw had just posted that her son Greg, a District Monitor, was nesting and a Cassandra had been found. A Seer.

I sat up, adrenaline chasing away my frustration. Could one of the two be my mate?

A few minutes of detective work revealed Gregory Shaw lived in Bent Oak, which was a little bit west of Austin.

I was on my way five minutes later.

CHAPTER 18
RENO

As we were on the way home, Cal texted that Jackson was awake, so we stopped to pick up four cheese pizzas. We could always order more if they needed them. Healing a severed neck had to take a lot of energy.

I'd left Simon in the car while I ran in to get the food. He was tired. I felt bad making him leave the house when he was recovering, but I could tell through the bond that he'd thoroughly enjoyed himself tonight. I'd have to make sure we got more social time now that the rogue vampires were dead. Maybe I should bring back the District picnics before the weather got too cold. We hadn't had one since I'd been acting DM.

When I got back into the car, Simon was fast asleep. I felt a surge of affection, and he smiled, even though he was passed out. Fuck, how long would it take me to fall in love with him?

I couldn't believe I'd known him less than a week. We'd barely had sex, and I'd been so stressed out about bonding at the time, I hadn't paid proper attention to Simon. He deserved all the attention.

I was making plans for waking up early tomorrow and talking Simon into morning sex when I turned onto my street. My groan woke Simon up.

"Wha's the matter?" He rubbed his face with both hands.

"Sorry to wake you, but we're almost home. My aunt is here." It was pretty late for her to visit, so I suspected she and her buddies had been out to dinner. Oh, shit. "Um, I told her we were bonded, so she'll probably want to hug you."

He froze, his fingers pressed into his cheekbones. "She will?"

"Guaranteed. Do you want me to head her off?" I pulled into the driveway next to Tia's car.

He shook his head, smiling. "No, I don't mind."

I made a mental note to hug Simon daily going forward.

We got out of the car, and I grabbed the pizzas from the back seat. Cal had the door open before we even made it to the front porch.

He took the pizzas with a grin. "Y'all need to go see what's happening in the guest bathroom. I already took some pictures, but you need to witness it for yourself before it's over."

I exchanged a bewildered glance with Simon, then I gestured for him to lead the way. Nicky waved from the kitchen table. Soledad was washing dishes, and she pointed us toward the guest bathroom. "Hurry. I'll meet your young man after."

Okay then. We were missing Jackson, Tia, and Rosita. Simon lengthened his stride, and I hurried to keep up. The bathroom door was closed, but we could hear splashing along with Tia and Rosita fussing. Simon knocked softly and opened the door a crack. With a laugh he pushed it wider.

Jackson, their panther form barely fitting in the tub, gave us pathetic puppy dog eyes from under a mass of shampoo suds. Tia and Rosita were splattered with water and soap.

"Welcome!" Tia beamed at us. "Simon, I'm so happy you're feeling better. I will give you a hug when I'm dry. We're almost ready to rinse."

I introduced Simon to Rosita, and after greeting her he edged into the room and leaned against the counter to stay out of the way. "Jackson, I'm sorry it never occurred to me that you'd need to bathe. I suppose I assumed you would just change form."

I wasn't sure where the dirt would go in that scenario, but Jackson nodded violently enough to dislodge some of the shampoo. Tia wasn't buying it. "They were lying on that floor for over twenty-four hours, and they had dried... stuff in their fur. Of course they needed a bath." Rosita took the shower-head sprayer out of its holder and flipped the handle to turn it on. Jackson hunched over and squeezed their eyes shut while they were rinsed.

I rubbed my mouth to hide my grin. "Did Jackson get anything to eat?"

"*Si*, we brought enchiladas."

"Great. Jackson, glad to have you back with us. Simon and I picked up some pizzas if you're still hungry after this, or we'll put them in the fridge for later." They seemed a little happier at that news.

The bathroom was too small for Simon and me to help dry Jackson, so we left Tia and Rosita to it. I stopped him in the hall before we got to the living room. "Do you need to sleep? Tia and her friends won't be upset. They can interrogate you the next time they drop by."

He smiled and kissed my cheek. "I'm fine for a little while at least."

"Okay. But if you feel like you need to lie down, just go. And one more thing." I went up on my toes and gave him a long, lingering kiss. "Can you delay your yoga until later in the morning tomorrow?"

He scrunched his eyebrows together, then he lifted them and a slow, seductive smile took over his face. "Are you suggesting I'm too tired to make love to you tonight?" He stepped closer to me, putting his lips next to my ear. "I can assure you, that will never happen."

I shivered, feeling my arousal and his boomerang through our bond. "Fuck." I slid my hands up to his chest and pressed until he stepped back again. "Why don't we play it by ear." I was mostly sure, his boasting aside, that he'd be asleep as soon as he got into bed. "You can get away with avoiding Tia and her friends tonight, but I can't."

He dropped his head back and stared at the ceiling. "If we have to wait until tomorrow, we'll need to set an early alarm. Do you know how many people will try to talk to us in the morning?"

"I'm not cutting your sleep short. We'll just remind them you're still recovering from your injury. It'll be fine." Or whoever interrupted us would regret it.

He grumbled under his breath as he took my hand and let me lead him to the kitchen. Cal had put the pizzas on the kitchen counter, and he, Nicky, and Soledad were sitting at the table having hot chocolate. I tugged Simon over. "Soledad, this is my mate, Simon."

She stood up. "Simon, you are the answer to our prayers. Come here." She opened her arms, and he bent over to give her a tentative hug.

Hoping he wouldn't ask the obvious question, I dodged around them to make glasses of ice water for me and Simon.

He broke the hug and stepped back. "Thank you. Um, why am I the answer to your prayers?"

Shit, he asked.

She threw me a contemptuous look, but I pretended to be absorbed in filling the glasses with ice. "Because Esperanza despaired of that one ever finding his mate. She worried he would grow old and die all alone, his final days steeped in bitterness and regret."

At the far end of the table, Nicky and Cal weren't bothering to hide their laughter. I groaned. Soledad loved her telenovelas. Though, to be fair, so did Tia and Rosita.

I set Simon's glass down on the table a little harder than I should've. "Soledad, thank you so much for bringing dinner over."

She shrugged to brush this away as she sat down again. "It was no trouble. Your Tia and Rosita shared in the work. We were so happy to be here when Jackson woke up."

Nicky sobered. "Me too. Their magic seemed to have recovered hours ago, so I was getting worried at how long they were unconscious." He wrapped his arms around himself. "I thought they were dead when it happened."

Shit, with all Nicky had been through, he did not need to lose any of us, especially right now.

Cal patted Nicky's back. "Don't forget they'd healed that rabbit shifter the day before. They may not have fully bounced back when, uh, they were injured, so it took longer for them to feel well enough to wake up."

He nodded. "I'm glad we won't have to worry about being in danger anymore, right?" I seconded that feeling with a vengeance.

"Right. No more vampires." Cal winked at Simon. "Except Simon of course."

I got a whiff of discomfort through our bond from Simon at this statement, but he didn't say anything.

Jackson came bounding out from the hallway at that moment, their fur glossy under the runes and a rhinestone tiara on their head. I had no idea where that had come from.

We all exclaimed over how nice they looked. Tia and Rosita followed them out more slowly, and I got up to take the wet towels from them. "Y'all seem a little worse for wear." Their clothes were damp, their hair was frizzy, and they exuded weariness.

Tia *tsked* and pointed at Jackson, who had hopped onto one of the chairs at the table. "That one made it much harder than it had to be." I headed for the laundry room as she switched her focus to her new target. "Simon, come here and give me a hug." She made cooing noises. "Welcome to the family, *mijo*."

"Thank you."

When I returned, Tia was still hugging Simon. He had his eyes closed, and even though he was hunched over enough that it had to be uncomfortable, he didn't look like he wanted the hug to end anytime soon.

Rosita winked at me, then she cleared her throat. "Let the young man go, Esperanza. I'm sure he'd rather have his mate in his arms."

Tia did release him, but Simon kissed her on both cheeks before stepping away.

"Everyone, sit. Who would like some hot chocolate?" Soledad got up to bustle around the kitchen. When Simon sat down next to me, I took his hand in mine.

Tia turned to him. "Young Nicky here told us you like to knit. We're more partial to crochet, but I'd love to see what you're working on sometime."

His eyebrows went up, and all I got was confusion through the bond. He glanced at me, then shrugged. "I—sure? It's just a blanket. I spend a lot of time in my minivan, so I need the warmth."

I squeezed his hand. "You *used* to spend a lot of time in your minivan. And, by the way, I hope you don't mind, but I moved all of your storage bins from your minivan into the house."

His eyes went wide to match his eyebrows. "You did?"

"Yeah." I held up my free hand. "I didn't look at anything, but it seemed wrong not having your stuff inside." I smiled, feeling all warm and fuzzy at having my mate's belongings close. More of that nesting instinct, probably, but now I was reveling in it. "I only put a couple of bins of your clothes in our bedroom closet for now, and I put the rest in the guest bedroom. I figure when you're feeling up to it, you can use your super strength to haul it all upstairs. I already moved a bunch of my clothes from the closet to make room for yours."

He stared at me for a few more seconds, and his eyes filled with tears. He let go of my hand and leaned over to throw both arms around me. "I haven't had a place to hang my clothes since I lived with Davi, and that was only for a few months."

Oh, fuck. I hadn't anticipated this. I pulled him closer, making his chair legs scrape across the floor. Through the bond I was getting a mishmash of love, gratefulness, disbelief, and awe.

"You have a home now. You're home." I rubbed his back as he tried to stifle his sobs.

Tia got up, came around the table, and hugged Simon with one arm, then kissed him on his head. "You have family and friends too. You're not alone."

Across from us, Cal appeared decidedly uncomfortable, as if he'd rather have been anywhere but here in the middle of all this emotion. Jackson's face was slightly scrunched up, and they kept glancing between Simon and Nicky. Nicky's lips were pressed together, and his eyes were shiny.

Oh. Oh, shit.

Simon must've felt my realization, because he sat back and wiped his eyes. "Sorry."

I smiled at him and brushed his hair out of his face. "You're entitled." I looked over at Jackson and Nicky. "The home thing? That goes for you two as well. I want you to stay as long as you like."

"Yes." Simon nodded emphatically as he sniffled.

"Really? You just got mated. Don't you want privacy?" Nicky's face turned pink.

I chuckled. "Maybe don't open our bedroom door without knocking first, but no. We don't need to be all alone in the house or anything."

Simon rubbed his chest. "Actually, I miss being with people. I would prefer it if you would stay. Both of you."

Jackson nodded, and Nicky grinned. "Okay."

"Great." I waved a hand at the living room. "You're welcome to continue sleeping in here, but we can get a TV for the guest bedroom. And once you're able to go up the stairs by yourself, Nicky, you should check out the attic and see if you'd prefer to live up there."

He looked thoughtful. "Thank you, I will."

Tia went over and gave Nicky a hug as well. Jackson got a kiss on the top of their head, and she gave Cal a pat on the shoulder. "We're heading home. Do you want us to bring you more food tomorrow?"

I shook my head. "I think we're good. But feel free to stop by if you like." Simon gave me wide eyes, and I backpedaled. "Um, in the afternoon would be better, though."

Cal faked a cough to cover his laugh. After I came back from walking Tia, Rosita, and Soledad to the door, he said, "Now that Jackson is okay, I'll be heading home in the morning."

"Thanks for coming, Cal. Really. Not to mention the vision that saved our lives."

He fidgeted under the praise. "I told you, I was just doing what I could to help."

"Well, it meant everything to all of us." Simon, Nicky, and Jackson all nodded and threw in their agreement.

We stayed up about an hour more, keeping Jackson company while they downed most of a pizza. They insisted Nicky eat one slice, and I made a mental note to make sure he was getting enough food. He could walk to the kitchen now, but could he stay steady on his feet long enough to make a sandwich?

For that matter, did Nicky know *how* to make a sandwich?

Shit, I should make a list of life things Nicky needed to learn.

I picked up my phone to make a note, and I didn't have any unread texts or Discord messages. I leaned into Simon. "Thanks for messaging the Wonders back."

He kissed me on the cheek. "My pleasure."

I went back to my note-making, but my thoughts started straying to the feel of Simon's shoulder where it pressed against mine. How his jaw was covered in a fine stubble that would feel oh-so-nice rubbing along my naked thigh.

Fuck. I couldn't get a boner at the kitchen table. I sat up, moving away from Simon. He made a barely audible noise of protest. Maybe it was time for bed. Except Simon needed sleep more than he needed sex, and I had to keep that in mind. My dick could wait until morning.

Finally the conversation wound down, and Simon and I escaped to our bedroom. I showed him where I'd made space for his stuff in the closet and the drawers, and we decided to see how everything fit before determining whether we needed another chest of drawers. We had room for a small one.

"Thank you for thinking to do this." He pulled me into his arms and gave me a kiss that made my entire body zing.

I groaned and pushed him away. "Stop it. You need to sleep."

"Nooo." His irises had a red cast to them, same as when we'd had sex for our bonding, and when he pouted, his lower lip stuck out between his fangs. It was fucking cute, and I had to walk away to keep from laughing. He called after me, "We said we'd see how I felt. And I feel horny."

I let out a breath but didn't turn around. "Okay, once I'm done in the bathroom, if you still want sex, we'll do it."

He muttered something about not being very romantic as I shut the bathroom door behind me.

My dick was half-hard, but hopefully brushing my teeth and getting ready for bed would take care of that. Sleep was more important for Simon than sex, and I was laying even odds that he'd be zonked out by the time I was done.

Though of course I wouldn't protest if he was awake and initiated something. He was right that I'd promised, and he knew his own body after all. Just thinking about his body had the image of Simon's naked skin consuming my brain.

My balls started to ache as I stripped down to my boxers. Shit, I needed to stop dwelling on sex. I put my clothes in the hamper and thought about doing laundry tomorrow, but it was no use. I could almost feel Simon's fingers spreading my precome down my shaft. My breathing was getting heavier, and I spread my legs apart as my dick began to stand up. My body was primed for Simon. Fuck, he'd know if I jerked off, but what if he was sleepy? How could I go out there with a raging boner and assure him he should just close his eyes and ignore me?

I opened the bathroom door a crack, half-hoping and half-ready to be disappointed that Simon had fallen asleep.

Well, he was in bed at least. But he'd pulled the covers down and he was naked, staring at me and stroking his cock.

I threw the door open the rest of the way and pointed at him. "You were sending sexy thoughts through the bond, you fucker!"

He widened his legs. "It's not my fault you didn't notice." He bent his knees and put his feet flat on the mattress. "Now get over here. I haven't been fucked since 1946, and you need to fix that." He lifted his balls and rolled them in his fingers.

I froze. Holy fuck. Even if Davi had liked to bottom, there hadn't been anyone else in all that time?

"What's the matter? Why are you anxious?" He started to sit up.

I raised my hands and rushed over to the bed. "No, sorry! Don't stop what you were doing." I sat down on the edge of the mattress and stroked his thigh. "I just had a little freakout. Some performance anxiety. I don't want to disappoint you."

He cursed under his breath and cupped my face in his hands. "I'm sorry. I shouldn't have said anything. But you have nothing to worry about. We're mates. Remember how you can feel what I feel and vice versa? Neither of us will be disappointed, I promise." He kissed me, and through the bond I got an enormous wave of lust and something a lot stronger than affection. It was too soon to be love, right? I'd felt hints of it before, but this seemed bigger.

I pushed myself into him, his sparse chest hair delicious against my nipples as his tongue and mine mimicked what I really wanted to be doing. I dragged a hand down his side to land on his hip. We should be lying down. This position didn't let me get close enough.

He pulled back, ending the kiss. I stared at him, my foggy, blissed-out brain not understanding why he stopped.

"We need lube, and I'll need prep."

"Lube," I repeated back to him, still staring into his eyes.

"Lube." He smiled at me like I was the most precious thing in the universe, and I melted against him.

"You're gorgeous." I ran my hand through his long auburn hair.

"Reno."

"Huh?" I dragged my fingers along his ear, then down his neck.

"Never mind. I'll check this drawer, shall I?" He scooted out from under me, and I barely kept myself from clinging to him like a koala. At least his dick, engorged and leaking, told me he was as turned on as I was. "It's okay. I'll be right back." He only moved far enough to let him reach the nightstand and yank open the top drawer.

"Ohhh. Lube. Good idea."

He chuckled. "Thanks."

My brain started processing again, and I took the tube from him. It was more than half full, so we'd be okay. At least for this round. I dropped it on the bed before lifting my hips so I could strip off my boxers.

Simon leaned back against the pillows, his hair mussed and his lips swollen from our kiss. His eyes were golden but tinged with red, and they looked at me with possessiveness and lust. Had anyone ever been more beautiful? He was so out of my league it wasn't even funny, but for whatever reason he'd picked me to be his mate. All I could do was make sure he never regretted it.

He lifted a hand and cupped my cheek. "I'd never regret you, Reno."

My face heating, I shook my head and focused on pouring lube into my palm. Simon lifted his knees to his chest, but I hesitated. "I didn't ask last time. Do you have anything, uh, that I should be aware of?"

He furrowed his brows and cocked his head to the side. "Like diseases? I can't catch human diseases, but we can use a condom if you'd prefer."

"No. Um, I mean... anatomical differences?"

His face eased into a smile. "No. Everything's very similar to yours."

I whooshed out a breath. "Okay, good." He laughed but stopped abruptly when I leaned forward and took his cock into my mouth. He might've said there weren't any differences between us, but I'd never met a human whose precome tasted like sparkly sunshine. I gently sucked the crown as I caressed his hole with my fingers. The feedback loop through our bond made my eyes roll back in my head. Holy fuck.

"Oh. Yes, please." His breathing was coming faster. He wriggled his hips to get me to go deeper, but I didn't let him hurry me. He whined. "Is this payback for teasing you earlier? Because I'm sorry!"

I pulled off and winked at him. "I'm not."

"Dammit, Reno! Next time I'm going to ride you, so I can be in charge of this part."

"You want to be in charge? You should've said." I teased him by pressing my finger inside, but only up to the first knuckle.

He snarled, and his eyes went full red. He bared his fangs at me. "Now!"

The feedback through our bond meant I was just as hard as he was, and my ass was all kinds of interested in being filled. If he changed his mind and wanted to top me, I wouldn't have hesitated.

I decided he'd begged enough, so I plunged the finger all the way inside him, careful to stay away from his prostate.

Simon threw his head back, exposing his throat. "More. I can take more." I wanted, needed to bite that throat. I might not be able to puncture his skin, but I could leave the biggest hickey anyone had ever seen. Marking him as mine.

I pushed a second finger into him, and he writhed, trying to take me deeper. He was flushed, tiny drops of sweat glistening all over his body. His dick slapped against his belly as he moved, leaving a dewy trail across his abs. He was enthralling. I couldn't tear my eyes away.

And it was me he wanted. Me he'd chosen. I was the luckiest man alive.

Simon sent back a wave of emotion so strong I couldn't put any label on it other than *love*. I gasped, and he smiled before jerking his chin at me. "I'm tired of waiting. Get your cock inside me."

I tore my gaze back to where my fingers entered his hole. "You're not ready. One more." My heart was still pounding from his almost-confession, but I shoved all that to the side to think about later. Ignoring his complaints, I added a third finger. He was too close to coming for me to try for a fourth, and thanks to the echo from our bond, he wasn't the only one. It didn't help that he was shouting, "In, in, in!" so loud that everyone downstairs could probably hear him.

I gently but swiftly eased my fingers out and guided my dick into his hole. That first push, so hot, so tight, was like coming home.

"Reno." Simon wrapped his arms and legs around me, leaving just enough space for me to thrust in and out.

The feedback through the bond told me exactly which angle felt the best, and it didn't take long before both of us were on the edge of our orgasms. "Can I bite you?" Simon's hot breath against my ear almost sent me over the edge.

"Yes! Do it."

His fangs cut my neck, and the first sucking pull made my dick even harder, my balls even tighter. The second pull made my orgasm explode through me. Simon came as well, and his orgasm threw me into an aftershock. I was in a trembling, quivering state for longer than I knew how to process.

When I resurfaced back into reality, I was splayed on top of Simon, my face in his neck and my spent dick no longer inside him. Between our bodies was a mess of cum, lube, and sweat. I groaned and inched to the side to roll off.

"No, not yet." He wrapped his arms around me and threw one calf across my ass to keep me in place.

I lifted my head and kissed his jaw, which was all I could reach. "Simon, you are the sexiest guy I have ever seen, much less been naked with."

He turned his head so he could kiss me back. "Thank you, my love. I feel the same about you."

I ducked my head back into his neck to avoid obsessing over the endearment he'd used. "But, you know what would make you even more attractive?"

He laughed out loud and hugged me tighter. "Let me guess. If I were wet and soapy in the shower?"

I nipped his neck where I'd wanted to leave a hickey earlier, and he sucked in a breath. "This bond thing is amazing. It's like you can read my mind."

He opened his arms and let me slide off him. I held out a hand to help him out of bed, and I kept hold of it while we walked to the bathroom and turned on the shower. Simon crowded me against the wall next to the tub and kissed me slowly and thoroughly. When he pulled away, he was smiling. "Speaking of reading your mind, I know you're not ready to say the words yet." I stiffened, and he kissed me again. "*Shhh.* Take all the time you need. I'm not in a hurry. *My love.*"

He kissed me again before stepping back, opening the shower curtain, and getting under the spray. Then he started singing Chappell Roan's "The Giver."

Stunned, I touched my lips, his *my love* bouncing through my brain like a rubber ball. The corners of my mouth turned up, and my chest felt fluttery and light. I laughed and peeled myself off the wall before getting into the shower with my mate.

With my love.

WIMBERLEY, TEXAS – APRIL 1 OF THIS YEAR

I tightened my fingers on the steering wheel, driving as fast as I dared on the poorly maintained roads north of the Build Barn where Cal's vision had put the next victim. The luchd-òl fola wouldn't park in the actual lot due to cameras and zero places to hide.

There. A white van. I passed it and parked in front of someone's house on the next block. I was already armed, so I just grabbed the tracking device and ran back. I wasn't planning on letting them leave with a victim, but I'd let at least one of them escape. I tried to calm my racing heart. This tracking device would lead me to their safe house, and there were few enough of the luchd-òl fola left that, if I planned things right, I could take them all out in one attack.

I double-checked that the tracker was secure and I could see it on my phone, then I took off for the Build Barn parking lot. I could hear yelling, so the fight had already started. In all the years I'd tracked the luchd-òl fola, no one else, until now, had figured out that Wonders were being systematically kidnapped, much less tried to do something to prevent it.

And even though none of the single District Monitors or Cal had turned out to be my mate, I was overjoyed to finally have some fucking help. And their online chatter about a sentient "Elven arti-

fact" made me think Prince Nicol's dèideag dìon *had made their way here too. I didn't believe in fate, but it was obvious things were coming to a head. I just needed to stay focused on the end goal and stick to the plan.*

Victory was close. I could feel it.

EPILOGUE
SIMON

JACKSON'S BAT CRACKED AS THEY HIT THE SOFTBALL. THE Wonders stacked on all the bases whooped and ran for home, Jackson bringing up the rear. Shirley, who was playing left field, shouted in frustration as she leaped for the ball but it still went over her head.

Beside me, Nicky jumped up and down as he cheered. His physical health had come a long way in the past few months, and he could manage the stairs to the attic multiple times a day just fine, but he wasn't up to playing an entire softball game. Shane had referred us to a Wonder who was a licensed therapist, and Nicky, along with his fellow ex-captives, had begun the long process of working through his trauma. He had his bad days and moments, but he impressed all of us with his perseverance and resilience.

On the pitcher's mound, Reno caught the ball Shirley threw to him, then he waited for the next batter, an eagle shifter named Rathbone, to step up to the plate. Reno's nose and the back of his neck were still a little sunburned from yesterday afternoon, when he and I had gone kayaking. I'd enjoyed slathering him with sunscreen this morning.

Nicky and I had prime seats, directly behind home plate. Reno, interestingly, had had a vision this morning of me and Nicky sitting in this exact spot on the bleachers, with everyone cheering around us. I hadn't picked these seats because of the vision though. I'd picked them because they were perfect for sending naughty thoughts to my mate as I admired how his shorts and slightly sweaty t-shirt clung to his body. We were also in direct view of Tucker's ass as he squatted behind home plate and raised his glove. Nicky, as he'd done each and every time this entire game, sucked in a breath.

On the one hand, I was thrilled Nicky's body was healed enough that his sex drive was surfacing. On the other hand, Elves reached sexual maturity in their twenties, so odds were his parents hadn't discussed the ins and outs of sex with him. Sure, he'd seen enough TV and movies, and he certainly had access to the internet, but I'd have to make sure he knew everything he needed to know. Especially about Elves and sex, because *that* wouldn't be anywhere online.

Around us, Wonders and their families—some of whom included humans like Emiliano Duran—chatted and laughed. Thomas and Anika, two of the Wonders who'd been rescued along with Nicky, were in attendance as well. We'd rented out most of the park for the afternoon and early evening. This was the first District-wide event to happen since Reno's cousin had died and he'd taken over as acting DM. I loved seeing everyone together, forming connections and having fun.

Some days I had trouble believing this was how I got to live my life now. After so many years alone, traveling constantly, suddenly having a home, friends, and a mate felt almost unreal. I still worried about Kinnon from time to time. Not knowing what had happened to him or whether he was out there harming Wonders was always a nagging worry in the back of my brain. But unless he announced his presence somehow, all I could do was keep a watch out online for news of missing Wonders.

With my computer skills, becoming a partner in Reno's private investigation business had been as natural as breathing for me, and Reno enjoyed the work more now that he could share the load.

To Reno's relief, I'd almost completely taken over the acting District Monitor role. I loved every minute of assisting the Wonders in navigating the mundane world, talking them through their problems, and giving advice. Reno, of course, loved every minute of not being the one to do that anymore.

I dreaded the day a magic carrier with DM abilities would come along and resonate with the District. I'd have trouble giving up being the person the Wonders relied on. Would the new DM remember to check in weekly with Portia Escobar, who would get so involved with her painting she'd forget to eat? Would they make sure Edward Bingham's family wasn't getting overwhelmed keeping up with his tendency to leave his seal skin near any pretty Wonder he saw?

Nicky nudged my arm. "What's the matter?"

"Oh, sorry. I was just thinking that someday these Wonders will get a real District Monitor, and I'd miss helping them."

Nicky made a face. "Why do they need a different District Monitor? They have you and Reno."

"But neither of us has the skills of a magic carrier with DM abilities. We can't hold enough connections, and we can't get emotions or locations through the connections we have."

His face went oddly blank. "Is that something either of you would want? To have those abilities, I mean?"

I huffed a laugh. "I promise you, Reno does *not* want to have DM abilities. Me? Well, if it were possible, I think I'd be pretty good at it."

"Okay. Give me your hand." He held one of his out, palm up.

"What?" Did he mean...?

He rolled his eyes. "I'm still genetically part of the royal family. I might not be able to do it at a distance like they did before the portal closed, but I know how to transfer magical talents. It's instinct."

Hesitantly I put my hand in his. Out on the field, Reno, who'd been preparing to pitch, straightened up and cocked his head at us. Nicky closed his eyes, then nodded and dropped my hand. "There you go." He looked back toward the game. "Why are they all staring at us?"

"I—" I gazed down at my core, where the wheel was spinning faster and faster. My magic burst out of me in a dazzling explosion, reaching out to the edges of the District.

Click. The magic retreated back into my body in a rush, and I snapped into place. Like I'd been unmoored and drifting my entire life, but now I was home and secure. Only my mating with Reno had been more emotionally satisfying.

I rubbed my chest as the connections I had with some of the Wonders in the District changed. I knew exactly where each of them was, and if I focused, I could get a general idea of their overall mood.

"Simon?" Reno was standing on the bleacher below us.

I wiped the tears from my cheeks and grinned at him. "The new District Monitor is here."

His eyes widened, and he looked between me and Nicky. "You? You wanted this?"

I nodded, and he stepped up to wrap me in a big hug. "Congratulations. I love you. We're the luckiest District in the world to get you as the DM." He sent happiness and pride through our bond.

"Thanks. I love you too."

As Reno shouted the news to all the Wonders, and they crowded around to congratulate me and start our connections, I knew it wasn't this District who was lucky.

It was me.

———

Thank you for reading *Wonder*! Don't miss my next urban fantasy series, *Singular Magics*, which kicks off with Manny's story, ***Unprecedented***!

ALSO BY BIX BARROW

BENT OAK, TEXAS

Holding On to a Hero (Will, Cole, and Jason's story)

Heart Me Up (Craig and Foster's story)

Head Over Feels (Felix and Malcolm's story)

What's Santa Got to Do with It (Steve and Baz's story)

We Don't Need Another Santa (Phillip and Lucas' story)

I Touch Hoses (Keson and Wesley's story) – Related novella

Last Mango in Palm Springs (Ford and Zachary's story) - Related novella

Voices Harry (Mitchell and Harry's story) – Free when you go to www.bixbarrow.com and sign up for my newsletter!

WONDERFALL

Seer (Cal and Greg's story)

Medium (Shane, Ellis, and Rory's story)

Wonder (Simon and Reno's story)

SINGULAR MAGICS

Magic Fate Ball (Elton and Rafferty's story) - Prequel novella

Unprecedented (Manny, Oz, and Arch's story)

Irreplaceable (Nicky and Tucker's story)

LOVE IN MAPLEWOOD (MULTI-AUTHOR SHARED WORLD)

Can You Feel the Maple Tonight (Drake and Finn's story)

ABOUT BIX BARROW

When Bix Barrow got an idea for her first book, it ended up turning into her second — and thus the first two stories in the *Bent Oak, Texas* series emerged. An aspiring author for most of her life, it took a foray into the MM romance genre to spark the humor, suspense, and blazing banter Bix now weaves into her novels. Accompanying her on her writing exploits are her two dogs and multitude of cats (six at last count). An avid traveler, Bix has started to view her expeditions as interviews for her future home. Born and raised in Texas, she is eager to move somewhere with fewer politicians, hurricanes, and flooding.

Join Bix Barrow's Boom Boom Room on Facebook for sneak peeks and fun conversation!

Sign up for Bix's newsletter and get a free novella! www.bixbarrow.com

facebook.com/bixbarrowauthor
instagram.com/bixbarrow
bookbub.com/authors/bix-barrow